Virginia Vineyards

BLIND LOVE

USA TODAY BESTSELLING AUTHOR

ASHLEY FARLEY

Copyright © 2022 by Ashley Farley

All rights reserved.

Cover design: damonza.com

Editor: Patricia Peters at A Word Affair LLC

Leisure Time Books, a division of AHF Publishing

All rights reserved. No part of this book may be used or reproduced in any manner without written permission from the author.

This book is a work of fiction. Names, characters, establishments, organizations, and incidents are either products of the author's imagination or are used fictitiously to give a sense of authenticity. Any resemblance to actual persons, living or dead, events, or locales is entirely coincidental.

CHAPTER 1
ADA

Ada is the last to arrive at The Nest, her family's ancestral sprawling estate built high above their vineyard in the Virginia Mountains. Parking her Mercedes sedan in the circular driveway, she gets out and strolls over to the car ahead of her in line—a baby blue Volvo convertible so old it will soon be eligible for antique license plates. The car's owner is the guest of honor at today's event. *Casey* lives here now. With *Ada's* father. In *Ada's* family's home.

Ada glances around. Security cameras are everywhere, but as far as she can tell, no human eyes are watching. A malicious smile spreads across her lips as she drags her apartment key down the side of the Volvo, from the driver's door to the rear headlight. Dropping the set of keys in her purse, she clicks her stiletto heels together and enters the house, sashaying down the center hallway toward the sound of murmured voices on the bluestone terrace.

Ada joins her two oldest brothers, Hugh and Charles, at the edge of the terrace away from the others. Nearby, a linen-draped banquet table sports champagne flutes and bottles of bubbly chilling in wine buckets. Their family's cook, Marabella, waits with knife in hand for a signal from Ada's father to cut the cake.

Written in script in pink icing on the chocolate sheet cake is the message *Welcome to the Family, Casey*.

Across the terrace, Ada's father huddles together with Casey and his youngest son, her third brother, Sheldon. Casey is a fairy-tale princess in a bubblegum pink wrap dress with a cascade of golden waves tumbling down her back. The sight of her father's hand resting on the small of Casey's back makes Ada's stomach sour.

Ada's gaze shifts from her father to his attorney, who is silently observing them from the doorway. She shivers. Horace Weaver creeps her out. He knows too much about their family's business, about the fortune that has passed down for generations. His beady eyes are always watching them, judging them as though deciding whether they're worthy of their inheritance. As if it's any of his business.

Ada's hat flops when she dips her head at the attorney. "Why is he here?"

Hugh shrugs. "Who knows? Dad asked him to come." He looks at Ada for the first time. "Why are you wearing funeral clothes?" He says about her all-black attire—wide-brimmed sun hat, tailored dress, Christian Louboutin heels.

"I'm in mourning," Ada says. "Our shares in the Love family fortune are about to shrink."

"Do you really think she's Dad's biological daughter?" Charles asks.

Ada peers at Charles over the top of her designer sunglasses. "Duh. Look at the three of them. Casey is a girl version of Sheldon, who is the spitting image of Dad, aside from a few gray hairs and crow's feet."

Hugh nods his agreement. "And they all have the same pale green eyes and cleft chin."

Truth be told, Ada has the most to worry about regarding the DNA results. Hugh and Charles have the same cleft chin and their mother's deep blue eyes. Her mother's dark chocolate hair is the only feature linking Ada to either of her parents.

She remembers her mother's whispered comments. *You're special, Ada. You're not like your brothers. One day, when you're old enough to understand, I'll explain everything.* But her mother never got the chance to explain. She dropped dead from a brain aneurysm when Ada was only fourteen.

Daniel motions for Ada and her brothers to move in closer. "Now that everyone's here, we can begin. Horace is joining us in an official capacity. I had the results mailed directly to him at his office. I have not seen them."

"And neither have I." Horace leaves the doorway and goes to stand beside Daniel. He produces a sealed envelope from the inside pocket of his suit jacket. "Do you want to do the honors, or should I?"

"I will." Daniel takes the envelope, tears it open, and reads the results out loud. "Hugh, match. Charles, match. Sheldon, match. Casey, match." He smiles over at Casey. "Welcome to the family, my dear." His eyes return to the paper. "And Ada . . ." His face falls. "Wait a minute. This can't be right."

"Give me that." Ada snatches the results from him and stares in horror at the words written beside her name. *No match.*

Ada feels eyes on her, burning her skin, waiting for her response. Her chest tightens, and she can't breathe. Spinning on her heels, she flees the terrace.

Her father's voice rings out behind her. "Ada! Wait! We'll do another test."

But Ada knows it's pointless. Another test will yield the same results.

Retracing her steps through the house, Ada closes the front door behind her and gulps in air until her breath steadies and the urge to vomit subsides. Stepping away from the house, she stares up at the stone facade of her childhood home. The memories rush back. Only a few are good. Her parents' stormy marriage put a damper on most of her youth. It dawns on her that her entire life has been based on a lie.

Ada gets in her car and speeds off. Tears blur her vision, and she misjudges the distance of the approaching tractor. She jerks the steering wheel, barely missing the tractor, and careens off the road. She slams on the brakes, and her car sinks into the moist earth.

Enzo hops down from the tractor and hurries to her aid. He knocks on her window. "Ada! Are you okay?"

She rolls down the window. "No, I'm not okay."

His dark brow knits at the sight of her distraught face. "What's wrong?"

She snatches up the DNA results from her lap and shoves the paper at him. "This!" There's no point in keeping it a secret. Word travels fast in a small town. The world will soon know she is not Daniel Love's daughter.

Ada punches the accelerator, and the tires gain traction, spinning dirt on Enzo as she navigates back onto the road. She forces all thoughts from her mind, her eyes glued to the road, during the short drive to her apartment in the nearby town of Lovely.

Tossing her bag on a chair, Ada goes straight to the kitchen, plunks a designer ice cube in a lowball glass, and pours Casa Dragones tequila over it. She takes her drink to the white leather sofa in the adjacent living room, where the serene decor calms her frazzled nerves.

Her apartment takes up the entire second floor of a renovated old building. The decor is crisp and clean with all white upholstery, accessories, and fluffy rugs scattered across the random-width pine floor. Wooden beams stretch across the ceiling and exposed brick walls provide a warm backdrop for her extensive contemporary art collection. On summer nights, Ada opens the floor to ceiling windows, letting the edgy music drift up from Blue Cosmos, the jazz club below.

Ada yearns to cry until her eyes are swollen and face blotchy. Anger and uncertainty have replaced her despair. She can cope with anger. She's been angry most of her life. But this lack of self-confidence is new for her. She's never been unsure about anything. She knows exactly who she is—the pampered only daughter of Daniel Love, the wealthy owner of the prestigious Love-Struck Vineyards. Now that honor belongs to Casey. *The little bitch.*

Ada's father is big on lineage. His Love ancestors founded the town over a hundred years ago. Daniel has plenty of legitimate offspring. He doesn't need Ada. She no longer meets genetic requirements to remain in the family. He'll fire her as his event planner and give her hush money to disappear before rumors scandalize the family. But where will she go? She has no other relatives. This morning she woke up as Ada Love. Now she's a nobody. In the blink of an eye, her life has drastically changed forever.

CHAPTER 2
CASEY

Daniel and the others clear out at once, leaving Sheldon and Casey alone at the food table.

"I've never seen a party break up in such a hurry. Even Marabella scurried outta here with her cake." Removing a bottle of champagne from a bucket, Sheldon peels back the foil and twist off the cork.

"What're you doing?" Casey asks, watching him fill two glasses.

"What do you think? We're celebrating." He hands a glass to her.

She eyes the glass as one might a live hand grenade. "How can we possibly celebrate after what just happened? It's not right. Your poor sister . . ."

"You're my sister too, Casey. The point of the party was to officially welcome you to the family. Here's to you." He clinks her glass, takes a drink, and smacks his lips. "Excellent. Dad splurged on the good stuff."

Casey takes a tentative sip. The wine is crisp, and the bubbles tickle her nose. "Seriously, though. Ada must be devastated."

Sheldon drains his glass in one gulp. "Actually, based on this new revelation, Ada is only my half sister. Even more cause for celebration. I'm enormously relieved to be genetically unrelated to such a cold-hearted woman. Come with me," he says, waving her on with the champagne bottle.

She follows him down the steps to the pool and sits down beside him on a chaise lounge. "Ada shouldn't be alone right now. Does she have a close friend she can call?"

Sheldon grunts. "Ada doesn't have friends. She raises venomous spiders as pets."

Casey can't help but laugh. "I'm not kidding, Sheldon. Ada's not my favorite person either, but I'm worried about her."

"Ada's a big girl. She can take care of herself."

"Where does she live, anyway?"

"In a swanky apartment in town. I'm sure she's there now, drowning her sorrows in tequila while she plots a way to get back at the world for Mom's indiscretion." Sheldon falls back in his chair. "Wow. I can't believe Mom had an affair. Even though our parents' marriage sucked, Mom was devoted to her children. She didn't seem the type to cheat on her husband."

Casey smooths her hair back into a ponytail, securing it with an elastic band from her wrist. "How old were you when she died?"

"Twenty. A brain aneurysm is not a bad way to go if you're the one dying. But it's brutal for the loved ones left behind. Our mom was here one minute, gone the next. Her loss left a hole the size of a crater in our lives. It was hard on all of us, but Ada was a hormonal fourteen year old. She was a basket case for years."

Casey kicks her feet up and stretches out on the chaise. "I feel sorry for her, losing her mom at such a vulnerable age and now finding out Daniel isn't her biological father."

"There you go again with your misplaced sympathy for Ada. If the situation was reversed, she wouldn't give you a second thought." Sheldon slips his sockless feet out of his loafers and nudges her leg with his big toe. "You're too nice for your own good, Casey. We need to toughen you up if you're going to survive in this family."

Casey kicks his foot away. "For your information, I don't aspire to be like your siblings. Their *toughness* has turned them into bitter people." She tilts her face to the sun and closes her eyes. "I should think about getting my own place."

"Why? These digs aren't good enough for you?"

"Are you kidding me? I love living here. Who wouldn't? But I intended for this arrangement to be temporary. Every time I mention moving, Daniel talks me into staying. I don't want to be a burden to your father."

"He's *our* father, Casey. And you're not a burden. The man doesn't lift a finger around here. His staff takes care of all his needs. When you get a boyfriend and start shacking up, then it might be time to get your own place."

"That's not gonna happen anytime soon," Casey says, her tone sarcastic.

"Right. I forgot. You're saving yourself for Jamie."

She rolls her head to the side and opens her eyes. "Like you're saving yourself for Ollie. Look at us. We're such losers."

Instead of refilling his empty glass, Sheldon takes a swig of champagne from the bottle. "Don't be such a defeatist. Jamie and Ollie are a match made in hell. They'll eventually break up, and when they do, you and I will be waiting in the wings."

"So, now I'm a defeatist. I'm glad to know you have such a high opinion of me."

"Actually, I have the *highest* opinion of you. You're one of the coolest girls I've ever met. I'm just saying you need to learn to fight for what you want."

She closes her eyes again, relishing the warmth of the sun on her face. "Where do you live, Sheldon? How come you've never invited me over for tea?"

"I live in a log cabin in the woods about three miles from here. It's a dump, not suitable for company or tea. But the rent's cheap, and I'm saving up to build a house. I'm working with an architect to design the plans."

Casey sits straight up. "No way! Where?"

His arm shoots out with a finger pointed at a spot above her head. "Up there. Dad gave each of us lots. He'll do anything to keep us close."

Casey cranes her neck as she looks at the wooded acreage on the mountain behind The Nest. "Nice. I bet the view from up there is incredible."

"It's amazing. Wanna see? It's only a short hike."

"I'd love that. But I need to change first." Casey swings her legs over the side of the chaise. "So do you. You can't go hiking in your good clothes," she says about his linen pants and starched white shirt. "Can you borrow something from Daniel?"

"No need. I keep a second wardrobe in my old room."

"Where is your old room? I don't remember seeing it in the main house."

"The wing to the left when you're facing the house." Sheldon stands and pulls Casey to her feet. "We call it the children's wing. When we were little, our parents banished us from the main house to live with our nanny."

Casey shields her eyes from the sun as she looks up at the house. "What's in the other wing, the one to the right?"

"More guest suites. Back in the day, Mom and Dad hosted elaborate fox hunting weekends. Their friends came from all over the state."

Casey scrunches up her brow. "Fox hunting? You mean with horses and hounds and riders dressed in red coats."

Sheldon laughs. "Yep. Dad hasn't hosted a weekend party in years, but he still hunts. He keeps horses in the stables. I assume you've seen them."

"I've noticed the stable, but I haven't been inside to see the horses."

"It's pretty cool, as far as stables go. I'll give you a tour on the way to my lot," Sheldon says and motions for her to go ahead of him up the stairs.

"Daniel has shown me the rose garden and trout stream. What else have I missed?"

"Tennis and pickle ball courts. That's pretty much it."

"You're right. This place is incredible. Why would I wanna live anywhere else? Daniel may never get rid of me." As the words leave her mouth, Casey has an ominous feeling of troubled waters ahead.

———

After touring the stables, Sheldon and Casey begin the hike up the hill to Sheldon's property. "Tell me about your house plans," Casey says.

"I'm going for a minimalist style with wide open spaces with walls of windows offering mountain views. The master suite is on the first floor, with lots of bedrooms upstairs for my children."

"You realize Ollie doesn't want children," Casey says, trailing along behind him.

Sheldon does an about-face. "You know this for sure?"

"Yep. Jamie told me. He's an open book. I know more than I want to about his relationship with Ollie."

"Shame on Jamie for talking about your boss behind her back." Sheldon turns around and continues walking.

When they reach the lot, they sit down on a boulder over-looking the mountains. Casey inhales a breath of clean air. "I could get used to this view."

"The lot next door is available if you're interested. Although that could present a problem if things are awkward between Jamie and Ollie after they break up." Sheldon removes his straw fedora and wipes the sweat off his forehead with the back of his hand. "Why doesn't Ollie want children?"

"Jamie says she's too preoccupied with her vineyard. She's not a spring chicken, you know. She's thirty-six. Her child-bearing years are quickly coming to an end."

"Damn! Really? She doesn't look that old. Jamie can't be over thirty. She's really robbing the cradle."

"Jamie's thirty-one, actually. And you're thirty-three, which makes you closer in age to her and Jamie in age to me. All the more reason for them to break up," Casey says with a grin.

"For sure. And time is of the essence. Ollie's biological clock is ticking. The sooner we figure out a way to break them up, the sooner I can make Ollie fall in love with me. Once that happens, she'll be putty in my hands. I'll convince her to have children, and we'll live happily ever after on our mountain." Sheldon elbows her in the ribs. "You and I need to put our heads together to devise a plan to break them up."

"Um, no. You're more like your siblings than I thought." Casey draws her legs beneath her chin. "What if Jamie and Ollie are destined to be together? Who are we to interfere with destiny? We should let things naturally progress."

"I'll remind you of that when we're all old and gray, you and I are still single while Jamie and Ollie are stuck in a dysfunctional marriage."

Casey rests her chin on her knees. "We both know Ollie doesn't love Jamie. But Jamie has it bad for Ollie. He'll be heart-broken if they break up. He'll settle for me and be miserable in a loveless marriage."

"It may take him a while to get over his obsession with Ollie. But when he does, he'll fall head over heels in love with you. Although, for the record, you can do much better than Jamie." Sheldon slides off the rock. "I suddenly have a powerful urge to see Ollie. Let's go to The Foxhole for a late lunch," he says, striding back toward the wooded path.

Casey hurries to catch up with him. "I'm not sure that's such a good idea. Remember, Ollie and I parted on bad terms when I quit."

"All the more reason for us to go. We'll invite her to join us for lunch. I can help smooth things over."

"Stop, Sheldon!" Casey grabs his arm, spinning him around. "You realize Ollie thinks of you as the enemy?"

"She thinks of my family as the enemy. Deep down, she knows

I'm a good guy. She has a thing for me. She's just not ready to admit it."

Casey laughs out loud. "You're awfully sure of yourself."

"You have much to learn about our family, Casey. Dad taught us to always appear confident, even when we're not."

Casey experiences a pang of jealousy at having been deprived of her father during her formidable years. "Whatever." She brushes past him. "I'll go with you. But only because I'm starving. And I want to see Fiona."

Casey's old roommate is the chef at The Foxhole. They didn't part on the best of terms either when Casey moved out. Casey misses her, and she doesn't want to lose Fiona as a friend. She hopes the time and distance will have eased the strain of their relationship.

CHAPTER 3
OLLIE

Ollie returns from working in the vineyard to find Jamie waiting for her on the screen porch. "Was I expecting you?" He stops by so often these days, she's never sure whether they'd planned a date or he's dropping in to say hello. Truth be told, these frequent visits are getting old.

The wounded expression on his baby face makes Ollie's heart melt. She can never say the right thing to him lately.

Her Apple watch vibrates her arm with a calendar notification for an upcoming event. *Lunch with Jamie at two o'clock.* "What I meant was, you're early. It's only one thirty, and I wasn't expecting you until two," she says, trying to cover for herself. But he knows she forgot. She always forgets.

He gestures at the wicker basket on the floor beside the door. "Delilah's packed us a picnic." The mention of Delilah's Delights, the gourmet market in town, makes her stomach rumble. She has to eat, and there's only yogurt in the fridge.

She forces a smile. "A picnic sounds nice."

"I thought we'd go to my favorite place, a shady spot by a trout stream about two miles up the road."

Irritation crawls across her skin. "Can't we eat here? I don't have much time."

"But it's Saturday," Jamie says with a huff. "Remember, we intentionally made the date for later so you could take the rest of the afternoon off."

"Right," Ollie says, even though she doesn't remember the conversation. She spreads her arms wide at the vineyard. "We have this whole big farm. We can find a peaceful spot here somewhere." She heads for the door. "We'll have fun. I'll grab the four-wheeler if you'll get the dogs out of the kennel."

Ollie leaves the porch before he can argue. She's jogging down to the barn when she notices Sheldon and Casey waiting in line for lunch at The Foxhole, her vineyard's new cafe tasting room. She's already in the doghouse with Jamie, and she hates to make him wait, but she doesn't want to be rude to Casey and Sheldon by ignoring them. She and Casey haven't spoken since Casey left Foxtail to work for Love-Struck. Besides, Sheldon's kilowatt smile makes her heart pitter-patter. Ollie reminds herself that he's the enemy as she makes her way toward them.

"The place is hopping," Sheldon says, and Casey adds, "I know you're thrilled."

"We're overjoyed. Fiona is cooking up a storm. Her recent specials have been over the top."

Casey smiles. "Good for her. She has mad talents in the kitchen. I'll stick my head in to say hello."

"Can you join us for lunch?" Sheldon asks Ollie.

"I wish I could. But Jamie's waiting for me." Ollie crosses her eyes. "Yippee! We're going on a picnic."

Casey and Sheldon exchange a look Ollie can't interpret.

Ollie squeezes Casey's hand. "It's good to see you. I'd love to catch up. I'll text you. We'll get something on the calendar." She tosses a wave over her shoulder as she continues on to the barn.

Ollie retrieves the four-wheeler and speeds back up to the house. Her Border collies, Chard and Rosé, run circles around Jamie as he stands in the driveway, tapping his foot with arms folded over chest.

Ollie slams on the brakes, screeching to a halt. "Sorry. I ran into Casey and Sheldon down at the Foxhole."

Jamie's blue eyes darken. "Naturally."

"What's that supposed to mean?"

"Do I have to spell it out for you? Sheldon's got the hots for you, Ollie."

"Be real, Jamie. He's just a friend." Ollie straps the picnic basket on the back and motions for him to get on. "Wanna drive?"

This brings a smile to Jamie's face. He's a boy at heart. "Sure!"

They head off into the vineyard with the dogs barking and running along beside them. They ride for fifteen minutes before they come to a large maple tree.

"How's this?" Jamie yells over the sound of the motor, and she gives him a thumbs up.

Jamie spreads a blanket beneath the tree, and while he unloads the contents of the picnic basket, Ollie stretches out and stares up at the canopy of sprawling branches, a gentle breeze rustling the tree's leaves.

"Let's eat," Jamie says when he has everything ready.

They pinch chunks of bread from a crusty loaf and snack on slices of salami and creamy Munster cheese.

"Great job on the picnic!" She smiles at Jamie. "It's all so French."

"Speaking of France, I brought champagne." From a portable insulated wine cooler, he removes a bottle of Veuve Clicquot.

Ollie frowns. "What're we celebrating?"

"Since you asked . . ." He sets the champagne down and gets to his knees, pulling Ollie up to face him. He produces a black velvet ring box from his pocket. "I love you, Ollie. And I want to spend the rest of my life with you. Will you marry me?" He opens the box to reveal a round diamond surrounded by a halo of smaller diamonds.

Stunned into silence, Ollie falls back on her haunches and buries her face in her hands. She didn't see this coming, and her mind races as she considers how to handle the situation. No matter what she says, Jamie will be hurt.

She drags her hands down her face and looks up at him. "I'm so sorry, Jamie. I thought I'd made it clear I don't want to get married. I've been married before, and I have zero interest in going that route again."

"An arranged marriage to your father's vineyard manager doesn't count," Jamie says.

"For your information, I chose to marry Sergio. I thought it would make my father happy. I wasn't ready to settle down, and I caused a lot of heartache."

Jamie sits down beside her. "It'll be different this time, Ollie. We're good together. We can have a happy life."

Ollie presses her lips thin. "There's one hurdle we'll never get past. I don't want children, and you do."

"I've come to terms with that. I can live without children," Jamie says in a reluctant tone.

"For now. Until your friends have children. Until they start teaching their sons how to fish and hunt and play baseball. You don't want to miss out on all that."

"We still have time. You may change your mind."

"And herein lies the problem. I won't change my mind. But you'll keep hoping I will. You'll grow resentful when I refuse to have children. Then we'll start fighting, and we'll both be miserable."

Jamie hangs his head in defeat, staring down at the ring.

"I'll be too old to have children in a few years anyway. I didn't think our age difference mattered at first. But I've come to realize it does. I shouldn't have let things go on between us for so long."

He snaps the ring box closed and jumps to his feet. "You're a psycho, Ollie."

"Why? Because I'm making a hard decision that is right for both of us?"

He ignores her. "Everyone knows you have an anger management problem. You need serious mental help." He storms off up the hill toward the winery.

She calls after him, "And you, Jamie, need to grow the hell up."

At the sound of her angry tone, the dogs scurry over, covering her face in licks. But their affections are short-lived, and they're soon once again chasing each other through the rows of grapevines.

Ollie grabs the bottle of champagne and scoots on her butt over to the tree. She pops the cork, takes a swig, and leans back against the tree.

When they met last summer, Ollie had been attracted to Jamie's boyish charms. But those charms had quickly worn thin. She'd stayed with him because she didn't want to be alone. She realizes now how unfair it was to string him along and give him false hope.

There's some truth to Jamie's words. *Everyone knows you have an anger management problem.* Ollie flies off the handle for no apparent reason, and she harbors misguided hatred for the Love family. Well, maybe not completely misguided. The older Love brothers have wreaked havoc on her life in their attempts to get their hands on her farm.

But Jamie calling her a *psycho* hit close to home. Ollie's brother, Alexander, is a bona fide psychopath. He set fire to their family's Napa Valley home, killing both their parents. He's currently in prison, serving two life sentences for murder. Chronic mental disorders can be hereditary. What if her problem is more than an anger management issue? What if she's prone to violent tendencies?

Relief rolls through Ollie as she cleans up the picnic. Jamie is out of her life. She can no longer hurt him. Ollie sucks at relationships. She's better off alone.

CHAPTER 4
ADA

The banging on Ada's door is incessant. Whoever it is refuses to go away no matter what obscenities she yells. She's not in the mood for company. Especially not if it's her father. Wait! He's no longer her father. Is she supposed to call him Daniel now?

If only she could cry. This rage is all-consuming. She's certain her head will explode, and she fears her pounding heart will fracture a rib. She spent the afternoon wallowing on the sofa, screaming insults at Casey into the pillow. She realizes her anger toward Casey is misplaced. But it makes Ada feel better to blame everything on Daniel's bastard child who appeared out of the blue and turned Ada's life on end. If Casey hadn't come to town, the secrets of the past would've stayed hidden. Where they belong.

More knocking is followed by a familiar voice. "Ada, it's Enzo. Open the door."

About a month ago, Ada had a drunken encounter with Enzo. She ran into him downstairs at the Blue Cosmos and invited him up to her apartment. Her face warms now, thinking about their hot sex. He'd wanted to spend the night, but Ada wouldn't let him. She'd made it clear it would never happen again. And they haven't spoken since.

"I know you're in there, Ada. Your car is in the parking lot. I'm not going away."

Wrapping the throw blanket around her like a cape, she plods in bare feet across the hardwood floor and swings open the door. "What're you doing here, Enzo?"

"I was worried about you. I came as soon as I got off work." He waves the DNA results. "This is devastating news. You shouldn't be alone."

"Well, I am alone. I've been alone all day." She strides across the room and snatches her cell phone off the coffee table. "Not a single member of my family has reached out to me. Shows how much they care about me."

"They care, Ada. They're respecting your privacy, giving you time to adjust."

"Ha. Shows you how little you know about my family. They don't respect anybody's anything." She checks Enzo out, liking what she sees—black knit shirt clinging to broad shoulders and faded jeans hugging his butt. If she were in a better frame of mind, she'd make a move on him.

Enzo enters the apartment, closing the door behind him. "Have you been drinking all day?" he asks, eyeing the empty tequila bottle on the coffee table.

"Damn straight! As you can see, I ran out." A thought strikes her. "Since you're here, you can go to the liquor store for me." She stumbles around the room, searching for her purse. She finds it hidden behind a pillow in a white leather barrel chair. She removes two hundred-dollar bills and shoves them at him. "Buy the biggest bottle of Casa Dragones you can find."

Enzo looks down at the money and then up at her. "The last thing you need is more booze. Have you eaten anything today?"

"I'm not hungry."

"You need food to absorb the alcohol." Enzo goes to the kitchen and opens the refrigerator.

"You won't find anything in there," Ada says, dropping to a barstool at the kitchen island. "I don't cook."

Enzo closes the refrigerator door and turns to face her. "Then we'll go to Ruthie's."

Daniel is a regular at Ruthie's. Not only is he the last person Ada wants to see, Daniel would have a coronary if Ada showed up with one of his field workers. "I told you, Enzo, I don't want food. I want tequila."

"You've had enough tequila."

Ada jumps to her feet. "Enough? Are you kidding me? All my life, I've been Daniel Love's only daughter. Then I find out I have a half sister. And that half sister is his biological child, not me. I could go on a month-long bender, and it still wouldn't be enough tequila to drown my sorrows."

Enzo inhales a deep breath and lets it out slowly. "Okay, fine. I'll make a deal with you. I'll grab us some sandwiches from Delilah's, and then we'll talk about getting more booze. What do you want on your sandwich?"

"Anything's fine. They have wine at Delilah's. Get a bottle of red." She's still holding the two hundreds. When she tries to give them to him, he waves the money away.

"Is pesto chicken okay?"

"Pesto chicken is fine." Ada waits for him to leave before going over to the window. She throws open the sash and lowers herself to the sill, watching Enzo cross Magnolia Avenue and disappear inside Delilah's Delights.

She considers swan-diving out of the window. She'll face plant on the sidewalk below, putting an end to her misery. She imagines the scene. First responders arriving, and their futile attempts to resuscitate her. A distraught Enzo reaching out to Daniel with the news of her demise. She doubts her former father would come to her funeral. He certainly wouldn't plan one for her. The absence of Love blood in her veins makes her unworthy of a plot in the family cemetery. Hugh will get the task of having her body cremated and dumping her ashes over the side of the mountain.

Ada contemplates her afterlife. She'll surely burn in hell for all the evil things she's done. She imagines the devil jabbing his pitchfork at her as flames lick at her body. Perhaps she should stay alive a little longer. Is it too late to make amends for her sins?

Enzo emerges from Delilah's with a white paper bag but no bottle of wine. As he crosses the street, she calls down to him, "You forgot the wine."

He yells back up, "I never agreed to buy any."

She grabs her purse and is headed out the door when he comes up the stairs.

"Where do you think you're going?"

"To get some wine." When she tries to brush past him, he hooks an arm around her, lifting her off the ground, and carries her inside the apartment.

"We eat first. Then we can talk about having a drink."

Ada stomps her foot on the hardwoods. "Ugh! You drive a hard bargain."

He hands her the bag of sandwiches. "They're both the same."

She takes the bag to the island, unwraps a sandwich, and sinks her teeth into the ciabatta bread. Despite having no appetite, she chokes down half the sandwich.

When music from downstairs drifts through the open window, she gets up and dances around the island. She gestures at his half-eaten sandwich. "Finish that, so we can go to Blue Cosmos. I'm ready to party."

"A minute ago, you were drowning your sorrows in tequila. Why the sudden change in moods?" He pops the last bite of his sandwich into his mouth and reaches for her second half.

"Because I'm free." She throws her hands in the air. "Daniel Love is a tyrant. And since I'm not his daughter, he can no longer order me around."

"Your father raised you from birth. It's difficult to sever such deep ties." He plucks a piece of lettuce off his sandwich. "Your situation isn't much different from someone who was adopted as an infant."

Ada stops dancing and falls back against the island. "Okay . . . so what if Daniel doesn't kick me out of the family? Which is highly unlikely, but for the sake of argument, let's pretend for a minute. There's a lot of money at stake here, Enzo. And my siblings are cutthroat. My brothers will jump all over the opportunity to get rid of me." She straightens. "I'm going to freshen up while you finish eating."

She leans against the wall for support as she makes her way down the hall to her bedroom. Ada stops short when she sees her reflection in the bathroom mirror. She makes a split-second decision to shower, which helps to sober her up. She blow-dries her hair, touches up her makeup, and slips on a black slinky dress that dips way down in the back.

Enzo has cleaned up from dinner and is sitting on the sofa, scrolling through social media when she emerges from the bedroom. He whistles and jumps to his feet when he sees her. Smiling, she takes him by the hand and drags him down the stairs.

The live ensemble, Twilight Groove, is rocking the house when they enter the jazz club. They make their way to the bar and secure two vacant stools. Enzo orders a beer from the bartender, and Ada asks for double tequila on the rocks.

Enzo leans in close. "Are you sure that's a good idea, Ada? You've already consumed a lot of booze today."

"Buzz off, Enzo." Ada sits back in her seat and crosses her long tanned legs. "I'm miserable company. Go find another pretty girl to flirt with. I can crawl my way back upstairs when I reach my limit."

Enzo gives his head a vigorous shake. "No way! I'm staying with you."

"Suit yourself. But if you start counting my drinks, I'm going to ask you to leave."

He taps his beer bottle to her glass. "Fair enough."

The music is too loud for them to carry on a conversation. Ada sips tequila while she watches Luke Ellington wow the crowd with his saxophone. He's smoking hot with dirty blond hair and piercing blue eyes. She's hit on him before, but he didn't seem interested. If Enzo wasn't nannying her, she might try again tonight. Although, the truth is, she *does* need a babysitter right now. She's too much of a mess. She doesn't trust herself. If only Daniel would call. She looks at her phone for the umpteenth time, but her screen is blank. She can't believe it. He's actually going to disown her. He's punishing her, as if any of this is her fault.

When the band takes a break, Ada orders another round of drinks. If he disapproves, he doesn't show it. He angles his body toward her. "I realize this is a touchy subject, but do you have any idea who your real father might be?"

Ada's throat swells as the tears finally arrive. "It doesn't matter who he is, Enzo. It only matters that he's not Daniel Love."

CHAPTER 5
CASEY

Late afternoon on Saturday, Casey is lounging by the pool, staring up at the puffy clouds floating in the sky across the vineyard, when the urge to paint strikes hard. Throwing on her cover-up, she hurries up to her room for supplies. She's gathering her oil paints when she changes her mind and grabs her watercolors instead. In recent months, she's strictly been sketching with colored pencils. She hasn't held a brush in her hand since her mother's cancer diagnosis three years ago. Watercolors will be less intimidating as she eases her way back into painting.

Casey sets her easel up on the terrace and loses herself in her work as the landscape comes alive on her paper—the winery and vineyard and late day sun descending beyond the mountain range. Her phone vibrates around seven o'clock, breaking her reverie.

"Girlfriend!" Fiona blurts. "Do I have some juicy gossip for you?"

Casey's spirits soar at the sound of her old roommate's voice. Fiona had been tied up when Casey stopped by the kitchen to speak to her during lunch earlier. "Talk to me."

"I will. In person. What're you doing tonight?"

Casey had planned to have dinner with Daniel. Mirabella left a crab casserole for them. But she hasn't seen him all afternoon, and he's been known to disappear without telling anyone his whereabouts. "I haven't gotten that far. What did you have in mind?"

"Come to Blue Cosmos with me. They're having a live band. Twilight Groove. I hear they're amazing."

Casey glances down at her cover-up. She's sweaty and greasy from sunscreen. "I need to shower first."

"Then get on it," Fiona demands. "I'll go early and grab us a table."

As she carries her art supplies back to her room, Casey wonders about Fiona's juicy gossip. Could it have something to do with Ollie?

She quickly showers, towel dries her hair, and slips on a yellow sundress with cowboy boots. She searches the house one last time before leaving, but Daniel's not in his bedroom or study, and his car is missing from the driveway. He must be devastated after discovering Ada is not his daughter. Wherever he is, she hopes he's not alone, that he has a friend to hang out with.

The Blue Cosmos occupies the ground floor of a renovated old building that once served as the town's bank. Back-to-back semi-circular banquettes with small round tables divide the jazz club in two. Casey fights her way through the crowd to the back, where Fiona is waiting at a table near the dance floor.

Casey slides onto the bench seat beside her old roommate, giving her a quick peck on the cheek. Fiona looks sweet in a floral sundress with her sandy pixie cut accenting her blue eyes. "Spill it! I'm dying to hear the gossip."

"You'll have to wait," Fiona says with a devilish grin.

Casey falls back against the banquette. "Are you kidding me? After you insisted I rush over here. What do I have to wait for?"

"Our drinks." Fiona's gaze shifts to the left of Casey's face. "And here they come now." A server appears with a tray bearing two flutes of champagne.

Casey softly claps her hands. "Ooh! Bubbles! What're we celebrating?"

"Ollie and Jamie broke up." Fiona raises her glass to toast. "To you, Casey! Your dream is about to come true."

Casey ignores her friend's toast. "I'm not heartless, Fiona. I think Jamie's adorable, and we have a connection. But I never wished for anyone to get hurt. What happened? Did Ollie finally break up with him?"

"You won't believe it!" Fiona gulps down some champagne and slams her glass down on the table. "So, Jamie invited Ollie to go on a picnic. He proposed to her, and she actually shut him down."

Casey's heart tumbles in her chest at the thought of Jamie buying Ollie an engagement ring and planning the proposal. He was going to marry her, and she turned him down. He'll be nursing a broken heart for the foreseeable future. He may never get over Ollie. "How did Jamie take it?"

Fiona shrugs. "I didn't see him. But Ollie said he was irate."

"What else did Ollie tell you?"

"Not much. Jamie brought a bottle of champagne with him on the picnic to celebrate their engagement. When he stormed off, Ollie drank the entire bottle by herself. She was downright giddy when she returned to the farm. She didn't admit it, but she appeared relieved to be rid of him."

"The breakup was long overdue," Casey mutters.

Fiona eyes Casey's phone on the table. "Text him. Now's your chance to make your move."

"No way! Jamie needs some time to himself. I'll check in with him tomorrow. If he wants to talk, I'll be happy to listen as his friend. But I won't throw myself at him. Besides, I can't compare to Ollie. She's beautiful and ballsy and I'm . . . I'm . . ."

"You're gorgeous. And way better suited for Jamie."

Casey cuts her eyes at Fiona. "Why do you say that? Because I want children, and Ollie doesn't?"

Fiona considers this. "That too. But mainly because you're

super sweet, and Jamie's a sensitive guy. Your personalities complement each other." She nudges Casey's arm. "Text him. You need to strike while the iron is hot."

"While he's down in the dumps? No thanks. I don't want to be his rebound person, Fi."

Fiona considers this. "You have a point. Wait until tomorrow, then."

Casey laughs. "Thanks for your permission."

Fiona catches the server's attention and holds up two fingers.

Casey grabs her arm. "Not for me. I'm driving."

"Aw, come on. You can crash with me. It's Saturday night. Let's have some fun. I've heard this band is killer."

The idea of spending the night with Fiona appeals to Casey. She could use some girl talk. Maybe they'll go home early and order a pizza. "Okay. I'll stay."

"Outstanding!" Fiona rises from the table. "Be right back. I'm going to run to the restroom before the band starts."

Casey waits until Fiona disappears in the crowd before calling Sheldon. He answers on the fourth ring with a garbled hello, and she hears water flowing in the background. "What're you doing, Sheldon? Swimming in the bathtub?"

"Ha ha. I'm fly-fishing," he says in a clearer voice.

Casey raises a brow. "In the dark?"

"There's still a little daylight, and fish usually bite at dusk," Sheldon says. "I can hardly hear you from the noise. Are you at a bar?"

"I'm at Blue Cosmos with Fiona. She just told me, and I thought you'd want to know, Ollie and Jamie broke up this afternoon."

He pauses a beat, and Casey imagines the grin spreading across his face. "And Fiona is certain about this?"

"Yep. She heard it from Ollie herself. Jamie proposed, and Ollie turned him down." Casey spots Fiona heading back from the restroom. "I gotta go, Sheldon. Let's talk tomorrow."

Fiona returns to her seat as the band members make their way onto the stage. All four appear to be in their thirties—a bald but bearded drummer, a guy with milk chocolate skin and spiky dreadlocks on the keyboard, and a guitar player with shoulder length blue hair. The saxophone player is by far the best looking, with strong facial features and mesmerizing blue eyes. Casey is captivated when he blows into his instrument. She can't take her eyes off him, and he notices her too. When she smiles shyly at him, he winks at her.

The crowd migrates onto the dance floor, hindering her view of the sexy saxophone player. But during the set, every time she glimpses him, those blue eyes are gazing back at her.

When the band announces they're taking a break, the dance floor clears except for one couple who continues to slow dance even though no music is playing. Casey, realizing the young woman is Ada, lowers her head and sinks down in her seat. "There's Ada. I don't want her to see me."

Fiona observes the couple. "She's drunk. That gorgeous guy she's dancing with is holding her up. Any idea who he is?"

Casey sneaks a peek. "I'm not sure, but he looks like Enzo, one of our field workers." She lowers her gaze again, and she's still staring at her lap when Fiona lets out a squeal. When she looks up again, Fiona is throwing her arms around a guy Casey has never seen before.

"What're you doing here?" Fiona asks, pulling the guy down beside her on the banquette.

"I wanted to surprise you. I hope that's cool."

"Way cool." Fiona plants a kiss on his cheek. "Will, this is my old roommate, Casey." She turns to Casey. "Will's the guy I told you about from Hope Springs, the one I went tubing with on the Cowpasture River last weekend."

"Right! Very nice to meet you, Will."

A popular song plays from the sound system, and Fiona drags Will off to dance, leaving Casey alone at the table. She notices the saxophone player at the bar, guzzling down a bottled water. He smiles at an attractive brunette and leans in to speak to her.

Casey's disappointed he doesn't stop by her table when he returns to the stage. But he puckers his lips at her, blowing her a kiss, when he picks up his saxophone.

Fiona and Will remain on the dance floor throughout the second set. Casey feels like a loser sitting at the table alone. She should leave. She's fine to drive. She's only had two glasses of champagne, spaced out over several hours. But she can't drag herself away from the saxophone player's mesmerizing blue eyes.

When the set is over, he stores his instrument in a case and makes a beeline to Casey's table. "Can I buy you a drink?"

She smiles up at him. "I'm driving, and I've had my limit, but I would love a bottled water."

"One bottled water coming right up." He drops his saxophone case on the floor at her feet and wanders over to the bar. When he returns with their drinks, he sits close to Casey on the banquette.

"Your performance was amazing," she says. "How long have you been playing the saxophone?"

"As long as I can remember. Do you play an instrument?"

Casey shakes her head. "I took a few guitar lessons as a child. But I never got the hang of it. I'm an artist."

"Hobby or profession?" he asks, taking a long pull on his beer bottle.

"Both. I'm a graphic designer. What about you? Do you have a day job?

"I'm an environmental attorney. I practice with a law firm in Hope Springs, but I live here in Lovely."

"Cool. I'm Casey, by the way." She offers a hand, but he kisses her cheek instead.

"And I'm Luke. Luke Ellington. Like the late Duke Ellington except with a L."

Casey bites down on her lip, stifling a laugh. "Is that a coincidence or by design?"

Luke chuckles. "Completely a coincidence. My parents were hippies. I'm not sure they even knew who Duke Ellington was." He stands suddenly. "Dance with me."

Luke pulls Casey to her feet and leads her onto the dance floor. He spins her into his arms and holds her tight. His chest is broad, his arms strong around her, and he smells like the outdoors, fresh air and pine forest.

Several songs later, when the bartender makes the last call, Casey tears herself away from him. "I should be going."

"Did you drive?"

"I did. I met my friend here." She looks around the dance floor for Fiona. "But I guess she left with her boyfriend."

"Then I'll walk you to your car." Slinging his saxophone case over his shoulder, he presses his hand against the small of her back as he leads her to the small parking lot out back.

She clicks her doors unlocked and turns to face him. "Nice to meet you, Luke."

"Nice to meet you, Casey." Her heart dances across her chest when he brushes his lips against hers. "Can I see you again?"

"I'd like that," Casey says, and calls out her number while he enters it into his phone.

Casey floats home on a cloud. She can still feel his hands on her hips, his muscular thighs against hers. Jamie's image pops into her head as she's brushing her teeth. After crushing on him for months, she finally has a chance to be with him. Just as Luke enters her life. Why is romance always so confusing?

CHAPTER 6
ADA

Ada wakes on Sunday morning with a splitting headache. She cracks an eyelid to see Enzo lying beside her. She closes her eyes again as she pieces together last night's events. The end of the evening is a blur. She remembers dancing with Enzo at the Blue Cosmos. And she has a vague recollection of him helping her up the stairs to her apartment. She threw herself at him. Did they have sex? She lifts the covers, relieved to see she's still wearing her black dress.

Propping herself on one elbow, Ada watches him sleep. He seems so peaceful, she wonders if he's dreaming. Enzo is the quiet and serious type. But she often senses a darkness in him, like a storm blowing in from the west. She can't help but wonder what makes this enigmatic man tick. But she enjoys his company. She'd like to get to know him better. After she sorts out her disastrous family life.

Ada rolls onto her back, and when Enzo stirs, she pretends to be asleep. He gently nudges her, but she doesn't budge. And she works hard not to smile when he kisses her forehead before slipping quietly out of the room.

She drifts back to sleep and doesn't wake again until nearly one o'clock. She drags herself out of bed in search of her phone, which she finds in her purse on the bathroom counter. She has no missed calls and only one text message. Not from Daniel or her brothers, but from Enzo. *How are you feeling? Do you want company?*

Ada doesn't respond. She needs to be alone as she mourns the loss of her family. She orders delivery from Ruthie's Diner—deluxe cheeseburger and large fries—and spends the afternoon binge watching Netflix. She's grateful there's no booze in the house. She needs a clear head when she faces Daniel at work tomorrow.

Ada rises early on Monday morning. After jogging five miles, she showers and dresses in black slacks and a white silk tank with a triple strand of Tahitian pearls around her neck. Daniel gave the pearls to her mother on their twentieth wedding anniversary. They make a statement, a reminder to Daniel that, regardless of who her real father is, Ada is still Daniel's wife's daughter.

As the vineyard's event organizer, Ada's primary job is arranging weddings. And Love-Struck Winery hosts a seemingly endless number of them. She meets with a diva bride and her cantankerous mother for most of the morning.

Early afternoon, she's in her office, typing up notes from her meeting when Daniel's assistant calls. "Mr. Love needs to see you in his office ASAP."

Maria's words are not lost on Ada. Daniel is *Mr. Love* to her now.

"I'll be there in a few," Ada says in a chipper voice despite the tightness in her chest.

She saves her computer document and leaves her desk. She takes a minute to check her reflection in the mirror, smearing on a coat of fresh taupe lipstick, before going down the hall.

Charles's and Hugh's offices are in a nearby building that was once the carriage house. The rest of the administrative offices are housed on the second floor of the winery. The front of the stately stone building is traditional, while the backside is more modern. Some offices provide better views than others. Daniel's sanctum offers the best. A sloping ceiling graduates from nine to fifteen feet, and the entire exterior wall is one giant window. When Daniel is out of the office, during a thunderstorm or when it snows, Ada likes to curl up on his burgundy leather sofa with a cup of hot tea.

Daniel sits at his massive mahogany desk, staring out at the mountains. He's unaware of her presence until she clears her throat. When he spins around, he's wearing a nostalgic expression that makes Ada wonder who or what is on his mind.

He gestures at the door. "Close the door."

Ada views this as a bad sign. Except for private meetings, Daniel strictly adheres to an open-door policy.

She does as she's told and sits down opposite him.

He steeples his fingers. "I value the work you do for the business, and I don't want to lose you. I hope you'll consider staying on. Your pay will not change. However, I'm revoking your interest in the business."

Ada's head jolts backward. "Are you saying you're taking away my shares?"

"You're very perceptive," he says in a sarcastic tone.

Ada springs to her feet. "You can't do that!"

"I can. And I am," Daniel says, a steely edge to his voice.

"I'm not an employee." She jabs her thumb into her chest. "I'm Ada, your little girl. You raised me."

"This family is about more than sons and daughters, mothers and fathers. Our ancestors built this vineyard. And it's our duty to keep ownership in the family. With the blood kin."

Ada realizes there's no point in arguing with him. The hard set of his jaw warns her he won't change his mind. Her throat swells and tears threaten, but she refuses to let him see her cry. Spinning on her heels, Ada storms out of his office, slamming the door behind her. She marches down the hall to the stairs and out the front of the building.

Hugh and Charles are meeting in Hugh's office when she bursts in. "Daniel just took away my shares."

Hugh shrugs. "You know how he is about Love blood," he says, using air quotes.

Ada stills. "You already know about this?"

"Dad called a meeting earlier to warn us," Charles explains.

Ada's stomach knots. "Was Goldilocks there?" When Charles doesn't answer, she shifts her gaze back to Hugh.

Hugh gives his head a solemn nod. "She was."

"We can't let him get away with this. The two of you have to help me come up with a plan."

Hugh folds his arms over his chest. "I'm sorry, Ada. But you're on your own this time. I already tried talking to him, but he's being stubborn."

Ada looks from Hugh to Charles, who averts his eyes. "Thanks a lot. What am I supposed to do?"

"Now might be a good time to make a change," Hugh says. "You're always talking about moving, about trying life in a big city."

Ada's jaw hits the floor. Never before as she mentioned moving to a city. "Grrr! This is so unfair."

She stomps out of his office, and she's barging through the exterior doors when she crashes into Sheldon. He grabs her arm to prevent her from falling.

"Get your hands off of me." She shoves him hard and scurries away.

"Wait!" He runs after her. "What's wrong?"

She cast a sideways glance at him but keeps walking. "Stop pretending like you don't know. Daniel kicked me out of the family."

Sheldon grabs her arm, stopping her. "You're being melodramatic. He didn't kick you out of the family."

She glares at him. "Like hell he didn't. This isn't my fault. Why is he punishing me?"

"He's not punishing you. You're just the target of his anger. Dad is pissed at Mom, and he's taking it out on you. He'll calm down, eventually."

"No, he won't. You should've seen him just now." She points a red lacquered fingernail at the winery. "He means business, and he's as stubborn as they come. His precious Love blood means more to him than his relationship with the girl he raised from birth. And since my blood is red and not blue like yours, my association with the family is now null and void."

"Seriously, Ada. Chill out. You sound like a whack job."

"Hugh thinks I should move. Is that what you think, Sheldon? That I should start a new life somewhere else?"

He shrugs. "You've got plenty of talent and experience. You could try something different. It doesn't have to be event planning. You'd make an excellent influencer. Your Pinterest boards and Instagram accounts will earn you whatever kind of marketing job you want."

She jerks her arm away and continues toward the parking lot.

"Where are you going?" Sheldon calls after her.

"To the city. To start a new life," she tosses back over her shoulder.

"Don't do anything rash until things settle down. I'll talk to Dad for you. I can be persuasive."

Ada gets in her car, but she doesn't start the engine. She palms the steering wheel. "To hell with all of them."

Ada has never considered moving to a new city. She's never wanted to be anywhere but right here at this vineyard. Her senior year in high school, she applied to only one college—Jefferson College over in Hope Springs. And she flunked out after one semester. Not because the academics were too challenging, but because she hated going to class. She couldn't stand the sorority girls with their phony smiles and frat boys who were only interested in sex. Over Christmas break, when she showed her father her grades, she begged him to let her work at the vineyard. Their wedding business was taking off, and they desperately needed an event planner. And she's made a name for herself. Thanks to Ada, Love-Struck has become a major wedding destination.

Ada rests her head against the seat. She has nowhere to go

except her apartment, and she doesn't want to be alone. Then again, she would be alone in a room full of people. Her mother is dead. The man she has called father all her life has disowned her. And her brothers are too self-centered to care about anybody but themselves. If she weren't such a bitch, she would have more friends. Might even be married. Perhaps she *should* make a fresh start with a clean slate. She has a small savings account. And Sheldon's right. She has an impressive resume. But she'd be a nobody working a menial job in a strange city and no family with which to spend holidays. There's something to be said about being a big fish in a small town. She can't let Daniel get away with punishing her for her mother's sins. Ada was never one to give up on a fight. And she has no intention of starting now.

CHAPTER 7
OLLIE

Ollie's day couldn't possibly get any worse. The tractor won't start, and The Foxhole's brand-new commercial ice maker isn't working.

She accuses Fiona. "What'd you do to the ice maker?"

Fiona gives her the stink eye. "Nothing! It's your fault for buying a subpar machine."

Ollie glares back at her. "It's in your kitchen, your domain, which makes you responsible."

Fiona bangs a pot down on the stove. "I'm tired of you blaming me every time something goes wrong around here."

Ollie turns her back on Fiona and storms out of The Foxhole. Up at the house, she slices a juicy summer tomato and dumps a spoonful of tuna salad on top. She sits down at the breakfast counter with her plate and stuffs a forkful of tuna salad into her mouth. But the tuna tastes fishy, and she spits it out into her napkin. Where did the tuna salad come from? Then she remembers she bought it at Delilah's over a week ago. No wonder it tastes fishy.

Ollie slides her plate away. She has no appetite anyway. Maybe she's having a delayed reaction to her breakup with Jamie. She misses him, and she's disappointed he hasn't called, even though she knows it's for the best.

Ollie's chest tightens with the old familiar panic. Her skin feels clammy and sweat trickles down her back. She can't breathe. She needs air. Sliding off the barstool, she stumbles through the open french doors onto the screened porch. Collapsing in a wicker rocker, she inhales and exhales until her breath steadies. She hasn't had a panic attack since she bought the farm. Why now? What triggered it? Is it the prospect of being alone?

Ollie hears the crunch of gravel in the driveway, and Sheldon's Range Rover comes into view. He parks beside the porch and gets out. When he sees her sitting with her head bowed, he crosses the porch and kneels down beside her chair. "What's wrong, Ollie? You don't look well. Are you sick?"

"Jamie and I broke up."

He strokes her arm. "I heard. Is there's something else bothering you?"

For someone who hardly knows her, Sheldon has an uncanny ability of reading her moods. "I'm fine." But as the words leave her mouth, tears well in her eyes and slide down her cheeks.

This is it, she thinks. *The breakdown that follows the panic attacks.*

"You are clearly not fine." Sheldon pulls her to her feet and holds her tight while she sobs. He strokes her hair and whispers encouraging words until the crying subsides.

Taking her by the hand, he says, "Come on! Let's go for a walk."

At least she no longer has to worry about Jamie seeing them together. His unfounded jealousy toward Sheldon had grown tiresome. Perhaps Jamie sensed the chemistry between Ollie and Sheldon, the undeniable attraction Ollie has been trying unsuccessfully to ignore for months.

She allows Sheldon to lead her off the porch and down the steps. Instead of going toward The Foxhole, they walk in the opposite direction toward the road. When they reach the farm's entrance, they turn around and look back at her property—the black split-rail fence lining the driveway to her gray farmhouse with its sunny yellow door.

Sheldon spreads his arms wide. "Look at all this. You're creating something special here. This boutique vineyard belongs to you. Think of it as your foundation. When something goes wrong, you grab onto it like a rock and hold tight. This place, your new home, will see you through the difficult times."

Ollie nods, but she doesn't speak for fear she might cry again. Sheldon gets it. He understands how she feels about the farm. The way she felt about Hendrix Estates, her family's home in Napa. The way Sheldon must feel about Love-Struck. Jamie never understood her devotion to this place. Foxtail is more than a business. It's the core of her existence.

They sit down on the ground in the shade of a cherry blossom tree with their knees tucked beneath their chins.

Sheldon leans into her. "Tell me the truth. Are you really upset about Jamie or is it something else?"

Ollie lets out a sigh and sags against the tree. "I don't know what it is, honestly. I can't seem to control my emotions these days. This anger has taken hold of me and won't let go. I don't know where it's coming from. As you just pointed out, I have everything I've ever wanted. Why am I not walking on air? I lashed out at Fiona earlier about a broken ice maker. And right before you came, I had a panic attack. I haven't had one of those since I bought the farm, and it scared me."

"Maybe this is a delayed reaction to your parents' deaths?"

Ollie shrugs. "Maybe. But it's been two years. Shouldn't I be over it by now?"

"Some people never get over great losses. And your brother's involvement in their deaths compounds your grief. Have you ever talked to a therapist about your anxiety?"

"So many I can't remember their names. They don't help."

"Then you haven't met Veronica Mason, the most renowned psychiatrist on the East Coast who happens to live in Lovely. Right over there."

She follows his gaze to the cluster of buildings atop the mountain on the next ridge over. "I've wondered about that place. It looks like some sort of compound."

"Those are Ronnie's swanky facilities for long-term patients. It's like a luxury wilderness spa for the mentally unstable."

Mentally unstable? Is that what I am? Ollie asks herself. And she's surprised at her answer. *Something is definitely off inside your brain.*

"How well do you know this Ronnie person?"

"Intimately. We dated in high school." Sheldon chuckles. "We broke up our senior year. I got tired of her trying to psychoanalyze me. We've remained close friends. Would you like me to provide the introductions?"

Irritation flashes through her. Why do the Loves think they own the universe? "I can introduce myself."

Sheldon pauses a beat. "I'm not like my brothers, Ollie. I'm a good guy. Stop being so stubborn and let me be your friend."

Ollie suspects he wants to be more than friends. But he's trying to help, and she's being unreasonably difficult. "I'm sorry, Sheldon. Stubborn is my middle name," she says in a teasing tone. "How about if I use your name as a reference?"

"That works. You can check out her website. Google Tranquil Mind, Peaceful Heart."

"Seriously? That's the name?"

Sheldon smiles. "Believe it or not. When you see the place, you'll understand why."

"I doubt any therapist can make my mind tranquil and heart peaceful." Ollie gets to her feet. "I need to get back to work."

Sheldon stands, and they start back toward the house. "Give it some thought. You don't have to decide anything today."

"Who would take care of Foxtail while I'm gone?"

"I could look after things for you," Sheldon volunteers.

Ollie grunts. "I'm sure that would go over well with your father."

"Dad would be all for it. He's eager to make amends for the rotten things my brothers have done to you."

"Thanks, but I'll figure something out," Ollie says. She's not at all comfortable with a member of the Love family running her farm. Not even Sheldon. Not even for a day.

Back at the house, Sheldon takes off in his Range Rover, and Ollie hurries to her office to google Tranquil Mind, Peaceful Heart. The gallery of photos is stunning. They offer private accommodations, and every patient receives daily group and individual therapy.

Ollie studies the faces of the patients in the photographs. Most appear clean-cut, but their woebegone expressions reveal their deep-seated sorrow. Ollie doesn't belong here. She can manage her problems on her own. Once she gets through her first harvest season, she'll treat herself to a long weekend at a real spa, complete with facials and massages and decadent food.

Ollie works in her office until midafternoon when she ventures down to The Foxhole to help Fiona clean up and reset for the next day.

"How was the lunch crowd today?" Ollie asks as they straighten the cafe.

"Fine." Shoving a chair under a table, Fiona barrels past Ollie and bursts through the double doors.

Ollie sighs and follows her into the kitchen, where Fiona is scrubbing the commercial griddle with a vengeance. "You're mad at me about the ice maker. And I don't blame you. I'm sorry. I was out of line. I'm not myself right now. Breaking up with Jamie is for the best. But it's still hard."

Fiona spins around to face her. "You've changed these past few weeks, Ollie. Your temper tantrums have gotten progressively worse. It's so bad now, I dread coming to work. Maybe some of your anger has to do with Jamie. But I think there's something else wrong. You need to figure it out soon, because I can't take much more."

Ollie holds her gaze steady. "Are you threatening to quit?"

"You may leave me no choice. This hostile work environment is really dragging me down."

Ollie gulps back fear. She can't afford to lose her chef. "I didn't realize you were unhappy. I'll do better, Fiona. Just give me another chance."

"One more chance," Fiona says, her finger aimed at the ceiling. "Then I'm out of here. You can't treat people this way."

"You're right. And I promise, I won't let you down."

Ollie and Fiona finish cleaning up in silence. Ollie has always avoided prescription meds in the past. She prefers to manage her anxiety with exercise and meditation. But neither work for her anymore. Her previous doctor prescribed sleeping pills and anti-anxiety meds. She filled the prescriptions but took none of the medication. Maybe if she sleeps better, she'll feel more rested and less on edge. She doesn't need a shrink. If she works harder, she can manage her anger on her own.

CHAPTER 8
CASEY

Casey holds her breath while Daniel studies her proposed label. Massaging his chin, he says, "It's um . . ."

"Boring." Casey snatches the mockup off the easel and returns to her seat across from Daniel at the conference table.

"Okay, well, maybe it's a little vanilla," he admits.

"I was going for simple elegance," Casey says, staring down at the graphic in her hands.

"Then you accomplished your objective. But I don't want simple elegance. I want extraordinary. Give me what you gave Ollie for Foxtail Farm."

"I created a mascot for Foxtail. Fancy the Fox works for them. I don't see us using pink hearts to promote Love-Struck."

"Most definitely not," Daniel says, his lip curling in distaste. "This is your first stab at the project. I trust you'll come up with the right concept."

Casey wishes she had as much confidence in her as Daniel does.

"How's the hiring going?" Daniel asks.

Casey flaps her hand. "So-so. Our charming town has a shortage of marketing experts. How do you feel about taking a chance on someone with no experience? I'm talking to a young woman tomorrow. She just got her master's degree in Commerce with a concentration in marketing from UVA."

Daniel pauses to consider the idea. "That could actually be a good thing. We can train her to our ways. I view her youth as a bonus as long as she has a fresh perspective like you."

"Or not so fresh as evidence by this," Casey says, tearing the mockup in half.

"Don't be so hard on yourself, Casey. It's a process. Discovering what we don't want will help us figure out what we do." Daniel stands and comes around to her side of the table.

As she gathers her belongings, Casey says, "Can't you give me some idea of what you're looking for? Something more substantial than extraordinary."

"Nope. I'll know it when I see it."

Casey smiles up at him. "Thanks for nothing."

She leaves the conference room and goes down the hall to her office, where she collapses in her desk chair. She's twirling a strand of hair, racking her brain for branding ideas, when Fiona appears in the doorway.

"Nice digs, girlfriend! And that view is amazing." Fiona comes around the desk to the window. "Is Love-Struck hiring?"

Casey stands beside her. "We are, actually. What do you know about marketing?"

"Aside from posting pics of food on Instagram, absolutely nothing."

"Too bad, because I could use some inspiration. The Fancy the Fox branding came to me out of thin air. But for the life of me, I can't come up with a concept that excites me for Love-Struck."

"The moods of our wines inspired you for the Foxtail labels. I assume you've tasted the wines here."

Casey glances at the door and lowers her voice. "I don't want Daniel to hear me say this, even though he knows it's true, but our wine sucks. He's hiring a new winemaker and revamping all the varietals. Hence the reason for the rebranding. But Daniel refuses to give me any direction. He says he'll know it when he sees it."

"Why don't you come up with a wide variety of designs? That would give you an idea of his tastes."

Casey considers this before responding. "Brilliant suggestion! Delilah's has a generous selection of wines. I'll go check out her labels," she says, retrieving her purse from her bottom desk drawer.

"I have a better idea." Fiona's thumbs fly across her phone's screen. She pauses, and seconds later, her phone pings with an incoming text. "Come on. We're going on a field trip." She loops her arm through Casey's and drags her out of the office and down the hall.

"A field trip where?" Casey asks when they reach the parking lot.

"To Hope Springs." Fiona starts her engine and puts the car in reverse. "The Inn at Hope Springs has an extensive collection of wines. Lucy, the sommelier, is starting a tasting for their guests at five o'clock."

Casey looks at her watch. "That's in ten minutes."

"We'll be fine. Lucy always conducts a tour of the cave before the tasting."

Casey glances down at her gray dress and matching heels. "I'm not dressed for traipsing around in a cave."

"The *cave* is how I refer to the basement wine cellar. It's seriously cool, although kinda creepy too." Fiona looks over at Casey. "By the way, I'm sorry for bailing on you on Saturday night. I had no idea Will was planning to come."

"No worries. I'm glad you found someone who lights your fire."

"He definitely does that." Fiona returns her attention to the road. "You'll be relieved to know my crush on you is officially over."

"You can crush me anytime. I was flattered in a weird way."

"So, how'd it go with the sexy saxophone player?" Fiona asks. "Did you hook up with him?"

"I don't hookup with strangers, Fi. Although he walked me to my car and kissed me. I gave him my number, but he hasn't called yet," Casey says with a long face.

"Duh. It's only Monday. Give him a chance."

"I realize that. And truthfully, the timing is all wrong. I don't want to mess up my chances with Jamie."

"I've changed my mind about you and Jamie. I think you should stay away from him. At least for now. He stopped by The Foxhole this afternoon to see Ollie. Thank goodness she was working in the vineyard. He's a total mess. I had to talk him off the ledge. He was going to beg her to give him another chance."

Casey's spirits tank. Making her move on Jamie might take longer than she expected. "That's not cool. How is Ollie taking it?"

"She's angrier than ever. You won't believe what happened this morning," Fiona says and tells Casey about Ollie's outburst over a broken ice machine.

"Whoa. She's really a loose cannon. Did she apologize?" Casey asks, staring out the window at the sights as they drive down Main Street in Hope Springs.

"Yes. And she seemed genuinely sorry. But I set her straight. Someone had to. I love Ollie, and I understand she's going through a difficult time, but she needs to get her act together before she runs off all her employees."

"Good for you for standing up to her. Ollie's hard-headed. A little tough love is exactly what she needs right now." Casey thumbs off a text to Sheldon, alerting him to this latest development.

They are turning into the entrance at Hope Springs Farm when he texts back. *I tried to talk to her this morning. I suggested a local psychiatrist who can help with her anger issues. Unfortunately, I'm not sure I got through to her.*

Fiona turns the car over to the valet attendant, and they enter the inn. She introduces Casey to her old friends at the front desk, and they take the elevator down to the basement. The ceiling is low and lighting dim. Wine racks line the narrow hall that stretches as far as the eye can see, and uncorked bottles of wine wait to be consumed on a large oak table.

The sommelier motions them over. "Just in time. We were getting ready to start."

Fiona and Casey join the other guests, making their way to the table. The sommelier's knowledge of wine is impressive, and Casey learns a lot during the hour-long tasting. Afterward, while the guests place orders for cases of wine, Fiona runs up to the kitchen to speak to her friend, Cecily, leaving Casey to wander the basement hall, studying the various labels. She takes pictures of the ones she likes best and makes notes on her phone of the ideas reeling in her mind.

"I have a little wine buzz," Casey says as they are waiting for the valet attendant to bring Fiona's car. "If you're not okay to drive, we can get a bite to eat while we sober up."

Fiona waves away her concern. "I only took small sips. Normally, I'd love to grab dinner, but I have some chores I need to do at home."

"That's cool. I need to get home anyway." The car arrives, and they climb into their respective sides. "Thank you for bringing me here. Not only did I learn a lot, I now have a ton of ideas."

Fiona smiles over at her as she pulls away from the inn. "Yay! Mission accomplished."

Casey accesses her photo app and scrolls through the pictures she took of the wine labels. She's staring at the screen when a text from Jamie pops up. *I need to see you. I'm really struggling. I'm worried I might hurt myself.*

Casey's skin turns cold, and she texts back. *I'm on my way home from a wine tasting in Hope Springs. Can you meet me at Love-Struck? I'll be there in ten minutes.*

He responds with a thumbs-up emoji. At least Jamie considers

Casey a good enough friend to reach out to her in his time of need.

He's waiting in front of Daniel's house when Fiona drops her off. He gestures at the gray SUV parked in front of her Volvo. "Is that your dad's Tahoe? Because I really don't wanna see anyone right now."

Casey doesn't blame him. He looks like walking death with a scraggly beard and dark circles under his puffy eyes. "Let's go out back to the pool," she says, and leads him around the side of the house.

He drops to a chaise lounge and buries his face in his hands. He lets out a blood-curdling cry that sounds like a wounded coyote. "This hurts so much, Casey," he sobs into his hands with shoulders heaving. "I was going to marry her. We were going to live happily ever after. Now she's gone, and I have nothing left to live for."

Casey's heart breaks for him, even if his is breaking for another woman. She eases down beside him and places her arm around his waist. "You have plenty to live for, Jamie. A loving family. A job you're good at."

"I hate selling houses," he snaps. "My plan was to quit real estate and work the farm with Ollie."

That would've been a disaster, Casey thinks. She pulls him in tighter. "You'll feel better soon. You just need to give it some time."

Jamie shoves her away. "What I need is a drink," he says, swiping at his eyes.

"A drink is the last thing you need. It'll only make you feel worse."

Jamie studies Casey's face for a long minute. His blank expression gives nothing away.

Casey remembers having suicidal thoughts when she broke up with her college boyfriend of two years. She'd run straight home to her mother, and they'd spent a snowy February weekend binge-watching rom coms. Her mother's undivided attention had gotten her through those dark days.

"What you really need is a reset. Why don't you stay with your parents for a few days? Let them fuss over you."

Jamie's face lights up, as though he hasn't considered this. "I might just do that. I could use a big dose of home right now. My parents never approved of Ollie. They thought she was too old for me."

Casey leans into him. "Funny how parents usually know what's best for us."

"Ollie and I had some issues. But I really loved her, and I thought we could overcome the obstacles." Jamie gets to his feet. "Thanks for being here for me."

Casey stands to face him. "What are friends for? You can call me anytime."

She walks him out, this time passing through the house on the way to the driveway. Casey waves as she watches him drive away. While he's clearly suffering, he appears to be coming to terms with his breakup. If Casey is patient and plays her cards right, their friendship might morph into a more meaningful relationship down the road.

CHAPTER 9
ADA

Ada is locking up the winery on Tuesday evening when she notices her father and Casey in the parking lot, standing beside a shiny white convertible Mercedes. They are close enough for Ada to read their lips.

"I can't. It's too much," Casey says, shaking her head.

Daniel places the key in her palm. "I want you to have it."

Casey bounces on her toes. "Thank you so much!"

Ada burns with fury as she turns away from the door. First a car. Next, it'll be a piece of jewelry, a diamond tennis bracelet or a pair of diamond stud earrings. Ada was once the recipient of expensive trinkets, tokens of her father's love. He's thrown Ada out like yesterday's trash, and Casey is now the sole object of his affection.

Ada pours a glass of Petit Verdot and takes it over to the window. She's deep in thought, watching the sky change from yellow to orange to pink, when Enzo pounds on the door.

She crosses the tasting room to let him in. "What're you doing here?"

"I saw your car out front, and I thought I'd check on you. How're you holding up?"

"Not so good." Ada returns to the tasting table and pours

more wine into her glass. "Daniel took away my shares in the company. He's allowing me to keep my job. But only because he wouldn't know what to tell his friends if he fires me. Goldilocks has basically taken my place in the family. A few minutes ago, he presented her with a new car."

"I'm sorry, Ada. I know this is hard for you. But getting drunk won't help." He takes the wine away from her. "Let me cook you dinner."

Ada arches a manicured eyebrow. "You know how to cook?"

"I'm Italian. Of course I know how to cook."

How scandalous would it be for her to go on a date with a field hand? Daniel would not be happy. All the more reason for her to go. "Where do you live?"

"In town. Not too far from your apartment, actually. We can drop your car off, and I'll walk you home later."

Ada hesitates. "Can we take the wine?" she asks, eyeing the Petit Verdot.

Mischief tugs at his lips. "I can offer you a much better selection of wine at my house."

Ada laughs. "That wouldn't be hard to do." She grabs her purse from the behind the bar. "Let's do it. Suddenly I want to put as much distance between Daniel Love and me as possible."

———

Enzo's moss green bungalow is charming, with a small front porch and tidy yard. He unlocks the front door, and they enter a living room with walls and trim painted a high-gloss navy blue and handsome furnishings and rugs.

Ada circles the room. "I can't believe your landlord let you paint such dramatic colors."

"I am the landlord, Ada," he says, and leads her into a chef's kitchen with stainless steel appliances and marble countertops.

"Whoa. Exactly how much are we paying you?"

Enzo's face darkens. He opens his mouth to speak and stops

himself. He removes a bottle from a wine refrigerator and unscrews the cork. "Now, for the wine I was telling you about. This time of year, I prefer the refreshingly light Albariño."

He pours a splash and hands her the glass. She takes a tentative sip. "This is delicious. I've never even heard of Albariño."

"It's grown mostly in northwest Spain and Portugal." He fills a glass for himself and begins dicing tomatoes.

"What can I do to help?"

"You can make a salad." He brandishes his knife at the refrigerator. "I have plenty of greens and vegetables."

"Where in Italy are you from?" Ada asks as she rummages for salad ingredients.

"Taranto, a coastal city in Pulia. Which is basically the heel of the boot in southern Italy."

"Do you have family in Italy?" Ada asks, tearing cos lettuce into a bowl.

"My parents died in a car accident a few years back, and I'm an only child. But the rest of my relatives still live in different parts of Italy." Enzo fills a pot with water and places it on the stove to boil. "I came to the states to find a new direction for my life. Waiting tables at an exclusive men's club in Richmond inspired me to become a sommelier. I figured I might as well learn the business from the ground up while I'm studying. Hence the reason I took the job at Love-Struck."

"I'm impressed," Ada says. She's also intrigued. There's more to this guy than meets the eye.

Enzo adds pasta to the boiling water. "When Daniel hires the new winemaker, I'm hoping he'll let me be his apprentice."

Ada brings a knife down on a cucumber, chopping the end off. "If you're buttering me up for a promotion, you picked the wrong daughter. I'm currently out of favor with Daniel. You should hit on Casey."

Enzo's dark eyes smolder. "I don't need a promotion, Ada. Any more than I need this job."

A pang of guilt tightens her chest. Why does she always put

her foot in her mouth? "I'm sorry, Enzo. You should know by now I have a bad habit of offending everyone around me."

An awkward silence settles over them as they finish preparing the meal. Ada sets two places at the kitchen counter with place-mats and flatware and a fat vanilla pillar candle. Enzo's pasta dish is simple but delicious with fresh tomatoes, garlic, basil, and mozzarella.

"Why do you do it?" he asks, twirling noodles around his fork.

She cast a sidelong glance at him. "Why do I do what?"

"Offend everyone around you?"

"It's a defense mechanism I learned from having three older brothers." She stabs her salad with her fork. "I take that back. I can't blame my brothers for my flaws. The truth is, Enzo, I'm just a bitch."

He chuckles. "I admire your honesty. And I prefer to think of you as ballsy. I also think you're unhappy."

Ada lets out a sigh. "Is anyone ever really happy, Enzo?"

"I was. As a child. Weren't you?" Enzo cuts his eyes at her as he stuffs a chunk of crusty bread in his mouth.

"Not really. My parents had a miserable marriage. They fought all the time. I was pretty lonely, living on the vineyard with no friends nearby to play with."

"We must always strive for happiness, Ada. If we lose hope of ever finding it, we're doomed to a life of misery." He gets up and carries his plate to the sink.

She joins him in rinsing the dishes and placing them in the dishwasher. "That really hit the spot, Enzo. You're an excellent cook. Thank you."

"You're welcome." He grabs the wine bottle. "Let's finish this outside."

She follows him through the back door to a small patio where four lounge chairs are grouped together around a fire pit. They sit side-by-side, listening to crickets chirp and staring up at the bright stars in the inky sky.

"You know what you need?" Enzo asks and doesn't wait for her to answer. "A distraction."

"Who? You?" A seductive smile spreads across her lips as she walks her fingers up his arm.

"I'll be your distraction anytime." He takes her hand and kisses the tips of her fingers. "But I was talking about your biological father. You should try to find him."

Ada jerks her hand away. "Why do you keep bringing that up?"

"Because it's a challenge, something to take your mind off Daniel and Casey."

They sit in silence for a minute while Ada considers looking for her biological father. "I guess I could start by sending my DNA to one of those genetic websites. Although that's a long shot."

"You never know until you try. You could also look through your mother's belongings. You might find a clue in a letter or diary."

"I'm not sure Daniel kept much, but I could search the attic." Ada thumbs the rim of her wineglass. "I'm afraid, Enzo. What if I find out my father is an axe murderer?"

Enzo chuckles. "You and I both know that's highly unlikely." He gets up and pulls Ada into his arms. "Even if you don't find your biological father, you might learn more about your mom and her relationship with Daniel. Something that might help you decide what it is you really want from your family. From your life."

"That would be helpful. Right now, I have no clue what I want." Ada looks up at Enzo. "How'd you get to be so smart?"

"I don't consider myself smart. But I have strong intuitions. And you and I are kindred spirits."

Ada rests her head on his chest. She can't remember her last meaningful relationship. It was with some local boy she dated for about six months in her early twenties. She doesn't even remember his name now. She could get used to evenings like this. A healthy dinner followed by a glass of wine under the stars.

Maybe a walk to town for an after-dinner drink at Blue Cosmos. Or watching a movie by the fire in the winter. Ada has never given much thought to having children. She always assumed one day she would. Enzo will be a loving father.

There's only one problem. Daniel has in mind for Ada to marry a doctor or lawyer, someone with the same social status as the almighty Love family. He would never approve of her marrying a blue-collar farm worker. Then again, she doubts Daniel will foot the bill for her wedding, let alone walk her down the aisle. Enzo's right. She needs to figure out what it is she really wants from her family. Or if there's anything left for her with the Loves.

CHAPTER 10
OLLIE

Ollie is a walking zombie. The sleeping pills give her a hangover. And while the Xanax takes the edge off her panic attacks, she's having to take increasingly more than the prescribe dosage to be effective. On the bright side, she's made it through two whole days without an angry outburst.

After spending the first part of the day in the vineyard, Ollie ventures down to The Foxhole on Thursday afternoon to help Fiona wrap up from the lunch rush. When she enters the cafe, she hears laughter coming from the kitchen. She tiptoes across the room and peeks through the window.

Jamie and Fiona are standing together near the griddle. He's smiling playfully at her, and she's flirtatiously batting her eyelashes at him while toying with the short hairs of her pixie cut. Are they seeing each other now? Ollie removes a pill bottle from her pocket and pops a Xanax in her mouth. She doesn't want Jamie, but she doesn't want anyone else to have him, either.

She kicks the swinging door open. "What's going on in here?"

Jamie freezes, and Fiona's eyes grow wide. "Nothing. We were just talking," Fiona says with a hint of irritation in her voice.

Jamie retrieves a Styrofoam container from the counter. "I

stopped by to pick up my take-out order. Thanks, Fiona. I'll see you around," he says and slinks out of the kitchen.

Ollie stares Fiona down. "Are the two of you hooking up now?"

Fiona's head jerks back as though she's been slapped. "What? No! I can't believe you'd think such a thing. You and I are friends, Ollie. At least I thought we were."

"We are. Which is why it wouldn't be cool for you to start seeing my ex so soon after we broke up."

"You have nothing to worry about. I'm dating someone. He lives in Hope Springs." Fiona turns away from Ollie and walks over to the sink.

Ollie goes to stand behind her. "Did Jamie ask about me?"

"Nope. He was only here a minute."

This hurts more than Ollie will admit. She wants what's best for Jamie, and that is definitely not Ollie. Still, she misses his company. "How was the lunch shift today?"

"Crowded. We broke our record of tables served." Fiona turns on the hot water and squeezes liquid detergent into a sink filled with dirty pots.

"That's good news! I'll go close out the register and see how much we made."

Returning to the tasting room, Ollie removes the money from the cash drawer and prints a tape of credit card charges. She sits down at a table to sort out the proceeds. The number of patrons who still pay in cash surprises Ollie. And today there is over a thousand dollars in the drawer. But as she adds up the sales receipts, she realizes a hundred dollars is missing.

"Fiona! Get in here!" she screams, her voice echoing in the vast room.

Fiona bursts through the double doors. "What's wrong, Ollie? Are you okay?"

Ollie shoots out of her chair like a rocket. "There's a hundred dollars missing."

Fiona places her hand on her chest. "You scared me. For a minute, I thought something really bad had happened."

"Stealing *is* really bad." She gets close to Fiona's face. "Did you take the money?"

"You're joking, right? You know I don't handle the money."

Ollie stares her down. "If not you, then who?"

"One of our four servers. Not that I think any of them would steal." Fiona tugs off her apron. "This is the final straw. I quit." She tosses her apron on the checkout counter and storms out of the cafe.

Ollie is too weary to go after her. She removes her prescription bottle from her pocket and drops back down to her chair. Unscrewing the lid, she spills the contents of the bottle onto the table and counts the white pills. She only has six left. She pops one in her mouth. Now five. At this rate of consumption, her supply won't last another twenty-four hours. With no doctor to prescribe more, she'll have to find another source. She's now, officially, a junkie.

Ollie plants her elbows on the table and sobs into her hands. She's crying so hard she doesn't hear Sheldon come in until she feels a hand on her shoulder.

"What's wrong, Ollie?"

"I'm such a mess," she cries. "I need help."

He picks up the pill bottle and reads the label. "How long have you been taking Xanax?"

Ollie drops her hands and gulps in deep breaths of air. "Only a few days. But my usage is already out of control." She snatches a handful of napkins from the dispenser and falls back in her chair, blowing her nose into the napkins. "I've tried everything. The pills were the last resort. They don't work either."

"Did you call Dr. Ronnie?"

Ollie shakes her head. "I looked her up online, but I thought I could handle it myself."

Sheldon eyes the neat stacks of paper currency on the table. "What happened that made you so upset?"

"The cash drawer is short a hundred dollars. I accused Fiona of stealing from me." Ollie chokes back a sob. "And she quit."

"That's not good. You need to do something." He slides his phone across the table to Ollie. "Call Ronnie."

Ollie slides the phone back to him. "You do it," she says and adds, "Please."

"I'll get her on the phone, but you have to talk to her." He clicks on a stored contact and waits while the call connects. When he reaches voice mail, he leaves a message. "Hey, Ronnie. My friend desperately needs your help. I'm with her now. You can reach us on my cell."

Sheldon hangs up and places the phone on the table between them. "While we wait for her to call us back, let's see if we solve the mystery of the missing money." When they tally the sales receipts and count the cash, they determine no money is missing. They check twice more with the same results.

"I don't understand. I must have miscalculated," Ollie says.

"It's probably the drugs. You must get hold of this now, Ollie. Otherwise, you'll risk losing everything you've worked for."

Ollie lowers her gaze. "I know."

When Sheldon's phone rings, he snatches it up and walks to the far end of the room. Ollie can't hear what he's saying, but his expression is grave as he paces in front of the fireplace.

He returns to the table and hands Ollie the phone. "Your turn."

Ollie takes the phone and, in a meek voice, says, "Hello."

"Hey, Ollie. Ronnie Mason here. I understand you're struggling with some pretty serious issues."

The psychiatrist's voice is warm, setting Ollie at ease. "I'm not sure what my problem is, honestly. It could be a delayed reaction to my parents' death two years ago," she says, and briefly explains about her brother starting the fire that killed their parents.

"Where were you at the time of the fire?" Dr. Mason asks.

Ollie inhales a deep breath and spits out the answer. "Passed out drunk on the sofa in the living room."

"Could you have gotten them out if you'd been sober?"

While the question takes Ollie aback, she approves of the psychiatrist's direct approach. "My ex-husband is the one who dragged me out of the house. He couldn't get to my parents. Flames engulfed the house. It went up like a tinderbox. My brother confessed to starting the fire. He intended for me to die as well."

"No wonder you're suffering, after all you've been through. We could try outpatient treatment, but based on what you've told me, I believe you'd benefit from a week of in-house therapy. I have an opening coming up on Sunday. I realize it's short notice. But you'll be home in time for the Fourth of July."

Ollie's mind races. "That's three days from now. I'll need to find someone to oversee my business while I'm gone. Can you give me until tomorrow morning to figure things out?"

"Of course. Let me know what you decide."

"Thank you so much, Dr. Mason."

"You're more than welcome, Ollie. And please, call me Ronnie. Everyone does."

Ollie thanks the doctor and ends the call.

"My offer still stands," Sheldon says. "I'm capable of overseeing the farm while you're gone."

"I have a potential solution to that. But I have an even bigger problem. My chef just quit on me, and I'll have to close The Foxhole, which could be catastrophic to business considering we only opened a few weeks ago."

"Come on, Ollie. Fiona's a good kid. She'll forgive you once she finds out you've committed yourself to a week of intensive mental therapy."

"I hope you're right. Excuse me a minute." Ollie pushes back from the table and goes outside to the terrace where she places a call to Melvin Bass, Foxtail Farm's previous owner. Ollie and Melvin became friends during the transfer of the farm's ownership. He insisted she call him anytime she needs help. She hopes he meant it.

Melvin answers right away. "Ollie, how wonderful to hear from you! I hope nothing's wrong."

"Everything's great at the farm," she says, and explains her situation. "I have an opportunity to spend a week at Tranquil Mind, Peaceful Heart. I was wondering if you'd consider overseeing the vineyard while I'm gone. I'll buy your airplane ticket and pay you a handsome salary for the week. I know it's asking a lot. But there's no one I trust more than you."

"Are you kidding? I'd be thrilled. It's hot as Hades in Arizona right now. I relish the opportunity to breathe in the cool mountain air."

"You're a lifesaver, Melvin. I can't tell you how much this means to me."

"Happy to help," Melvin says.

"I've hit rock bottom," Ollie admits. "I'm actually looking forward to a week of being psychoanalyzed."

Melvin chuckles. "You're in excellent hands. I had a few sessions with Ronnie myself after my wife died. I'll text you my flight information when I have it."

Ollie feels pounds lighter as she pockets the phone and returns to Sheldon. "Melvin's coming to run the vineyard in my absence."

Sheldon appears relieved. "That's the perfect solution."

"Can I count on you as backup if anything goes wrong?"

"You've got it. Would you like me to drive you over to Tranquil Mind, Peaceful Heart on Sunday?"

Tears of gratitude fill her eyes. She's never been more afraid or alone. "Please."

Sheldon pulls her into his arms and holds her tight. As though reading her mind, he says, "I've got your back, Ollie. You're not alone. I will see you through this."

Ollie relishes the comfort of his muscular arms. He's so different from Jamie. He's confident and assertive. He's a man.

She draws away from him. "Okay then," she says, swiping at her eyes. "Let me lock up here so I can track down Fiona."

Sheldon retrieves the pill bottle from the table and stuffs it into his pocket. "You won't be needing these anymore. You'll be busy the next couple of days, getting things ready for Melvin. Call me if you need help with anything."

"I will." Ollie walks out with him, locking the door behind them.

They walk in silence up to the house, parting when they reach their cars. Panic tightens Ollie's chest as she drives to town. What if Fiona won't give her another chance? She grips the steering wheel, willing away the anxiety. She won't take no for an answer.

Fiona swings the door open and steps onto the porch. "What do you want?"

"I'm so sorry, Fiona. I'm really struggling. I have a history of crippling anxiety and panic attacks. And they've come back in full force these past few weeks. No matter what I do, I can't seem to shake the past."

Fiona walks to the edge of the porch, placing her back to Ollie. "I'm sorry for you, Ollie. I realize you've been through a lot. But I can't work under these conditions."

"And you shouldn't have to. I'm getting help." Ollie tells Fiona about her upcoming stay at Tranquil Mind, Peaceful Heart.

"Sounds like mental therapy camp for adults," Fiona says.

Ollie chuckles. "That's pretty much what it is. Melvin will run the vineyard for me. I'd be forever grateful if you'd stay on at The Foxhole. At least until I return."

Fiona turns to face her. "I'm glad you're getting help. I'll manage The Foxhole while you're gone, but I can't make any promises after that."

"I understand. I'm taking one day at a time right now." Ollie's shoulders sag as the tension leaves her body. "Coincidentally, I recounted the cash. There's no money missing. It was my error. I'm sorry I accused you."

"I'm sorry too," Fiona says, going inside and closing the door.

A horrible thought strikes Ollie as she drives away. What if Ronnie Mason can't help her? What if the anxiety is part of her genetic makeup and she's doomed to a lifetime of panic attacks? Fiona will quit for good and take the rest of The Foxhole staff with her. The vineyard workers may quit too, when they find out their boss is mentally unstable. It's difficult finding loyal employees these days, especially in a town the size of Lovely.

The stakes are high. Ollie can't afford to screw this up. She might not get another chance.

CHAPTER 11
CASEY

Casey is working at her desk late afternoon on Thursday when Daniel sticks his head in the door. "I have exciting news. I've decided to host a Fourth of July party."

"Sounds like fun. But that's less than two weeks away."

"I've booked the band and a professional fireworks company. We'll handle everything else in-house."

Casey gets up from her chair and comes around the desk. "Are you thinking of a traditional Fourth of July picnic with fried chicken and potato salad? Or a barbecue with hamburgers and hot dogs?"

"Neither," Daniel says with a snort. "We'll have linens and candles and a spread of food fit for royalty. We'll invite everyone who's anyone in the Commonwealth of Virginia."

"Sounds like a lavish affair. What's the occasion? Aside from the obvious."

"I haven't hosted a party in years. Just seems like a good time." They step out into the hall together. "I'll need you to handle the invitations. My admin is working on the guest list. With the short notice, we'll have to send Evites."

"How many people will you invite?" Casey asks.

"Best guess, four or five hundred."

Casey's brow hits her hairline. "That's a lot of people, Daniel."

"Ada can handle it. She's used to organizing large parties."

Maybe so, Casey thinks. *But I doubt she'll be too happy about it.*

Daniel palms Casey's cheek. "Look at the bright side. The party will provide plenty of photos for your new social media bunny. What's her name again?"

"Avery. I'm going to meet with her now. She'll be thrilled about the party," Casey says and heads off down the hall toward the marketing department.

Her father had gone bug-eyed when Casey introduces him to the new blonde bombshell addition to their marketing team. Avery is drop dead gorgeous with long blonde hair and curves in all the right places. And she loves photographing herself, which makes her the ideal social media marketer.

"I have a project for you," Casey says to Avery when she enters the marketing office. "We need to design an email invitation for our Fourth of July party."

Avery's eyes grow wide as Casey shares the details of the party. "Do we get to attend?"

"Of course. You'll be taking photographs for social media. In terms of the invitations, think elegant. Not red, white, and blue. Maybe gold and white." Casey checks her watch. "I'm leaving in a minute for an appointment. Take a stab at the design, and we'll discuss it more in the morning."

Casey returns to her office for her things and heads out to the parking lot. Her appointment is actually a dinner date with Luke. Much to her delight, he called earlier in the day and invited her to his house for dinner. He's expecting her in forty-five minutes, which gives her just enough time to change and freshen up.

Casey is rummaging through her closet for something to wear when Fiona calls. "Rapunzel, Rapunzel, let down your hair."

Casey barks out a laugh. "I'm afraid to ask what you're talking about."

"I'm standing in front of this stately manor you now call

home. I have something important to tell you. Two things, actually. Can I come in?"

"Sure! The front door is open. Take a right at the top of the stairs. My room is the last door on the left." Tossing her phone on the bed, Casey stands in front of her full-length mirror with two dresses—a black low-cut number and a periwinkle shift that buttons up the front and dances around her thighs.

The door swings open and Fiona strides in. "I wasn't sure you were here. Where's your car?"

"In the driveway. Daniel bought me a new car."

Fiona's blue eyes pop. "You mean that fancy white convertible is yours? God, I want your life."

Casey holds up the dresses. "Which one should I wear?"

Fiona tilts her head as she studies Casey's reflection in the mirror. "Depends. Where are you going?"

"Luke is cooking dinner for me at his house?'

"Definitely the blue." Fiona gives Casey a playful shove. "You go, girl! Why didn't you tell me Luke asked you out?"

"I haven't had time. He only called a little while ago."

Fiona turns away from the mirror to face the room. "Check out these digs." She circles the room and belly flops on the king-size bed. "I could get used to this."

Casey strips off her work clothes and slips on the periwinkle dress. "I don't have much time, Fi. What's so important you had to tell me in person?"

Fiona follows her into the bathroom. "Ollie hit rock bottom today. She accused me of stealing from the cash drawer."

Casey freezes with a tube of lipstick poised near her lips. "She accused *you* of stealing? You're the most honest person I know."

"Ollie apologized. She's not thinking straight. Turns out there was no money missing." Fiona slides onto the marble countertop. "Sheldon introduced her to some hotshot shrink. She committed herself to mental therapy camp."

Casey scrunches up her nose. "What's mental therapy camp?"

Fiona shrugs. "Who knows? Some place where she'll get

psychoanalyzed for a week. The program starts on Sunday. She's flying Melvin, the vineyard's previous owner, in to manage the vineyard while she's gone."

"Good for her! Sounds like she's getting the right help." Casey swipes the lipstick across her lips and rubs them together. "I trust Sheldon. He wouldn't lead Ollie astray." She returns the lipstick to her cosmetics bag and runs a brush through her wavy blonde hair. "What's your second bit of news?"

"I think I'll wait until after your date with Luke. I wouldn't want to influence your feelings for him."

"You can't drop a bomb like that and hold out on me." Casey takes Fiona by the arm and marches her out of the room. "But I need to get going. You can tell me on the way to the car."

"Jamie came by The Foxhole today," Fiona says as they're descending the stairs. "He asked me if I thought you'd go out with him."

Casey's heart skips a beat. "And? What did you tell him?"

"That it was too soon after Ollie, but maybe one day."

"That's the perfect answer." When they reach the driveway, Casey turns toward Fiona. "I don't know why you were hesitant to tell me. Am I not allowed to have a crush on two guys at the same time?"

"You can. As long as it doesn't get messy."

———

Luke lives down a winding road on a mountain slope about three miles on the other side of town. A sign bearing the name *Ellington Estates* marks the entrance to the property. The house is a sprawling, one story Spanish hacienda with stucco exterior walls and a terracotta roof.

Luke greets her at the arched front door. "Welcome."

"You didn't tell me you live on a vineyard," Casey says.

Luke smiles. "I inherited the estate from my parents. I was

raised in Richmond. When I left for college, my parents bought this farm. This was their retirement project."

"It's lovely," she says in a soft voice.

"You're lovely." He gives her a peck near her mouth.

Casey's stomach somersaults, all thoughts of Jamie temporarily forgotten.

Luke gives her a brief tour of the house, the bedroom wing at one end and his study at the other. An informal living area makes up the middle with a sitting room and adjacent kitchen. Luke pours two glasses of white wine and hands one to her. "Shall we walk through the vineyard before we eat?"

"Yes, please! That sounds nice."

They stroll through the rows of grapevines to the winery. As they walk through the barrel room, Luke explains, "We're a small boutique operation. We only have two varietals, a red and a white from which we produce a few hundred bottles a year."

Casey lifts her glass. "Is this your white?"

He nods. "Do you like it?"

"Very much. But I'm no expert."

Luke chuckles. "The experts like it as well. We've won several local awards. We only sell by the case, and we have a long waiting list of clients."

As they start back toward the house, Casey asks, "Have you considered expanding the vineyard?"

"No way. This was my parents' dream. I pay people to keep the winery running. While I enjoy living on a vineyard, I have no interest in making it my career."

When they return to the kitchen, Luke sets about preparing dinner. He drizzles olive oil over asparagus and places the sheet pan in the oven. While it's roasting, he reheats the mushroom risotto he made earlier in the day and sears tuna steaks in a skillet on the stove.

When the meal is ready, they take their plates out to the terrace where Luke has set the small table with placemats, flatware, and candles.

"Is this Twilight Groove?" Casey asks about the soft jazz playing in the background.

Luke points his knife at her. "You have a good ear. We produced a demo tape about a year ago, just for kicks."

"Do you have aspirations of becoming famous?" Casey asks, a mischievous smile creeping across her lips.

Luke laughs. "Nope. We all have successful day jobs. We only do weekend gigs for fun. Speaking of which. We're playing again at Blue Cosmos on Saturday night. I hope you can come."

"I'll try. I haven't figured out my weekend plans yet," Casey says casually so as not to appear too eager.

Luke cuts into his tuna steak. "You haven't lived in town long, have you?"

"Only a few months. How'd you know?"

"I never forget faces. Especially one as pretty as yours. What brings you to Lovely?"

"I'm originally from New York. I never knew my father. My mother kept his identity a secret until she passed away last spring. I came here to meet him. He's Daniel Love of Love-Struck vineyards."

Luke smiles. "I know Daniel. I did some legal work for the vineyard not too long ago. He's a good man. I imagine it was a shock having you show up out of the blue."

While they finish dinner, she tells him how generous Daniel has been in opening his home to her and offering a job as head of his new marketing department. Luke is easy to talk to, and she confides in him about her trouble with her new half siblings.

"Except for Sheldon," Casey says. "He's been amazing."

"That doesn't surprise me. I worked with Sheldon on the case. And I got to know him pretty well."

Once the dishes are put away, Luke offers her more wine, but she asks for a cup of hot tea instead. They return to the terrace to watch the sunset. They talk for over two hours about their careers and families and their dreams for the future.

When Luke sets his piercing blue eyes on her, Casey feels like he's looking deep into her soul, and she can't remember ever revealing so much about herself.

It's almost ten o'clock when he walks her to her car. Opening her car door, she says, "Thank you for a wonderful evening."

"Thank you for coming. So . . ." He twirls a strand of her hair. "Can I expect to see you on Saturday night?"

Casey stares down at the ground, kicking at the gravel with her sandal. "I'm not sure. I don't know many people in town, and I'd feel awkward going alone."

He runs a finger down her cheek. "But you won't be alone. You'll be with me."

She smiles. "Only you'll be performing."

He cups his hand behind her head and draws her face close to his. "I'll save you a seat at the bar," he says, his breath a whisper on her lips.

"How will that work in a crowded bar?"

"Easy." He pulls his phone out of his back pocket and snaps a photograph of her.

Casey giggles. "What're you doing?"

"I'm taking your picture. I'll show it to Rich, the bartender, and he'll save you a seat." He stuffs the phone back in his pocket and takes Casey in his arms. "Please, say you'll come. I really want to see you again."

"And I really want to see you as well. I'll be there."

When Luke presses his mouth to hers, the earth falls away beneath them.

CHAPTER 12
ADA

Ada thinks a lot about happiness. Whether she's ever actually experienced it and whether she could achieve it in her future. Her gut intuition tells her Enzo could be the key to her happiness. She has a chance with him, if she can avoid screwing it up like she's screwed up every other relationship in her life. As difficult as it may be, she decides to stay away from him until she sorts herself out.

Ada asks her brothers in passing if she was mean as a child.

Hugh laughs and jokingly says, "You've always been a brat."

Charles, in his usual sullen manner, says, "I don't remember."

But Sheldon, when he stops by the tasting room for coffee on Friday morning, takes the time for a discussion. "I wouldn't say you were mean. You were quiet, often inside your own head. You enjoyed riding more than hanging out with your friends."

"That's because horses don't cause drama. My friends were always stirring up trouble."

Sheldon laughs. "That's true. As best I can remember, you were a normal kid. Mom dying was a turning point. You were so hurt and angry. We tried to help you, but no one could ever reach you."

Ada refills his to-go cup with coffee. "Do you think people can change?"

"Of course, Ada. We're human. We all make mistakes. God wants us to try harder, to always strive to do better."

Ada remembers what Enzo said about striving. *We must always strive for happiness, Ada. If we lose hope of ever finding it, we're doomed to a life of misery.* Is it possible the act of striving to do better, to be kinder, is, in itself, the root of happiness?

Ada comes around the counter to hug him. "Thanks for the advice, bro."

Sheldon appears taken aback by her sincerity. "Anytime, sis. By the way, I talked to Dad on your behalf. I got him to listen, although there's no guarantee he'll give you back your shares."

"Thanks for trying. You're not such a bad guy, Sheldon. Perhaps I was wrong about you," she says with a wicked grin.

"Maybe I was wrong about you too, Ada."

As she watches Sheldon leave the tasting room, Ada wonders if there is hope for a relationship with him after all. They've never gotten along. As children, they were always vying for their mother's attention. And Sheldon, being a mama's boy, usually won out.

Ada returns to work. Around noon, she's finishing up a tasting with a rowdy group of wealthy business executives from Texas when her father's assistant calls. "Your father would like to see you as soon as possible."

"Say again, Maria. I can't hear you over the noise."

Maria raises her voice. "Your father wants to see you as soon as possible."

"Tell him I'm finishing up with a group of VIPs, and I'll be there as soon as I can."

So, he's *her father* again. Does this mean he's giving Ada back her shares in the company?

Ada returns her attention to the businesspeople. As she takes orders for cases of wine to ship to their homes in Texas, she imagines the scene with her father playing out. He'll beg her forgiveness and assure her genetics don't matter. Ada will always be his daughter, no matter what.

Thirty minutes later, she floats on air up the stairs to the administrative offices. When she enters his office, Daniel doesn't stand to greet her, which she interprets as a bad sign. "It's about time. What took you so long?"

"I was hosting a group of wealthy Texans. Didn't Maria tell you?"

"Right." He slides a notepad and pen across his desk to her. "Sit down. You'll want to take notes. I've decided to have a Fourth of July party. I've taken care of the heavy lifting by booking the band and organizing the fireworks display. I assume you can handle the catering."

Lines appear on Ada's forehead. "That's only ten days away. I hope you're planning to serve hot dogs and hamburgers."

Her father folds his arms on top of his desk. "On the contrary. I want the best of everything: seafood and beef and booze. Servers and bartenders and tables set up on the lawn with linens, china, and candles."

Ada crosses her legs, taking notes as he rants on about the elaborate details for the party. Finally, he sits back in his chair. "I think that about covers it."

"Are you sure? We could construct a champagne fountain or fly in exotic orchids from a tropical rainforest in South America."

"Cut the sarcasm, Ada. Just be sure to spare no expenses. I want our guests to still be talking about this party at Christmas."

"Who are these guests anyway? Have the invitations been mailed?"

"Casey's department is taking care of that. The guest list comprises old friends and business associates from across the state. I doubt you know many of them. You can come if you want, but I'm sure you have better plans," he says in a tone that lets Ada know he doesn't want her at his party.

Ada straightens, holding her head high. "I'll cancel my other plans. I'd rather be here. Thanks for inviting me."

Daniel's lip curls as though he smells something rotten. "Suit yourself. Coincidentally, I spoke with Sheldon, and he reminded me how much you've grown the wedding business. Against my better judgement, I've decided to let you keep your shares. Although you will have no voting rights. If you ever decide to get rid of them, you must agree to sell back to a family member."

"I understand," Ada says, as tears sting her eyes. She should be thrilled. But what's the point in keeping her shares if she has no voting rights? Daniel once asked for Ada's opinion about everything relating to the business. But he no longer values her input. She's not his daughter anymore. She's merely the hired help.

Ada gets to her feet and scurries out of the office before she embarrasses herself.

She spends the afternoon putting the party plans in motion. She meets with their head chef, who grumbles about them not having enough time to prepare for such a lavish event. While she manages to placate the chef, finding rentals proves to be even more of a challenge. Late in the day, she gets a lead on a new high-end party rental firm owned by a young woman who recently left her job as head event planner at Hope Springs Farms. She leaves a message for Presley Ingram who calls her back right away.

"It'll be tight," Presley says. "We have a large wedding that weekend, but if we pick up from that event on Sunday, we can drop off your rentals first thing Monday morning. I realize that's cutting it close for you, since your party is Monday night, but that's the best I can do."

"I'll take it! Thank you, Presley. And I look forward to doing lots of business with you in the future."

Ada is leaving the office when Enzo calls. "Can you join me for dinner at Belmonte's? I booked a reservation for seven."

Ada yearns to see Enzo, but she vowed to keep her distance until she can give him her best self. But first she needs to determine what that best self is. "I wish I could, Enzo. But I'm working tonight. Daniel is throwing a last-minute Fourth of July party and guess who gets to plan it?"

"Duty calls," Enzo says, sounding disappointed. "Let me know if you change your mind. Or if you want company later."

"Will do. Thanks for understanding."

Ada picks up a salmon Caesar salad from Delilah's on the way home and spends the evening devising the dinner menu for the party. She goes to bed early and rises at dawn on Saturday morning with a hankering to go riding.

Ada much prefers the western saddle, even though her mother always insisted she ride English. She dresses in jeans, a short-sleeved plaid shirt, and her cowboy boots. She hasn't been to the stables to see Glory, her dapple-gray thoroughbred, in over a month. Riding has always reduced her stress and boosted her confidence. She makes a mental note to carve out more stable time in the future.

Ada knows the trails around the property like the back of her hand. She becomes one with the powerful animal as she takes off on a dirt path through the woods. When she reaches her lot, she's shocked to see the land has been cleared and earth movers parked near a mountain of downed trees. What is Daniel up to now?

Ada digs her heels into Glory's side. The horse picks up a trot, and they return to the stable via the road. She turns the horse over to a stable hand and continues on to the house, where she finds Daniel drinking coffee and reading the newspaper on the terrace.

When she approaches the table, her shadow blocks his sun, and he looks up. "Why are you having my lot cleared?"

"Good morning to you too, Ada." He folds his paper and lays it on the table. "It's *my* land. I can do what I want with it. I'm giving you a bigger lot further down the road."

"How much further down the road? In West Virginia? You gave me Glory for my twenty-first birthday. Are you taking her back too?"

Her father stands, forcing her to take a step backward. "I don't have time for your hysterics, Ada. I have a tee time in twenty minutes."

She follows on his heels into the house and down the center hall to the driveway. "I have a right to know what you're building on my lot. You gave *me* that land instead of the boys, because you wanted *me*, your daughter, close to you."

"I'm building a guest house. Not that I owe you any explanations."

Ada twirls around to face the house. Spreading her arms wide, she says, "Why do you need a guest house when you have a mansion full of guest suites?"

He gets in his Jaguar and speeds off, leaving her standing in the driveway staring at his taillights. She yearns to scream and stomp her feet but having a tantrum will solve nothing. Daniel is pushing her away, and there's not a thing she can do about it.

Returning to the barn, she spends the rest of the morning grooming Glory and cleaning her tack. But the afternoon drags by at a snail's pace. She's never been a fan of Saturdays and Sundays. She prefers the structure of the weekdays.

Around five o'clock, Enzo texts her for a date, but she ignores him. She has the urge to get drunk. The last thing she needs is him trying to control her consumption.

CHAPTER 13
CASEY

Casey arrives at Blue Cosmos around nine thirty on Saturday night. She fights her way to the bar and signals for the bartender.

Recognition crosses his face when he sees her. "You're Casey. I'm Rick. I've been on the lookout for you. I saved you a seat." He gestures toward the end of the bar, where the only empty seat offers an unobstructed view of the stage. "I've been fighting off the crowd all night."

"I'm sorry to be so much trouble," Casey says, easing on to the barstool.

"No trouble at all for a pretty woman like you. What can I get you to drink?"

Casey opens her mouth to order wine and *tequila* comes out instead. "Casamigos on the rocks, please. And make it a double."

Casey usually drinks wine, but something about the night feels magical. Perhaps it's the anticipation of kissing Luke again. Her drink arrives, and she angles her body toward the stage where Luke is playing his heart out on Saxophone. His music stirs feelings deep inside of her. Casey hasn't been with anyone since before her mother's cancer diagnosis, and she's long overdue a hookup. And Luke is a fine candidate. She imagines him taking her home to his hacienda and making love to her in his king-size bed.

The thought of having sex again after so long both excites and terrifies Casey. She drains the tequila and signals to Rick for another.

She's nursing her second drink when Ada stumbles over to her. "You've gotta be kidding me! Are you the special someone Luke was saving this barstool for?"

"I'm sitting here, aren't I?" Casey gives Ada the once over. She's a vamp, a seductress on the prowl with lipstick the same blood red color as her clingy dress.

Ada's eyes travel from Casey to the stage. "How long have you been seeing him?"

Casey tosses her blonde hair over one shoulder. "We've had a couple of dates. Not that it's any of your business."

Ada turns up her nose at Casey. "You're nothing special. I don't get what everybody sees in you."

"I have a heart. And you're a spiteful bitch."

Ada gets close enough to Casey's face for Casey to smell her sour breath. "You're the new girl in town, and everyone wants you to sit at their lunch table. Men love their toys while they're shiny and new. But that newness eventually wears off."

Casey laughs. "I wouldn't count on that happening anytime soon. Daniel was in love with my mother. Not yours. I remind him of the best months of his life. And you remind him of his troubled marriage."

Ada's face darkens to a deep red. "Why, you little bitch?"

Casey doesn't see Ada's hand coming until it lands on the side of her face. She's numb from the tequila, and instead of crying out in pain, Casey laughs in Ada's face. Which enrages Ada even more.

Ada's getting ready to strike again when Rick comes from behind the bar. "That's it, Ada. You've had too much to drink. I should've kicked you out an hour ago." He summons one of his bouncers. "Please escort Ada upstairs to her apartment."

"Yes, sir," the bouncer says, and manhandles a squirming Ada through the crowd to the door.

Rick goes behind the bar and fills a glass with ice, handing it to Casey. "Here. Hold this against your face. She really clocked you. You'll likely have a bruise, anyway."

Casey presses the glass to her cheek. "I'm sorry, Rick. This is partially my fault. I egged her on."

"I'm sure she deserved it. She's never started a fight before, but she drinks too much every time she comes in here."

Casey is proud of herself for standing up to Ada. She gives the tequila credit for the liquid courage. "Can I have another tequila, please?"

She sips the new drink instead of slurping it down, but she's a lightweight, and by the time Luke comes down off the stage, her head is buzzing.

"Someone's tipsy," he says in a teasing tone.

She giggles. "Maybe a teensy bit."

Luke grins. "I guess that means I'm driving you home."

Casey slides off the barstool and into his arms. "You can drive me to your home." She doesn't care if she's being aggressive. Satisfying her burning desire to feel his body pressed against hers is the only thing that matters.

He grins. "In that case, what are we waiting for?" Slinging his saxophone over his shoulder, he takes her by the hand and leads her out of the jazz club.

On the way to his house in his pickup truck, she babbles on about his talent and how much she loves hearing him play. He smiles and thanks her for the compliment. When he unlocks his front door, Casey jumps him, covering his face with kisses and trying to drag him down the hall to the master suite.

"Not so fast. You need to sober up a little first. The fresh night air will help." Scooping her up, he carries her outside to the terrace and deposits her on a lounge chair. "Don't move. I'll be right back."

He disappears inside and returns with a tall glass of water for her and a bottle of beer for him. He stretches out on the chaise lounge beside her.

"So, what happened between you and Ada tonight?"

Casey rolls her eyes. "She smacked me. I deserved it, I guess. I provoked her."

"No one ever deserves to be hit in the face, Casey. Or anywhere else for that matter."

"Whatever. It was worth it. I got in a few insults."

He fingers her cheek. "Your face is still red. You may have a bruise."

She rolls her head to the side to look at him. "Will you blow your horn for me?"

"Seriously? I've been playing on night."

"Just one song." She presses her hands together. "Please. Pretty please. Then I'll be sober, and you can have your way with me."

Luke laughs out loud. "I doubt you'll sober up that fast."

He goes back inside and returns with his saxophone. "I'm not much of a songwriter, but I've been working on this one piece."

He lifts his instrument, and seductive music fills the quiet night. Casey closes her eyes and drifts off to sleep.

She wakes the following morning, fully clothed and alone in Luke's bed. Snippets of the previous evening rush back. The confrontation with Ada. Casey throwing herself at Luke. Him playing his saxophone for her on the terrace. She sits bolt upright and scrambles from beneath the covers. She pads in bare feet down the hall to the kitchen where Luke is at the stove frying bacon.

"Morning," Casey says shyly.

He smiles at her over his shoulder. "Morning."

"I'm sorry about last night, Luke. I rarely drink hard liquor. I guess it creeped up on me. We didn't . . . um, you know?"

He chuckles as he forks bacon onto a paper towel. "I prefer for my lovers to be conscious."

"Ha ha. Have you seen my purse?"

"Right there." He dips his head at her bag on the island.

"Oh. Duh." She sits down on a stool and slides her phone from her bag. She expects her phone to be blown up with calls and texts about her fight with Ada. But she only has one text from Jamie inviting her to brunch today. Flutters dance across her chest. Is he asking her on a date?

Casey texts back. *Sure! Where and when?*

He responds right away. *Ruthie's Diner at eleven.*

Casey looks up from her phone to find Luke staring at her. "Is everything okay?"

"Sure! Everything's fine," Casey says, sliding her phone back in her bag.

"Good! I couldn't read your expression. I thought maybe something was wrong." Luke cracks eggs into a bowl, scrambles them, and pours them into a skillet. "Would you like to spend the day together? We could pack a picnic and go for a hike."

A dreamy expression overcomes Casey's face as she imagines them lazing beneath a large tree beside a rolling stream. He'll bring his saxophone along and make beautiful music. Afterward, he'll take off her clothes and run his hands across her naked body. She shivers with desire at the thought of them making love out in the wide open.

Casey jerks back to reality. What is wrong with her? Jamie and Luke stir very different emotions in her. Jamie is her friend. But Luke makes her feel like a woman.

"Well?" Luke asks as he scoops eggs onto two plates.

"Well, what?" Casey says, eyes narrowed.

Luke brings the plates over to the island. "The hike and picnic. Can you go?"

She lets out a disappointed sigh. "I wish I could, but I can't. I promised a friend I'd have brunch with him."

"Is he the one who sent you the text?" Luke asks, sitting down beside her.

"Mm-hmm. He just broke up with his girlfriend, and he's

down in the dumps. He needs cheering up," Casey says, unable to look Luke in the eyes.

"I'm not playing games here, Casey. If you have feelings for him, you need to tell me now."

Casey forces a smile. "Jamie and I are just friends. I promise."

The lie weighs heavily on Casey as she picks at her eggs. Why didn't she just tell Luke the truth? Her feelings for him scare and confuse her. He's an attorney. A musician. A man. He's out of her league. But Jamie is comfortable, like her favorite pair of running shoes. She owes it to herself to give him a chance. If she doesn't, she might always wonder what might have been.

CHAPTER 14
OLLIE

Ronnie Mason's program is based around meditation and self-reflection. Which is torture for Ollie, who spends much of her time running from her thoughts.

When they aren't in therapy sessions, the patients take wilderness hikes, soak in hot tubs, and practice yoga. They aren't allowed to speak while conducting these group activities. The point is to be inside their own heads as much as possible.

On Monday afternoon, Ollie goes for her first private session with Ronnie, who is an attractive redhead with dazzling emerald eyes. When Ollie enters the office, the psychiatrist comes from behind her desk.

"Welcome, Ollie. We can either sit in here." She gestures at the seating area that includes a leather sofa and velvet chaise lounge. "Or we can go outside to the patio."

Ollie smiles at her. "I prefer the outdoors. Besides, we should enjoy this pleasant weather."

Ronnie waits until they are seated in comfortable lounge chairs before asking, "How are you finding your stay at Tranquil Mind, Peaceful Heart so far?"

"Everything's been great. Although I will say this place gives new meaning to deafening silence."

The doctor places a reassuring hand on Ollie's arm. "Facing demons is hard work, Ollie. We learn something about ourselves when we're forced outside of our comfort zones."

Ollie takes in the stunning view of the mountains. "I'm impressed at how much you've accomplished at such a young age."

"I had a lot of support from my father." Ronnie lets out a sigh. "Two assailants killed my mother during a home invasion when I was eight. I witnessed them beat her to death."

Ollie gasps, her hand flying to her mouth. "That's awful. I'm so sorry."

Ronnie's lips part in a sad smile. "I was a basket case afterward. At the time, the best child psychiatrist on the East Coast lived in Lovely. My father sold our house and moved us down here from Philadelphia."

"He must love you very much to make such a sacrifice."

Ronnie shrugs. "I'm his only child. Neither of us could stand to live in that house after what happened anyway. We found the natural beauty of this area therapeutic."

"I love living in the mountains. Although I'm still waiting for them to work their magic healing powers on me," Ollie admits.

"Have you opened your heart to them?"

Ollie considers the question for a long minute. "Not as much as I should have, I guess. Did your child psychiatrist inspire you to become a therapist yourself?"

Ronnie nods. "Eula Cannon saved my life. From the time I was old enough to think about my future, I knew I wanted to help others as she'd helped me."

"Sheldon mentioned you used to psychoanalyze him when you two dated in high school."

The doctor chuckles. "I'm sure he also told you that's why he broke up with me."

Ollie grins. "He may have mentioned that. Is your father still living?" she asks, thinking about her own father and how supportive he'd been.

"Yes. But he lives in the Florida Keys now. When he moved down there several years ago, he turned this property over to me and provided the funding for the buildings. And here we are. Now you know my sad history. Let's talk about yours."

For an hour a day for the rest of the week, the doctor and Ollie dissect her life one piece at a time. While the process is painful, the doctor helps her put certain events into perspective. Slowly, but surely, she feels better.

On Wednesday afternoon, Ollie is discussing her breakup with Jamie in group therapy when she suffers a panic attack.

Krista, one of the group therapists, moves her chair next to Ollie's. "Tell me how you're feeling?"

"I can't breathe, and my heart is racing." Ollie's eyes dart around the room as she searches for an exit. "I need to get out of here."

"You're in a safe place," Krista says in a soft voice. "You're amongst friends, and we won't let anything happen to you. I want you to take deep breaths as you count to ten."

Ollie inhales and exhales as she counts. By the time she reaches ten, the panic is subsiding.

"There now." Krista gives Ollie's leg a pat and straightens in her chair. "Most of us have experienced panic attacks. Some more crippling than others. What's the worst thing that can happen when you have a panic attack?"

"You could die?" says Roger, a middle-aged man with leathered skin and white hair.

Krista shakes her head. "You may feel like you're dying when you're suffering a panic attack. But clinically speaking, death does not occur from panic attacks. The goal is to eliminate panic attacks by determining what triggers them. We'll be working on that in here. In the meantime, if you feel one coming on, close your eyes and go to a safe place in your mind. Breathe deeply and count to ten, as Ollie just did. Focus on your senses, what you hear and see, anything to divert your attention from the attack."

In Ollie's mind, no place on earth is safe. But later that

evening, when she feels another panic attack coming on, she stares it down. She reminds herself it won't kill her and counts her breaths until the panic subsides.

"Tell me about your marriage," Ronnie says at the beginning of Thursday's session.

Ollie lets out a sigh. "Sergio worked for my father for decades. He was like a second son. I thought marrying him would make my father happy. Sergio tried to tame me, and I wasn't ready to settle down."

"Relationships rarely work when one person attempts to control another."

"Ours certainly didn't." Ollie snatches a tissue from the box and wipes her damp eyes. "Sergio felt I owed him something for the trouble I caused him. He sued my family for a fourth of the winery, which was half of my half. The lawsuit was bogus, and the judge ruled in our favor, but our lives were in turmoil for more than a year."

"How did that make you feel?" Ronnie asks.

"Guilty as hell. Guilt is the only emotion I seem to feel, Ronnie." Ollie blows her nose into the tissue. "Fortunately, Sergio and I are friends again. I wouldn't have made it through my brother's trial without him."

Ollie talks at length about the fire, her parents' deaths, and her brother's incarceration. When she discusses her relationship with Jamie, she's surprised to discover the anxiety she's recently been experiencing is more about him than her family.

Ollie confesses, "I never loved him. I knew from the beginning we weren't a good match. He desperately wants a family, and children aren't a top priority for me. I used Jamie as a crutch to avoid being alone."

"Your time together wasn't wasted, Ollie. You learned something about yourselves, and that knowledge will help you make better choices in the future."

Ollie plucks a hot pink petunia from the container beside her. "Why did the panic attacks get worse after I broke up with him?"

"Perhaps because you felt guilty for hurting him. In my experience, people who have guilt are empathetic people. Being concerned about others' feelings isn't a bad thing. I want you to learn to recognize your feelings and cope with them before they spiral out of control."

"I suck at relationships. I've sworn off men for good."

Ronnie doesn't respond. She waits until Saturday, Ollie's last full day in the program, before broaching the subject of Sheldon. They are eating lunch at the small round table on the doctor's patio. The psychiatrist scoops up a forkful of chicken salad. "So you claim you've sworn off men for good. Does that include Sheldon?"

"What does Sheldon have to do with anything?" Ollie asks over the rim of her sweet tea glass.

A smirk tugs at the doctor's lips. "Your face goes soft and rosy whenever you mention his name. You have feelings for him, whether you're ready to admit it."

"I told you how his brothers have treated me."

"His brothers, Ollie. Not Sheldon. He's proven his friendship to you many times."

Ollie eats in silence while she ponders her relationship with Sheldon. "My feelings for Sheldon are confused. One minute I want to strangle him. The next I . . . "

"You what? Want to kiss him?"

"Maybe." Ollie has imagined doing more than kissing Sheldon. Her attraction to him is strong, unlike anything she's ever experienced.

"What's holding you back?"

Ollie doesn't know how to answer. "I'm not sure, honestly."

"Don't deprive yourself of happiness, because you're afraid to try again."

Ollie pushes her plate away, her food barely touched. "Are you encouraging me to seek a relationship with Sheldon? Because I don't see how I can make someone else happy when I'm not happy myself."

Ronnie dabs her lips with her napkin. "You're closer than you realize, Ollie. You've come to terms with losing your parents and your brother's involvement in their deaths. You'll eventually forgive yourself for stringing Jamie along. And when the time is right, you should look for love again. After all you've been through, you deserve a happily ever after."

Ollie stares down at her folded hands. "What makes you think I could have that with Sheldon?"

"Because I know Sheldon. He's one of the good guys, and he truly cares about you."

Ollie's heart skips a beat. "How do you know that?"

"He told me. Sheldon buys me coffee once a week. In exchange, I counsel him on a number of things. He's been smitten with you since you moved here. You're young, Ollie. You practically have your whole life ahead of you. Give yourself permission to live it to the fullest."

CHAPTER 15
CASEY

Casey politely declines Jamie's invitation to be his date for the Fourth of July party. They've seen each other nearly every day for the past week, meeting for coffee and lunch and even twice for dinner. She gave it an honest try, but Jamie doesn't light her fire like Luke does.

Because she's been spending so much time with Jamie, Casey has ignored Luke's texts and calls all week. Luke, a business associate of Daniel's, was invited to the party, and Casey was thrilled to see his name on the acceptance list.

Casey takes extra care with her appearance in getting ready for the party. She blow-dries her wavy golden hair until it dances around her shoulders, and the simple white sundress she chooses shows off her bronzed skin. Slipping her feet into strappy gold sandals, she glides on air over to the winery.

The expanse of lawn in front of the building is decked out for the party. Tables are draped in white linens with small arrangements of blue hydrangeas and pillar candles in hurricane globes stretching down the centers. The stage for the band and dance floor are off to the right with a fully stocked bar and food tables to the left. Somewhere off in the vineyard, a fireworks expert waits to fill the night sky with explosions of color. Mother Nature has blessed them with temperatures in the seventies and zero percent chance of rain.

Avery takes a break from snapping images for social media to join Casey for a pregame glass of wine. "Let me know if you have any special request for pics," Avery says.

"You're the professional," Casey says. "Just be sure to get at least one of Daniel with the governor."

Avery winks at her. "You know it."

Promptly at six thirty, Casey and Daniel position themselves at the edge of the lawn near the parking lot to greet their guests. She meets the governor and a senator, as well as many business associates and winemakers from all over the state. So many faces. Too many names to remember. But none of them are Luke.

Casey mingles with the crowd until seven thirty when Daniel appears on stage, ringing a handbell and tapping on the microphone. "If I could have your attention, please," he says, and waits for the guests to gather around. "The Fourth of July is always a good time to have a party, but tonight, I have even more reason to celebrate. I'm delighted my daughter has come into my life, and I wanted to throw a party in her honor for all of you to meet her. Not only has she brought me much joy, Casey has sparked new inspiration in me I never thought possible at this stage in my life. Casey." He sweeps an arm in her direction. "Please join me."

Casey's face warms as she makes her way onto the stage. Daniel embraces her, and she stands on her tiptoes to kiss his cheek.

"Isn't she lovely?" Daniel turns Casey to face the crowd, one arm still draped around her shoulders.

Casey scans the guests, her gaze landing on Ada, who glares back at her with pure hatred. Casey doesn't blame Ada. If the situation were reversed, Casey would hate her too. Just beyond Ada, Casey spots Luke standing near the bar, smiling his sexy smile at her.

Avery photographs Daniel and Casey as they exit the stage

together. The post will be all over social media by morning. The wording will read, *Isn't She Lovely?*

Casey is making her way through the crowd toward Luke, when Jamie pulls her off to the side. "You look amazing. I've been dying to do this all week." Cupping the back of her head, Jamie brings her face close and covers her mouth with his.

His lips are slobbery, his tongue fat and hot in her mouth, and Casey fights back the urge to gag. Her revulsion is confirmation they are not suited for each other. How could she have been so wrong about him?

When Casey finally breaks away, she sees Luke staring at her with shock and disappointment. He does an about-face and takes off toward the parking lot.

"I'm sorry, Jamie. I've gotta go," Casey says and hurries after him. "Luke! Wait!"

Luke increases his pace.

She catches up to him as he's getting in his truck. "You don't understand. It's not what you think."

"Seriously, Casey? You expect me to believe that? You've been avoiding me all week, and I just saw you lip-locked with that dweeb."

"I admit a had a crush on him while I was working at Foxtail. But he was with Ollie then. When they broke up, I felt like I owed it to myself to give Jamie a chance."

Recollection crosses Luke's face. "Jamie's the guy you were texting on Sunday morning. You lied to me. You promised me you were just friends."

"I didn't lie. Jamie *is* my friend. That's all we are. We've spent some time together this week, but that's the first time he kissed me. Believe me, there's no chemistry."

"How old are you, Casey?"

"Twenty-seven. Why?"

"Because I'm thirty-two. Age is important at this stage in our lives. You're too young and immature to know what you want. And I don't have time to wait around while you figure it out." He hangs his head. "You're a special girl, and I'm sorry it didn't work out between us." He gets in his truck and speeds away.

Tears sting Casey's eyes as she wonders back into the crowd. She yearns to go home and have a good cry, but for Daniel's sake, she must stay and entertain his guests. She fills a plate from the buffet and sits down at the end of a table across from people she doesn't know.

Only five minutes pass before Jamie finds her. He spills some of his beer on Casey when he sits down beside her, and she can tell he's borderline sloppy drunk.

"Sorry." He rubs at the stain on her dress with a napkin. "Who was that guy?"

"Stop," she says, brushing his hand away. "He's someone I've been seeing. I'm sorry, Jamie. I thought maybe there was something between you and me, but I'm not feeling it. I hope we can still be friends."

Jamie's shoulders slump as he deflates. "I guess so."

Casey eats a few bites of salad and excuses herself. She's relieved to see Jamie leaving the party with his parents a few minutes later.

The band begins playing while the guests are finishing dinner. By the time the tables have emptied, the dance floor is full. Casey is watching Ollie and Sheldon swing dancing to *Dancing in the Moonlight* when Daniel comes to stand beside her. "They make a nice couple," he says.

Casey nods enthusiastically. "Agreed. He's really into her. Looks like she's finally giving him the attention he deserves."

"I have a surprise for you."

Casey angles her body toward him. "What kind of surprise?"

"I'm building you a house. I've given each of my children a lot on the Love-Struck property. Yours is the closest to The Nest." Daniel is talking loud enough to be heard over the music, and Casey isn't the only one who hears him. Ada is hovering nearby, the yellow flecks in her eyes blazing with anger.

Casey shakes her head. "No, Daniel! I can't accept such an outrageous gift."

"Too late. They've already cleared the land. The contractor will start digging the footings in the next couple of weeks." He pulls her in for a half hug. "I'm so proud of you, Casey."

Casey risks another glance in Ada's direction, only to discover she's gone. "I don't know what I've done to make you proud. I can't even come up with a brand you approve of."

"Listen to me." He takes her by the shoulders, holding her at arm's length. "I approve of every design you've shown me. They all have merit. We just haven't found the right one for Love-Struck. But we will. And I'm not in a hurry." He gives her a gentle shake. "Stop pressuring yourself so much. Relax. Get out of your office more. Stroll around the property. Mingle with the guests in the tasting room. Understanding our business on a more personal level will give you a better feel for our brand."

There's that *feel* word again. She came up with the Foxtail Farm brand by feeling the wine. Maybe Daniel is right. She needs to connect with the land and the wine and the patrons. "I'll get right on it."

Casey's spirits soar. She has a new direction for her work. As disappointed as she is about Luke, she's better off forgetting about romance for the time being. She'll focus on creating the new brand, and if the opportunity presents itself, she'll work toward bridging the gap with Ada. Despite her mean streak, Ada deserves better than the way Daniel is treating her. Regardless of who her biological father is, Daniel raised her as his child. He can't just kick her out of the family for something she didn't do.

CHAPTER 16
ADA

Ada eases away from Daniel and his new plaything. Casey has officially taken Ada's place in their family, in her father's life.

When she turns to flee, Ada runs smack into Enzo's chest. His strong arms steady her. "Easy there, Ada. Where are you going in such a hurry?"

"To get some air. I feel claustrophobic." She breathes in his scent. His musky cologne is both seductive and mysterious. "Although the air smells pretty darn good right here. I've missed you, Enzo."

"Oh yeah? Then why have you been avoiding me all week?" he asks, a playful smirk tugging at his lips.

"I've been busy." She spreads her arms at the party. "Planning an event of this magnitude normally takes months. I did it in ten days."

"Well, congratulations. You did a stella job."

Dressed in black, Enzo stands out among the other attendees, who are wearing summer attire. "What're you doing here? I don't remember seeing you on the invitation list."

"I'm part of the cleanup crew. My primary job is to help with takedown after the party ends. For the time being, I'm collecting empty glasses." He gestures at a tray of empty glasses on a nearby table.

"Dance with me." Before Enzo can protest, Ada drags him onto the dance floor.

Enzo takes her in his arms, and they move rhythmically to *Lean on Me*. She notices Daniel at the edge of the dance floor, watching them with face set in stone. She hooks an arm around Enzo's neck and pulls his head down, pressing her mouth against his. He responds by tightening his hold on her.

The kiss lasts long enough for those around them to take notice and stare, aghast. When they finally pull apart, Enzo says, "What's gotten into you?"

"I told you, I missed you."

"And I missed you." Enzo's dark eyes smolder, as though he'd like to take her to bed. But then his gaze shifts in Daniel's direction. His face falls, and he drops his arms from around her. "I should've known this had something to do with your father. I refuse to be a pawn in your chest game, Ada."

Enzo leaves her standing alone on the dance floor, but she doesn't go after him. She accomplished her mission. She finally got Daniel's attention. Now is her chance to checkmate her opponent.

Ada heads off the dance floor in Daniel's direction. "Hello, Daddy. What do you think? The party turned out well, if I say so myself."

"Come with me." He grabs Ada's upper arm and marches her away from the crowd. "What're you trying to prove? Are you trying to get back at me by marrying a field hand?"

Ada lets out an indignant huff. "I'm not marrying Enzo. I'm just having a little fun."

"By acting like a slut? Making out on the dance floor with a field hand is beneath you. Have some pride in yourself, Ada. You can do better." His jaw tightens. "Or maybe you can't. Maybe it's in your blood. Maybe your mother was slumming with one of my field hands when she got knocked up with you."

Fury rages through Ada. "If you'd been nicer to her, paid her more attention, she wouldn't have been looking elsewhere for love."

"So now it's my fault," Daniel says, throwing up his hands.

"It's certainly not all hers. Mom is not the only one who ended up with an illegitimate child. No matter how many parties you throw her, or how many houses you build her, Casey will still be your bastard."

"How dare you?" Daniel rears back his hand as if to smack her.

Ada goes rigid, bracing for impact. "Go ahead, Daniel. Hit me. I'll have you arrested so fast your head will spin. And I have three hundred witnesses to your assault."

Daniel lowers his hand. "You're just like your mother. Never happy. Always demanding more."

"If that's true, it's because *you* spoiled me." She stabs a red-lacquered nail at his chest. "I was your pampered little princess. You were so proud of *me*. And now, because we're unrelated genetically, you want to get rid of me. Here's a news flash for you, Daniel. I'm not going anywhere."

Brushing past him, she crosses the lawn to the bar, demands a bottle of tequila from the bartender, and retreats to her second-floor office in the winery. Without turning on any lights, she grabs a glass from her bar, sits down at her desk, and pours herself two fingers of tequila. The band's music vibrates through the window and lights from the party dot the landscape below. She'll have a front-row seat for the fireworks when they start.

Ada forces herself to take tiny sips of tequila. She's been careful to avoid overindulging since her drunken encounter with Casey at Blue Cosmos. It hasn't been easy, considering the stress she's under. But spending time with Glory and riding the trails around the vineyard has helped clear her head and put her life into perspective. She's been contemplating finding her biological father. After tonight, she's ready to move forward with the process.

Daniel's words rush back to her. *Maybe it's in your blood. Maybe your mother was slumming with one of my field hands when she got knocked up with you.* That may very well be the case. But considering her mother's social circles, her biological father is more likely a prominent member of local society.

Ada opens her top desk drawer and removes the test kit she ordered weeks ago from 23andMe. First thing in the morning, she'll fill the test tube with saliva and drop the return package in the mail. She'll have to wait two weeks for the results. She realizes the likelihood of her discovering her biological father is slim. She'll only be matched to him if he's previously submitted his DNA sample. If she's lucky, she'll be linked to a first cousin or aunt or uncle. There's a very good chance this will prove to be a dead end.

She remembers Enzo's suggestion about looking through her mother's belongings for a clue about her father. Ada was furious when Daniel paid someone to haul off her mother's beautiful clothes—the Chanel evening gowns and St. John knits. She had to beg him to let her keep her mother's Italian made riding boots and the triple strand of pearls. Daniel locked away the rest of her mother's jewelry for safekeeping. Ada hasn't thought of the jewelry in years, but she needs to get it back before he gives it to Casey.

What had become of the contents of her mother's small study? Her riding trophies and extensive collection of historic fiction? Lila had been responsible for paying the household bills. Her father would've kept those documents, at least for a few years. The thought of exploring the contents of her father's vast attic in the summer heat is discouraging. But she's willing to suffer if it means turning up a clue. All she needs is a name.

CHAPTER 17
OLLIE

Ollie has never had so much fun on the dance floor. Sheldon twirls her around and dips her low until she's giddy. When the band takes a break, Sheldon and Ollie go in search of liquid refreshment.

Ollie trips along beside him on the way to the bar. "You have some serious dance moves. Where did you learn to swing dance like that?"

"My mom insisted we attend cotillion," Sheldon says, mopping sweat from his face with a blue bandana. "We can watch the fireworks from here, or I can take you to my favorite spot for a better view."

"Do we have time to get there before the fireworks start?"

"Sure! It's just up the hill from Dad's house." Sheldon grabs a bottle of champagne and two glasses from behind the bar. "Follow me but stay close. It's dark."

They cut across the rolling lawn behind Daniel's stone mansion to a metal utility building. "Hold these." Daniel hands her the champagne and glasses and disappears inside the building. A minute later, she hears the rumble of a small engine. Headlights blind her as Sheldon emerges from the building on a utility gator. He pulls up beside her. "Get in."

Ollie hops into the passenger seat, and he speeds off up a gravel road. They've gone about a half mile when he swerves off the road to the left and navigates the gator down a wooded trail to a small clearing. He removes a stack of blankets from the back of the gator and spreads them out on the ground in front of a large boulder. He pops the champagne cork as the first rockets splatter the night sky in brilliant color.

Champagne in hand, Ollie settles with her back against the rock. "Tell me more about this place, your favorite spot."

"My dad gave each of us a piece of land on the vineyard. I'm biased, of course, but I think mine's the best. I'm working with an architect to develop house plans. I hope to start construction by the end of the summer."

"How exciting," Ollie says, although she's not sure living so close to his father is such a good thing.

They watch the rest of the fireworks show in comfortable silence. After the finale, Sheldon refills their glasses and leans against the rock beside her. "You seem calmer, more at peace with yourself. I assume your time with Ronnie was productive."

"Very much so. I owe you one for the recommendation," Ollie says, touching her glass to his. "Anxiety will always be an issue for me. But I'm learning what triggers it and how to cope with the panic attacks. I feel more carefree, like the young woman I was before I married Sergio. But I'm older and wiser now. I know what I want out of life."

He scoots closer to her. "Oh? And what's that?"

"To run my vineyard to the best of my ability, and to find my happily ever after with the man of my dreams."

Sheldon's pale green eyes twinkle. "If you're accepting applications, I'd like to submit mine."

Ollie angles her body toward him. "Why would you after the way I've treated you?"

"Because I realize you were just taking your anger at my brothers out on me."

"But you didn't give up on me. And that means more to me

than you'll ever know." Ollie runs her thumb across his lower lip. "I've had just enough champagne to say this. I sense something intoxicatingly delicious between us. My feelings for you are so intense, they scare me."

"Welcome to my world," he says, leaning in close, his lips a whisper on hers. The kiss stirs something deep inside, and she's disappointed when he doesn't kiss her again.

Placing an arm around her shoulders, he pulls her close and they talk well into the night. About the house he's designing and her plans for the vineyard, as well as their deepest secrets and dreams for the future.

They are gazing up at the starry sky, and Sheldon is giving Ollie a constellation lesson when she drifts off to sleep. The first rays of dawn are peeking over the horizon when she wakes. Sheldon is propped on one elbow, staring down at her.

"Please tell me you haven't been watching me sleep all this time."

"Long enough to know I can't live without you," he says in a voice husky with desire.

Ollie forces him onto his back and rolls on top of him. "And I can't live another second without feeling you inside of me."

His teeth nibble at her lower lip. "Are you sure this is what you want?"

"I've never been surer of anything in my life. But I warn you, Sheldon, I have more than my share of problems. I'm an extremely flawed human being."

"Then, baby, that makes us a perfect match."

———

Ollie is alarmed to find Melvin in her kitchen, removing a muffin tin from her oven, when she arrives home around eight o'clock. "Shouldn't you be at the airport? Did you miss your flight?"

"I did. On purpose." Melvin places two mini quiches on a

plate, adds a scoop of cantaloupe balls, and slides it across the counter to a place set with flatware and a glass of orange juice.

"What's all this?" Ollie asks, gesturing at the breakfast.

"I'm buttering you up. I have something I wanna talk to you about."

Ollie's stomach grumbles as she takes a seat at the breakfast counter. "This looks delicious. I hope you're joining me."

"If you insist." Melvin fixes his plate and sits down beside her.

Ollie takes a bite of muffin. "This is amazing. What's in here?"

"Eggs, sausage, cheese. All the artery clogging ingredients that taste so good," Melvin says and pops a whole muffin into his mouth.

Ollie sips her orange juice. "And freshly squeezed. I'm impressed. I didn't realize you were such a good cook."

Melvin smiles, revealing tobacco-stained teeth. "I've been honing my skills. I occupied my time in Arizona by cooking for my son's family."

"Whatever you're buttering me up for must be huge."

Melvin hangs his head. "I'm not ready to leave Virginia, Ollie. In fact, I don't think I'll ever be ready. I tried Arizona. But I don't like it out west. Living with my son and his family isn't working out for any of us. They don't complain, but I can tell I'm in their way."

The hairs on Ollie's neck stand to attention. "Are you asking to buy back the farm?"

Melvin chuckles. "Even if I wanted to, I couldn't run the farm with my rheumatoid arthritis. But I'd like to continue to work here. You don't have to pay me. But this farm is all I've ever known. When I moved to Arizona, I left my heart and soul in these mountains. Being here this last week has made me realize what a mistake I made in leaving."

Ollie studies his weathered face. The lines around his eyes are deep from decades of squinting in the sun. His cloudy blue eyes have witnessed much over the years. "Where would you live?"

"With your approval, I'd like to fix up the caretaker's cottage."

"You don't need my approval to clean up that eyesore. But I insist on paying you. The farm will benefit from your wisdom and expertise. I'm knowledgeable when it comes to growing grapes, but my winemaking skills are lacking. I've been contemplating expanding our offerings. I don't need to be a marketing expert to realize we need a rosé. But I want something different, bold and funky. Not like the sweet swill they sell next door."

Melvin stabs a forkful of melon balls. "I have just the thing in mind. A full-bodied Syrah blend with notes of white pepper and cherries."

Ollie's grin is wide. "Yes! That's exactly what I'm thinking." She holds her hand out to Melvin. "Welcome home, Melvin. We're gonna make a brilliant team."

Melvin gives her hand a firm shake. "I came close to producing the Syrah rosé once. The world wasn't ready for it at the time, but the varietal has grown so much in popularity in recent years, I believe rosé enthusiasts will be receptive."

While they eat, they discuss other potential additions to Foxtail Farm's collection. Melvin is finishing his coffee and Ollie is rinsing the dishes when she feels his eyes on her.

"I don't need to ask how the party went?" He says with a snicker. "Your rosy glow gives you away. If I didn't know better, I'd say you're a woman in love."

She looks up from the sink. "What does that mean? Am I not allowed to fall in love?"

"Of course you are. But you're fresh out of mental rehab. It seems a little soon."

Ollie's skin prickles. "Don't judge me, Melvin. I've been through a lot the past few years. I'm looking for happiness wherever I can find it."

Melvin's gray, bushy eyebrows become one. "Of course you are. I will never judge you, Ollie. I just want you to be careful. And to find someone who deserves you."

Ollie places the last plate in the dishwasher and closes the door. "I doubt you'll approve. He's Sheldon Love."

His smile reaches his twinkling blue eyes. "I approve whole-heartedly. Sheldon's not like the rest of the Loves. I've known him all his life. He was a good boy who grew into an honorable man."

Relief washes over her. "I'm glad you think so." Melvin's approval is important to her. He's an older and wiser version of her father. Having him back on the farm will ease the pressure. The combination of his experience and her drive will enable them to accomplish great things together. And Ollie has a very long list of goals she yearns to achieve.

CHAPTER 18
ADA

Searching her father's attic for Ada's mother's belongings is a painstakingly slow process. To avoid a confrontation with Daniel, she waits for him to leave for work in the mornings. And with the summer sun beating down on the slate roof, she can only stand the heat in the attic for a couple of hours.

Starting at the north end, she meticulously searches through every container and box. She rummages through trunks packed with elbow-length white kid gloves and beaded dresses from the roaring twenties. When she locates the family's collection of heirloom Christmas ornaments, she spends hours reminiscing about Christmases past—snowy mornings by the fire opening presents and elaborate gifts from Santa, dirt bikes and ponies and stereos.

On the second Thursday of July, Ada is tiptoeing up the stairs to the second floor, when Daniel's sharp voice stops her in her tracks. "Ada! Where do you think you're going?"

Turning to face him, she retreats down the stairs. "There you are! I didn't know you were here. Your car's not in the driveway."

"My car's in the shop," he snaps. "Did you need to see me about something?"

Ada has her story ready in the event she runs into him. "I want to talk to you about Mom's jewelry. I'm old enough to take care of it, and I'd like to have it. No sense keeping it locked in a safe when I could be enjoying it."

Daniel stares down his nose at her. "It's not all yours, Ada. Lila was your brothers' mother as well. I'm sure they would like their wives to have a few pieces. She certainly had plenty to go around."

"Fine. But as her only daughter, I should have first dibs."

"You maybe her only daughter, but I am not your father. I handpicked each piece of jewelry and gave them to her as gifts for birthday, anniversaries, and Christmases. Which means I get to disperse the jewelry as I see fit."

Ada is surprised he gave her mother anything, as miserable as their marriage was. "Gift is the operative word here, Daniel. You gifted Mom the jewelry, which means it belonged to her. She would want me to have my choice of it. I'll arrange a meeting with my brothers. I'd like to settle this as soon as possible. Before you give it to Casey like you've given her everything else that belonged to me."

"That's not entirely true. I'm letting you keep your horse."

"How generous of you," she says, brushing past him and storming out of the house.

Ada speeds down the road to the winery. She parks in her reserved space but remains in the car. She waits until she sees Daniel enter the winery before returning to The Nest, this time parking behind the stables.

Daniel may be onto her now. She must speed up the process. When she reaches the attic, she paces up and down the wooden floors, shining her phone's flashlight at the labeled boxes. She finds what she's looking for tucked under an eave at the far end of the attic. The chicken scratch writing on the box identifies the contents of Lila's study. She tears open the box. Inside are office supplies—paper clips and sticky notes and the bold point gel pens her mother preferred. Buried beneath the bric-à-brac are appointment books dating back from the time of Lila's death to the late 1980s. Bingo.

A wave of excitement rolls over her, and she can hardly wait to dive in. She wrestles the heavy box down the stairs to her car. On the drive back to town, Ada calls her assistant to let her know she'll be working remotely today. At her apartment, she digs out the appointment book for 1994, the year Ada was conceived. She flips through the pages to the summer months when her father was having his affair with Casey's mother in Napa.

Nothing jumps off the pages at first. There are monthly hair and nail appointments. Lila's annual mammogram and visit to her gynecologist. She met her friend Julia for tennis on Wednesdays. Often lunched with Janice and Renee. But under closer inspection, she notices frequent instances of the letter R written in her mother's curlicue script. R for coffee. R for cocktails. R in the afternoon.

Who the heck is R? It must be a man, otherwise she would have written out the name as in the other entries. Is it possible R is one of Daniel's friends? Grabbing her computer, she accesses the guest list from the Fourth of July party and scrolls through the names. None start with R. Closing the laptop, she falls back against the sofa cushions. From her early childhood, Ada remembers a vineyard worker named Ramon. He used to speak Italian to Ada. She never understood what he was saying, but she found his accent fascinating. Lila was too dignified to sleep with a field hand. Or was she? Ada would never have considered hooking up with a field hand. Until she met Enzo.

Ada has more questions than ever. But she knows just the person who could answer them.

Beatrice has never been one to show emotion, but the dour old housekeeper sounds excited to hear from Ada. When the Love children were growing up, Beatrice was more nanny than housekeeper. While she doted on Ada, she was strict with her brothers. Maybe Beatrice realized the boys needed discipline. Or maybe she doesn't like men, regardless of their ages.

Beatrice lives in a small yellow house in the less desirable section of town. She comes to the door in her pink housecoat with her gray hair in rollers. "Have a seat." She motions Ada to a metal glider on the front porch. "I'll get us some lemonade."

Lowering herself to the chair, Ada stares out at the tidy yard with its luscious green grass and impatiens lining the sidewalk. Unsure of how to broach the subject, when Beatrice returns, she blurts, "There's no easy way to say this. But I've recently learned Daniel Love is not my biological father."

If this surprises Beatrice, she doesn't let it show.

"I need to know who my father is, Bea. Is there anything you can tell me that might help?"

Beatrice hesitates, as though gathering her thoughts. "You already know your mama was miserable with your father. She begged him for a divorce, but he wouldn't let her leave. He threatened to take custody of you children and to cut her off without a cent. A good divorce attorney would never have let that happen, but Miz Lila was too afraid of losing everything."

"So, she suffered instead," Ada says, understanding for the first time how much her mother sacrificed to keep her family together.

A faraway expression settles on Beatrice's face. "There was that one summer Mr. Love spent in California. Miz Lila seemed genuinely happy then. I always assumed it was because your father was away, but maybe there was another reason for her sudden happiness."

Beatrice removes a bundle of envelopes from the pocket of her housecoat. The envelopes are notecard size and tied with a pale blue ribbon. "Your mother asked me to give these to you. She said I would know when the time was right." She fingers the satin ribbon. "I didn't question her, but I found it strange. I've often wondered if Miz Lila sensed something would happen to her."

Ada takes the bundle from her. "Who wrote them?"

"I wouldn't know," Beatrice says in an indignant tone.

Of course Beatrice never read them. She was loyal to Ada's mother even after her death.

"Maybe they're from my biological father." She brings the

bundle to her nose and sniffs. The paper smells musty from being stored away for decades.

Beatrice points an arthritic finger at the notes. "I'm sure you'll find clues, maybe even some answers written in those."

Ada slips the notes in her purse. "I hope you're right."

Beatrice places her hand on top of Ada's. "I know this is hard on you, Ada. I can see it in your face. If you ever need to talk, you know where to find me. You're welcome here anytime."

"Thank you, Bea. That means a lot." Ada stands and kisses Beatrice's cheek. "I'll be in touch."

Eager to read the notes, Ada hurries down the sidewalk to her car and speeds off. She drives a mile, pulls over to the side of the road, and removes the bundle from her purse. Untying the ribbon, she opens the envelope on top and scans the messy script. The writer's words are beautiful, like poetry, and the message so intimate Ada's face warms as she reads. Whoever wrote this loved her mother very much. He speaks of the impossibility of their situation, about hurting their children if they were to leave their spouses.

One by one, she skims the rest of the letters but learns little about the man's identity except that his name begins with *R*, which is how he signs the notes.

Why did her mother ask Beatrice to give Ada the letters? Because Lila wanted Ada to understand how much she had loved her biological father. So Ada could understand the choices Lila made? Ironically, Ada understands even less about her mother's affair with her biological father than she did an hour ago.

Ada was born on June fifteenth, which means she was conceived in mid-September. Daniel came home from California in late August. The last note is dated November second. The man's last words: *I hate for our relationship to end like this. If you change your mind, you know where to find me.*

Ada assumes Lila told him she was pregnant, although she can't be certain. It appears as though Lila was the one who decided to pass Ada off as Daniel's daughter. But it doesn't sound like the man put up much of a fight.

Ada's head spins, and she yearns for a drink. She envisions the unopened bottle of tequila in her pantry. But getting drunk before noon won't solve her problem and will only make her more depressed. She needs someone to confide in. Someone she trusts. Only one person fits that bill.

She checks the clock on the dashboard. It's almost lunchtime, and Enzo often comes home from work to eat. She drives over to his house, prepared to wait for him, but his car is already parked in the driveway.

Ada knocks on the door, and when he answers, she says, "You're home for lunch early."

"I'm not home for lunch, Ada. I'm home because your father fired me."

Ada's jaw falls open. "For what reason?"

"He claims I stole a case of rosé from the winery. But we both know your father fired me because he doesn't want me anywhere near you." Enzo tightens his grip on the doorknob. "Why are you here, Ada?"

She rakes her hand through her dark hair. "I'm a mess, and I could really use a friend. But I can tell you're upset with me. I'm sorry. I made a mistake in coming here."

When she starts back toward her car, Enzo grabs her by the arm. "I have a right to be angry. You used me to get back at your father, and it cost me my job. But I'm not heartless. Come inside. I'll fix you a grilled cheese."

Enzo puts a southwest spin on his grilled cheese by using thick slices of Colby jack cheese, poblano peppers, cilantro, and sliced tomatoes on sourdough bread. While they eat, Ada brings him to speed about her search for her real father.

"Ramon was our vineyard manager for decades. He's the only man I know whose name begins with a *R*. The more I think about it, the more I'm sure it's him," Ada says and is grateful Enzo doesn't point out the irony of mother and daughter sleeping with field hands.

"Are you going to reach out to him?" Enzo asks.

"I have to find him first. If it's not Ramon, I'll keep looking. I'm desperate to find my father, Enzo. Knowing him will help me know myself."

CHAPTER 19
OLLIE

Ollie throws caution to the wind and jumps headfirst into a relationship with Sheldon. She can't help herself. She finds him so irresistible. For the next ten days, she spends all of her free time with him. They eat most meals together, take the dogs for long walks in the evenings, and pass lazy weekend afternoons picnicking and hiking on the nearby mountain trails.

The sex, steamy one minute and tender the next, boggles Ollie's mind. Sheldon knows how to turn her on and take her to heights she never imagined possible. Ollie has never felt so close to anyone before. Not even her ex-husband.

Ollie works hard to keep her anxiety under control. Twice a week, she goes for hour-long sessions with Dr. Ronnie. She meditates often and attends regular yoga classes at a studio in town. Sheldon is an enormous asset in helping her avoid panic attacks. He recognizes when something is bothering her and instinctively knows what to say to talk her off the ledge.

Ollie is sailing along on a smooth course, but the waters are uncharted, and her nagging intuition warns her of trouble on the horizon.

On Thursday afternoon of the second week of July, Ollie and

Fiona are meeting on the cafe's terrace to discuss issues relating to The Foxhole when Fiona blurts, "I'm worried about you, Ollie. You've jumped from the frying pan into the fire. Shouldn't you take some time for yourself before committing to another serious relationship?"

Ollie pauses, taking deep breaths to shake off her rising irritation. "I'm a big girl, Fiona. I can take care of myself. Besides, why waste time when Sheldon and I are meant to be together?"

"How can you be so sure of that? You hardly know each other."

Ollie opens her mouth to lay into Fiona, but the young woman's forlorn expression warns her off. "Is something bothering you, Fiona? You don't seem like yourself."

"I'm fine," Fiona snaps. "Aside from being worried about you."

"Well, I'm fine too. So let's both stop worrying."

That's easier said than done for Ollie. The seed Fiona planted in Ollie's brain grows. Is she rushing things with Sheldon? While they've been together for less than two weeks, she feels like she's known him for a lifetime. Until now, she hasn't let herself think about the many obstacles ahead if they stay together. Where will they live? Ollie has a farmhouse, and Sheldon's building his dream home. Ollie owns a vineyard, and Sheldon's family is her major competitor. And what about his brothers? She can't imagine sitting down to Thanksgiving dinner with Hugh and Charles at the table. Sheldon hasn't forced his family on her yet, but she senses it's coming.

When Sheldon invites her to lunch the next day to discuss something important, Ollie has a sneaking suspicion whatever he wants to talk about has to do with his family.

Ollie suggests they eat at The Foxtail. "Fiona wants feedback on her new sandwich items."

"That's cool with me. I'll be Fiona's guinea pig anytime. I'll see you around noon."

Ollie makes her way down to The Foxhole a few minutes

before noon and snags a table for two on the terrace ahead of the lunch crowd. Their server, Steve, appears, and she places an order for the two new menu items.

Ollie is scrolling through emails on her phone when Sheldon arrives ten minutes later. "Sorry. I got hung up on a business call." He kisses the top of her head and sits down across from her.

She smiles at him. He's handsome in a blue striped golf shirt that makes his pale eyes pop. "No worries. I ordered for us. I hope you don't mind. There are two new sandwiches, a roasted turkey Ruben, and the other rare roast beef with grilled onions and provolone cheese. I figured we'd share halves."

Sheldon places his napkin in his lap. "They sound delicious. I'm starving."

"The key ingredient for both sandwiches is Fiona's signature sriracha aioli sauce. It's flavorful without being too spicy." Ollie folds her hands on the table. "What did you want to talk to me about?"

"My father has invited us to dinner tonight at The Nest. It'll just be the three of us." Sheldon holds up his hand before she can protest. "He's not so scary once you get to know him."

Ollie lowers her gaze. "Must we do this so soon? We've only been together for such a short time, and I feel safe in our little bubble. Why upset the apple cart?"

"My father is very persuasive. He refuses to take no for an answer. I'm—"

Steve interrupts Sheldon when he arrives with their order. Ollie takes half of his roast beef and gives him the other half of her turkey Ruben. They sample their sandwiches and moan in approval.

"This is amazing," Sheldon says with his mouth full. "I vote for making both permanent menu items."

"I agree. I will tell Fiona you endorse the sandwiches. Maybe she'll name one The Sheldon," Ollie says with mischief in her aqua eyes.

"And the other The Ollie. But I get to be the roast beef," he says, taking another bite of sandwich.

"That means I'm the turkey." Ollie sets down her sandwich and wipes her lips. "And this turkey would like to postpone dinner with your father. At least for another week or two."

Sheldon's expression grows serious. "My feelings for you are rock solid, Ollie. Neither of us is getting any younger, and I want to start planning our future together. The first step is for you to get to know my father. I realize he can be difficult. And he certainly has plenty of flaws. But he's my best friend, the most important person in my life other than you."

His sincerity tugs at Ollie's heartstrings. "How can I possibly say no to that?"

Sheldon's face lights up. "Do you mean it, really?" He reaches for her hand. "I promise we'll have fun. Dad's planning a casual summer supper on the terrace. Totally low key."

Her eyes travel to the stone mansion on the hill. "I admit I'm curious to see the famous Nest."

"Wear comfortable shoes, and I'll give you the tour." Sheldon's phone vibrates the table with an incoming call. "I need to talk to this wine distributor. I've been waiting for his call for weeks. Do you mind if I cut out on you?"

"Go," Ollie says, shooing him away. "I'll see you tonight."

Sheldon takes the rest of his roast beef sandwich with him when he leaves the table.

Seated with her back to the cafe, Ollie doesn't see Jamie approach until he's seated in Sheldon's vacated chair. "You and Sheldon are awfully chummy. You didn't waste any time finding someone new after we broke up."

Anger surges through her. "Because I was ready to move on, Jamie. I was emotionally unattached to you, almost from the beginning. I was stringing you along, because I was afraid of being alone." Ollie realizes her mistake, but she can't take the words back.

"Is that why you're with Sheldon now? Because you're afraid to be alone?"

Ollie glares at him. "I'm not discussing this with you, Jamie. Why are you even here?"

"I came to see Fiona." Jamie takes a potato chip off Sheldon's plate and pops it in his mouth. "You realize Sheldon's using you."

Ollie rolls her eyes. "Using me for what?"

Jamie's jaw slackens. "Really? I guess love really is blind."

"Stop talking in riddles, Jamie. What is it you're trying to say?"

"After what that family has put you through, you of all people should realize how desperate they are to get this land." He taps the table with his finger. "What better way to get it than marrying you?"

"You have no clue what you're talking about. Now, please leave my table."

"Gladly," Jamie says, grabbing a handful of chips before scurrying away.

———

A sense of impending doom settles over Ollie as she moves through the afternoon. Is it possible Sheldon's using her to get his hands on Foxtail Farm? The prospect seems extreme. Then again, the Love family *is* extreme.

Ollie, wearing a pale blue linen sheath, is waiting when Sheldon arrives promptly at seven to pick her up. Nervous about meeting his father, she says little on the ride over. The treelined driveway meanders behind the Love-Struck winery to the stone mansion, which Ollie finds way more imposing in person.

She marvels at the priceless antiques in the center hallway as they pass through the house to the back terrace, where Daniel is pouring a drink at a bar cart.

"Welcome to The Nest," he says, kissing Ollie's cheek. "What can I offer you to drink?"

"I'll have whatever you're having."

"Vodka and soda it is." Daniel turns to Sheldon. "What would you like, son?"

"Same," Sheldon says with a nod of his head.

When the drinks are served, Daniel raises his glass. "To new beginnings."

A plump woman with caramel skin emerges from the house with a tray of canapes. "Ollie, this is our cook, Marabella. She's been with us for decades."

The women exchange smiles. "Nice to meet you, Marabella."

"Nice to meet you as well, ma'am."

Daniel and Ollie decline the canapes, but Sheldon gobbles down the entire tray.

Marabella lets out a deep, throaty laugh. "You need to come around more often to see me, you naughty boy," she says, smacking him on the behind with her empty tray. "I sure have missed that appetite of yours."

Sheldon rubs his belly. "I'm watching my figure. I can only afford to eat your cooking every so often."

They all laugh, and Marabella disappears inside.

Daniel rests a hand on Ollie's shoulder. "Once again, I'd like to say how sorry I am for the way my older sons have treated you. Their behavior is reprehensible, and I've warned them I will not tolerate it."

"Thank you, Mr. Love. Things have been much quieter since you returned to work."

"Please, call me Daniel. How *are* things at Foxtail?"

"Things are going well. Business at The Foxhole has really taken off, and Melvin has returned from Arizona."

Daniel narrows his pale green eyes, an older and wiser pair than Sheldon's. "That's surprises me. Is he pressuring you to sell the farm back to him?"

"No, sir!" Ollie says in a more forceful tone than she intended. "I have no intention of selling Foxtail to Melvin or anyone else. I had to be away from the farm for a week back in June, and I asked

Melvin to look after things while I was gone. Retirement didn't agree with Melvin, so he's decided to stay. He's a genius at wine-making. We have some exciting new varietals in the works."

Daniel's jaw tightens, but he doesn't respond.

When Marabella returns with the salad course, they move to a small table set with fine china, linens, and a bouquet of multicolored roses. While they eat, Daniel questions her about her family's vineyard in Napa, which leads to a discussion about the process of making wine. Daniel pours white and red wine with every course, and by the time they finish their entrees, Ollie is tipsy.

Marabella clears the dinner plates, and while they're waiting for dessert, Sheldon excuses himself to use the restroom.

Daniel leans in close to Ollie and lowers his voice. "I try not to play favorites with my children. But personalities often dictate relationships. Sheldon and I have always been close. He has a special place in my heart. If the two of you were to marry, after more than a hundred years, the feud between our two vineyards will end." He chuckles. "That's a fairy tale if ever I've heard one."

Ollie's skin prickles. "Sheldon and I have only been dating a couple of weeks. It's too soon to be talking about marriage."

"Maybe so, but I recognize true love when I see it. The possibilities are endless. A merger between our two vineyards would make us the largest vineyard in Virginia."

Ollie's body goes still. Is he out of his mind? Or have Daniel and Sheldon been planning this all along? Jamie's words rush back to her. *What better way to get it than marrying you?*

"As far as I'm concerned, the feud ended when I bought Foxtail Farm. As I said earlier, I will never sell my vineyard. And that includes a merger."

Sheldon returns from the restroom. "What'd I miss?" he asks, as though sensing the hostility between Ollie and Daniel.

"Your father can tell you." Ollie pushes abruptly back from the table. "I'll wait for you in the car."

Tears sting her eyes as she makes her way through the house.

Sheldon catches up to her as she's getting in the car. "What did Dad say to make you angry?"

Ollie swings around to face him. "As if you didn't know."

"I have no idea what you're talking about."

"I'm such a fool," she cries. "I believed your lies. But you don't want me. You're after my land. Your father suggested we merge our vineyards after we're married."

Sheldon presses his lips thin. "He actually said that?"

"Yes! I made a huge mistake in letting you into my life. I made a vow to never marry again. And I plan to keep it. Now, please take me home."

"If that's what you want." Sheldon goes around to the driver's side of the car. Starting the engine, he pulls away from the mansion. "I'm sorry, Ollie. Dad spoke out of turn. He and I have never discussed marriage or mergers."

"Whatever. I don't want to talk about it anymore."

When they reach the main road, Sheldon makes a right-hand turn toward Foxtail Farm. "You're angry, and I don't blame you. Please don't throw away what we have because of what my father said."

They ride the rest of the way in silence. When they reach the farmhouse, Sheldon parks and opens his car door to get out.

"I need to be alone tonight, Sheldon. I have a lot to think about."

"Please, Ollie," he says in a desperate tone. "Let me come inside. Let's talk this through."

"I made a terrible mistake in trusting you. I can't be with you, Sheldon. Your family is too screwed up. Your brothers are vindictive and your father controlling. I'm glad I figured it out now, before it's too late."

She slams the car door and runs inside, where she crumbles to the living room floor. Her chest constricts, and she struggles to catch her breath. This isn't a panic attack. This is the pain of a breaking heart.

CHAPTER 20
CASEY

Late Saturday afternoon, Casey is painting at her easel in front of the stable when Fiona drives up. She toots her horn and gets out of her car. "There you are! I've been looking all over for you." She peers over Casey's shoulder at the watercolor. "Ooh! That's so pretty. I love the perspective of the horse sticking its head out of the window."

"Thank you." Casey admires her work for a second before putting down her paintbrush and turning to face Fiona. "What're you up to?"

"Not you, Casey. *We*. We're going on a road trip."

"Another one? Where to this time?" Casey asks as she packs up her art supplies.

"Hope Springs. I think Will is seeing someone else. And I want to catch him in the act."

"Since when are you two exclusive?" Casey asks as they walk toward the mansion.

"We're not. But we had a date planned for tonight, and he canceled on me at the last minute. He claims his dad is sick, and he's driving over to Roanoke to see him. But he's been acting kinda weird lately, and I suspect he's lying about tonight."

"Do you even know where to find him?"

Fiona bobs her head. "According to Cecily, one of their friends is having a birthday party at Town Tavern. Cecily's not going because she has to work, but she thinks Will will be there."

"Unless his dad really is sick." When they arrive at the house, Casey reaches for the front doorknob. "I have to put my supplies away and change. Wanna come inside?"

"No thanks. I'll wait in your car."

"In *my* car? Why am I driving when it's your boyfriend we're spying on?"

"Because I'm too upset. I might wreck. And I'm dying to ride in this seriously cool sports car. Can we put the top down?"

Casey laughs. "Yes, we can put the top down. I'll be right back."

She disappears inside and returns a few minutes later wearing a blousy pink top over white jeans with her hair piled in a messy bun. Peeling back the convertible roof, they head off to Hope Springs.

"I haven't seen you in forever," Fiona says, checking her reflection in the visor mirror. "What have you been up to?"

"Working," Casey says in a disgruntled tone. "I've been trying to get a better feel,"—she hooks her fingers in air quotes— "for the vineyard. I've spent days in the fields, learning about the process of growing grapes. I've taken the winery tour too many times to count. I've attended wedding ceremonies and receptions, and I've planted myself at the tasting bars for hours on end, listening to patrons express their opinions while drinking flights of wine."

Fiona giggles. "That sounds like a lot. Has any of it helped?" she asks, folding up the sun visor.

"No!" Casey palms the steering wheel in frustration. "Daniel approves of my work. I just can't seem to nail the brand. I have one more concept I'll share with him this week. After that, I'm fresh out of ideas."

"I have faith in you, Casey. You're extremely talented. You'll come up with something."

"I wouldn't be too sure about that," Casey mumbles.

"How're things going with Luke?"

"I haven't seen him since the Fourth of July. He was furious when he saw Jamie kissing me. He called me immature and said our relationship won't work because of our five-year age difference. Never mind that I told him I'm not interested in Jamie. It sucks, because I really like him," Casey says as tears fill her eyes.

Fiona removes a travel package of tissues from her purse and hands one to Casey. "Are you sure there's nothing going on between you and Jamie?"

"Positive. There's zero chemistry between us. And I got tired of listening to him whine about how much he misses Ollie."

Fiona laughs. "Right? I flat-out told him to stop talking about her. He's gotten better about it lately. I honestly think he's trying."

Casey glances over at her passenger. "Sounds like you've seen a lot of Jamie."

Fiona shrugs. "He stops by The Foxhole almost every day. I think he's lonely. If you really like Luke, go after him. Prove to him you're not into Jamie and you're not immature."

Casey lets out a humph. "Easier said than done."

"There you go with that defeatist attitude again. Seriously, Casey, I question whether you truly have Love blood in your veins. Your siblings fight dirty, and you turn tail and run at the first sign of a challenge."

"Since when is avoiding confrontation a character flaw? Never mind. Let's change the subject." Casey spots the city limit sign for Hope Springs. "We're here anyway. Can you direct me to Town Tavern?"

"Sure. It's easy. Town Tavern is just ahead on the right."

"Got it." Casey turns right at the restaurant and parks in the lot behind Town Tavern.

"Here," Fiona says, tossing a black baseball cap to Casey. "Wear this so Will doesn't recognize you."

Casey throws the hat back to Fiona. "I am not wearing a baseball cap. Besides, I only met him the one time at Blue Cosmos. I seriously doubt he'd recognize me."

"Suit yourself," Fiona says, pulling a cap low to hide her face.

Town Tavern is crowded with a large party occupying a long table in the far back corner. Locating seats at the bar, Fiona flags down the attractive female bartender for a double vodka tonic.

The bartender turns to Casey. "What can I get you, miss?"

"I'll have club soda, please. And I'd like to see the menu."

The bartender slides the card stock menu across the bar. "Today's special is buffalo chicken wings. If you have a sensitive pallet, I wouldn't recommend them."

"Thanks for the warning." Casey quickly scans the menu. "I'll have the kale salad with grilled chicken."

"Got it." The bartender's blonde ponytail dances around her shoulders as she saunters off.

Casey's back is to the birthday party, but Fiona can't take her eyes off the attendees. "Do you see Will?"

Fiona shakes her head. "He's not here yet."

"Or he's not coming. He's probably on his way to visit his sick father. You said he's been acting weird lately. What makes you so sure he's seeing someone else?"

Fiona sags in her chair. "We had plans to have dinner at the inn tonight. He'd booked a reservation and everything. We were both excited. Then, boom. He cancels, just like that." She snaps her fingers. "He didn't even call me. He just sent a text."

"Which makes sense. He's upset about his father," Casey says.

The bartender returns with their order. Fiona is taking the first sip of her drink when her blue eyes suddenly go wide. "There he is. And he's with a perky little blonde." She ducks her head. "Let's get outta here before he sees me."

Casey hands Fiona her car key. "Wait for me in the car. I'll pay the check."

Fiona slides off the barstool and scurries away. Casey shovels salad in her mouth while she waits for the bartender to process the credit card charge. When she gets to the car, Fiona's thumbs are flying across her phone's screen. "Are you texting Will?"

"Yes." Fiona sends the text and looks up at Casey. "But don't worry. I bowed out gracefully. I told him I'm not feeling it, and I don't think he is either."

Casey starts the engine and drives down Main Street. "You never cease to amaze me, Fi. I thought you'd be more upset."

Fiona drops her phone in her bag at her feet. "I'm not really. Will's fun to hang out with. But the sex was only so-so. I'm holding out for the real deal. I want chemistry that sparks an explosion."

Casey laughs. "Good luck with that."

Fiona stares out the window. "Are you sure you're not interested in Jamie?"

Casey glances over at Fiona. "Positive. Why?"

"Because I might be. If you don't care. I don't want to infringe on your territory."

"Go for it," Casey says, picking up speed as they leave the outskirts of town. "I've never thought about you and Jamie as a couple. You'd be cute together. Just be sure he's not using you to get back at Ollie."

"Don't worry. I sense there maybe something brewing between us. But I plan to take it slow."

"You're fickle, Fiona. First, you declare your undying love for me. Then Will, and now Jamie."

Fiona sticks out her tongue at Casey. "At least I'm not afraid to explore my options like some people I know."

Casey watches the road as she lets this sink in. "I prefer to think of myself as cautious. Keep in mind, I spent the past three years nursing my sick mother. I'm still adjusting to the real world. Do you blame me for being a little gun-shy?"

"Not at all. But I'd hate for you to miss out on your chance with Luke if he's the one."

Fiona and Casey ride the rest of the way in silence, each lost in her own thoughts. What if Luke is the one? Casey's only chance at true love? She should at least give it one more try.

They're approaching Lovely when Fiona says, "Do you mind dropping me at my house? I'll get my car tomorrow. I can't wait to crawl in my bed and cry myself to sleep."

Casey risks a glance at her. "Wait? I'm confused. So you are upset about Will."

Fiona examines her fingernails. "My feelings are hurt more than anything. Being dejected is never fun, regardless of whether you liked the person."

Casey turns down Fiona's street and parks in front of her house. "In that case, why don't I stay for a while? You shouldn't be alone. We can watch a scary movie or something."

Fiona gathers her belongings. "I'm fine. Trust me, you don't want to see me ugly cry."

"Instead of wallowing in self-pity, why don't you give Jamie a call?"

Fiona aims a finger gun at Casey. "Good idea. I might just do that."

Casey blows her an air kiss. "Call me in the morning. I'll pick you up and take you to get your car."

"Sounds good. And thanks for going on my spy mission with me."

Casey waits until Fiona has gone inside before driving off. As she's passing through town, she notices a chalkboard sign on the sidewalk in front of Blue Cosmos. Twilight Groove is performing tonight. On a whim, she whips into the parking lot and enters the jazz club. As she's making her way through the crowd, she notices a striking woman with silky black hair perched on the stool at the end of the bar, her sultry dark eyes watching Luke's every move. She wants him, and based on her determined expression, she aims to have him at whatever cost.

Rich comes from behind the bar with a glass of champagne for her. "Long time, no see. Where have you been hanging out?"

"I've been working, mostly. Who's that woman?" Casey dips

her head at the dark-haired beauty. "Is she Luke's date for the night?" Her tone comes across as jealous instead of teasing as she intended.

"That's Brooke, his ex-girlfriend. I have no clue what he's doing with her. She's a real drama queen. She made his life miserable when they were together. She begged him to give her another chance. Truth be told, I think he's hung up on you. Every time he comes in, he asks if I've seen you."

"She's more his type," Casey says, her eyes still on the woman.

Rich's brow shoots up. "How so?"

"She's sophisticated and drop-dead gorgeous. And she's closer to his age."

"That may all be true, but he doesn't look at her the way he looks at you."

Casey drags her eyes away from the woman. "I should go. I made a mistake in coming here." She hands Rich the untouched champagne.

"Should I tell Luke you were here?"

"Please don't. Let him work things out with Brooke."

Casey holds back the tears as she fights her way to the exit. But she bursts out crying when she gets in her car. Wild thoughts run through her mind on the way home. Luke will play his saxophone for Brooke tonight, dancing with her under the stars on his terrace. Why does this hurt so much when she barely knows him?

Casey went out on a limb by going to Blue Cosmos, but it wasn't enough. She should've waited until the band took a break. Should've insisted Luke talk to her and begged him for another chance. Instead of fighting dirty, she did exactly what Fiona accused her of. She turned tail and ran.

CHAPTER 21
OLLIE

Ollie ignores Sheldon's calls and texts on Saturday, but she can no longer avoid him when he shows up at the farm just after lunch on Sunday.

"Ollie, please! Just hear me out."

"You have five minutes. Start talking," she says and drops to the porch steps.

Sheldon remains standing in front of her. "I've spoken to my father. He didn't mean to upset you. He wants nothing more than peace between Foxtail Farm and Love-Struck. He would never ask you to give up control of your business. Is it possible you took what he said out of context?"

Ollie has replayed her conversation with Daniel over in her mind dozens of times. "I'm willing to admit I may have overreacted. I warned you I wasn't ready to have dinner with your father, yet you pushed me. You upset the apple cart. I know you want more, Sheldon. But you need to understand I've just gotten out of a relationship. I spent a week in mental rehab to sort through my anxiety problems. I'm extremely vulnerable right now."

"What are you saying, Ollie?"

"That everything is happening too fast, and I need some time to myself."

Sheldon lets out a loud sigh. "There's no one else for me, Ollie. I've loved you since the first moment I saw you. And I'm willing to wait as long as it takes for you to sort out your life. But I won't beg. When you're ready, you'll have to come to me."

When he turns back toward his Range Rover, she resists the urge to go after him. Tears fill her eyes as she watches him drive away. She loves him too, with her whole heart. If she's meant to be in a relationship with someone, Sheldon is the one. But it's too soon. She doesn't trust herself enough yet. And she's not sure she's cut out for a lifetime partnership.

She feels the world closing in around her. Not in a panicky way, but in a way that warns her she needs space. She wants to give Sheldon her best self, and she's certain she'll get there with Dr. Ronnie's help. But who knows how long it'll take? Weeks? Months? Sheldon said he'd wait for her. Time will be the test of their love.

Ollie is still sitting on the steps, contemplating her future with Sheldon, when a black pickup truck she doesn't recognize pulls up. She stands to greet the nice-looking young man who gets out.

"Afternoon, ma'am," he says, tipping his hat at her. "Are you Ollie Hendrix?"

Ollie presses her lips into a tight smile. "I am. And you are?"

"I'm Enzo Medici. If you have a minute, I'd like to talk to you about a job. Actually, I'm interested in an unpaid internship. I'm studying to become a sommelier. I'm learning the winemaking industry from the ground up."

Ollie looks more closely at his handsome face. There's an intensity in his dark eyes that intrigues her. "Have you ever worked at a vineyard?"

He shifts his weight to the other foot. "Yes, ma'am. Most recently, I worked the fields at Love-Struck."

Ollie arches a brow. "Oh? And what happened? Did you quit?"

"Actually, no. Daniel Love fired me over a personal matter."

Leaning back against his truck, Ollie folds her arms over her chest. "I'm all ears."

"I was dancing with his daughter at the Fourth of July party—"

"And he didn't approve of his daughter dating a field hand," Ollie says in disgust.

"Right. Funny thing is, we aren't even dating. We're just friends. Ada's going through a tough time, and I'm helping her figure out her life." Enzo rakes his hands through his thick, dark hair. "I don't care so much about the job at Love-Struck anyway. I was ready to move on anyway. I've learned as much as I want to know about growing grapes. I understand Melvin Bass is back from Arizona. He's a legend. I'd worship the chance to study winemaking under him."

Ollie chuckles. "I agree. Melvin *is* a legend. I wish I could help you, Enzo, but I wouldn't be comfortable with you interning here while you're spending time with Ada Love."

He drags his finger across his heart. "I swear on my life. I don't need to know your secret formulas. In fact, I'd rather *not* know them. I just want to learn. And Melvin is the master."

Ollie shakes her head. "I admire your enthusiasm, but this is too risky. I don't trust the Loves."

"Then we have that in common." In a pleading tone, Enzo says, "Please, ma'am. I'll do anything you ask. I'm strong and resourceful. I'll help in the field and the winery and wash dishes in The Foxhole. I promise I won't get in your way. It won't be forever. Only a couple of months."

Ollie massages her chin as she scrutinizes him. Despite his good looks, he has an innocent way about him. "How old are you Enzo?"

"Twenty-nine." He snatches his baseball cap off his head and holds it to his chest. "Please, ma'am. I'd be ever so grateful for the chance."

He's just a kid. And so earnest. How can she possibly tell him no? "I'll consider it. As long as you stop calling me ma'am."

Enzo's face beams red. "I'll try. But my parents raised me to respect my elders."

"So did mine. But I'm not that much older than you." Ollie pushes off the truck. "I think I'll let Melvin make this decision. He's sprucing things up at the caretaker's cottage. I was just on my way down there to help him paint. If you have a minute, we can talk to him now."

"For Melvin Bass, I have all the time in the world. I can't wait to meet him."

Enzo steps in line beside Ollie, and they stroll together down the gravel driveway to the carriage house where they find Melvin rolling the living room walls in linen colored paint. When Ollie introduces their visitor, Melvin sets down his roller and shakes Enzo's hand. Ollie explains about Enzo's request for an internship and his association with the Love family.

Melvin's face brightens as the two men talk about Enzo's studies. "Your enthusiasm for the wine industry is contagious," he says, slapping Enzo on the back. "I would be delighted to work with you."

"Does is friendship with Ada Love not concern you?" Ollie asks.

Melvin waves away her worry. "He seems like a trustworthy young man. Besides, no way can he replicate our varietals without the magic ingredient."

Ollie flashes Melvin a knowing smile.

Enzo looks back and forth between them. "What magic ingredient?"

"You'll learn in time," Melvin says, an arm around Enzo as he walks him to the door. "I'm flying to Arizona tomorrow to collect my furniture. I'm driving my truck back, and I won't get here until the end of the week. I'll need the weekend to get settled, and we can start on Monday."

"That sounds great." Enzo shakes Melvin's hand again. "Thank you so much for this opportunity. I won't let you down."

Ollie stands with Melvin in the doorway, watching Enzo disappear up the drive.

"I have a good feeling about him," Melvin says.

"And I trust your intuition, although I'm not sure I want him to know about our magic ingredient. How is it that our soil is so different from Love-Struck's when we're located so close together?"

"It's all about topography, my dear." Melvin closes the door and returns to painting.

Ollie slides a roller brush onto the metal handle, dips it in the paint tray, and drags it down the wall opposite Melvin. "Tell me more about the feud between the Basses and the Loves. I've heard bits and pieces, but never the entire story."

"Well, as you know, the Basses settled here first. We were just a small family working a multi-purpose farm, minding our own business when the caravan of Loves came to town. Daniel's ancestors settled next door while the rest of them established the town."

"The Loves quickly became envious of our lush green crops while everything they grew wilted and died. They made an offer on our land, and we refused. And hence, the fighting began. They stole our cattle and horses. Burned our fields. One Love man ran off with a Bass's wife. And a Bass kid got a Love teenager pregnant."

"Was there ever a peaceful time between the two families?"

Melvin finishes his wall and moves around the doorway into the dining room. "Things were quiet when I took over the farm and remained that way until Daniel Love retired. Then Hugh got it in his cockamamie brain to build a resort on my land and started making everyone's lives miserable."

Ollie pauses to wipe sweat off her forehead with the back of her hand. "Things are better now that Daniel's back at the helm. I think he put Hugh and Charles in their places."

"I feel sorry for Charles. He's always been Hugh's shadow, never allowed to think for himself. Ada is feisty. Reminds me a lot of her mother. But Sheldon's a good kid. He and my youngest were friends growing up. Sheldon spent a lot of time over here. From a young age, I could tell the land was in his blood." Melvin peeks around the doorjamb at Ollie. "Speaking of Sheldon, I haven't seen him around much lately. You two have a falling out?"

"Not a falling out. A misunderstanding." Ollie covers the last strip of white wall in paint and joins Melvin in the dining room. "Things were happening too fast. I need some time to catch my breath."

"I tried to warn you about that," Melvin says, pointing his roller at her.

"It's not just me needing space." She attacks another wall with her roller. "Sheldon is looking for commitment, and I'm not marriage material. I've always been adamant about not wanting children. It was part of the reason I broke up with Jamie. The maternal instinct is not part of my genetic makeup. I'm finally running my own vineyard, doing what I've always wanted to do. A child doesn't fit into my vision of the future."

Melvin retrieves two bottled waters from the refrigerator and hands one to her. "Traditional families were the norm when my children were coming along. My wife gladly stayed at home with the boys while I worked. But things are different these days. Both my son and his wife have demanding careers. They are equal partners in parenting in every sense of the word. I admire how they juggle their schedules and divvy up the duties. You and Sheldon can too, as long as he's in on the same page. How does he feel about wanting a family?"

Ollie shrugs. "We haven't discussed it. But if he wants them, and I don't, we can't be together."

Melvin freezes, his bottle pressed to his lips. "I hate to tell you, Ollie. Love doesn't work that way."

Ollie shoots him a look. "What do you mean?"

"When people love each other, they make these tough decisions together. You should at least discuss it with Sheldon. Maybe he doesn't want children. Then you don't have a problem."

"Good point." Ollie takes a swig of water. "Thank you, Melvin. You're a good listener."

"One of many skills I learned from parenting. For the record, you would make a fine mama, Ollie. Plenty of young woman lack maternal instinct when they first become parents. But you develop it over time. Don't let your fear prevent you from having a child. Children are God's greatest gifts to us. Trust in Him, and it'll all work out."

CHAPTER 22
ADA

Ada tracks down Ramon's current address, and on Thursday afternoon, she makes the trip to Orange, a small town on the outskirts of Charlottesville, to pay him a visit. During the ninety-minute drive, her mind travels back in time to her childhood.

Ramon's family lived in a small house on the Love-Struck property. Ada had girl crushes on his twin daughters, Gabriella and Isabella, who were several years older with boyish figures and long manes of silky black hair. His wife was a plain but kind woman, always cooking something on the stove when Ada visited their home.

Ramon lives on a small farm on the outskirts of Orange. The crops appear well-tended, but paint is peeling from the white farmhouse. Even though Mrs. Delgado hasn't seen Ada in twenty years, she recognizes her right away when she comes to the door.

Mrs. Delgado brings her fingers to her lips. "My Goodness, if it isn't Ada Love! What a lovely creature you turned out to be. Just like your mama, God rest her soul." Her face softens as she speaks of Ada's mother. If Ramon had an affair with Lila, Mrs. Delgado was not aware of it.

Ada kisses the woman's plump cheek. "It's nice to see you,

Mrs. Delgado. Is your husband around? I have an urgent personal matter I need to discuss with him."

Mrs. Delgado fingers her rosary bracelet. "Yes, of course, dear. He's out back in the barn. I can make a fresh pot of coffee, and we can visit when you return."

"I wish I could. But I'm pressed for time today. By the way, how are Gabriella and Isabella?"

"Wonderful. Gabriella lives in Charlotte, and Isabella in New York City." She giggles. "They both have jobs in finance. It's all over my head. But they are making handsome salaries."

"I'm glad to hear it. Please tell them hello for me." Turning away from the door, Ada retraces her steps off the porch to her car.

Her stomach is in knots as she navigates the bumpy dirt road to the barn. She's thought long and hard about what she'll say to him, but when she finds Ramon mucking out a stall, her mind goes blank.

Unlike his wife, he doesn't recognize Ada. "Can I help you, miss?"

"It's me, Ramon. Ada Love."

"Well, I'll be darned." He leans his pitchfork in the corner and emerges from the stall.

Standing face-to-face, they study each other more closely. Age has not been kind to him. His skin is like leather from years spent working under the harsh sun. Other than his dark hair, Ada sees nothing of herself in him.

Ada inhales a deep breath. "This is awkward. I had a speech rehearsed, but it'll be easier if I just say why I'm here. I have reason to believe you might be my biological father."

Ramon barks out a laugh that sends Ada crashing backward against the wall.

"Oh, Lord." He takes hold of her arms to steady her. "I'm so sorry, honey. I startled you with my outburst. But you took me by surprise. What you say cannot possibly be true. I love my wife dearly. I have never cheated on her."

Disappointment overcomes Ada, and she wrenches free of his grasp. "Are you sure?"

"I'm positive. I would remember such a thing. Your mother was a glamorous woman. As close to a movie star as I've ever seen. Even if I had been attracted to her, she never gave me a second glance. I was way beneath her. Where on earth did you get such an idea?"

Ada sags against the stall. "It's a long story. A genetic test revealed that I'm not Daniel Love's child. I found love letters written to my mother and signed with the initial R. You're the only person I could come up with."

Ramon furrows his brow. "That's odd. Names beginning with Rs are common."

"Her affair happened the summer my father spent in Napa. Do you remember anything strange about my mother's behavior during that time? Anything at all that might help me track down my biological father?"

He hesitates a long minute before shaking his head. "I'm sorry. I worked long hours in your father's absence. I hardly had time for my own family."

Ada hands him a business card. "Please call me if you think of anything."

"Will do." He walks her to her car. "It's good to see you despite the circumstances. I hope you figure things out."

"Me too," she says and drives away.

Ada waits until she reaches the interstate before calling Enzo. He answers on the first ring. "What happened? Is he your father?"

"Nope. He literally laughed in my face when I asked him."

"And you believe him?" Enzo asks.

"I do. He loves his wife very much. I don't think he'd cheat on her. He has no clue who my father might be. What am I gonna do, Enzo? It could be anyone. What if it's one of Mom's old high school boyfriends? She grew up in Texas. How will I ever find him?"

"You're getting way ahead of yourself, Ada. One step at a

time. Focus on the highway. Get yourself back to Lovely safely. Stop by here on the way home, and we'll come up with a plan."

"All right. See you soon."

Ada rolls back her sunroof and cranks her classic rock tunes. But her mind is in turmoil, and the drive is tedious.

Enzo is waiting for her on his terrace with a slightly chilled bottle of pinot noir and a small tray of thinly sliced prosciutto and Asiago cheese. Ada collapses in the chair beside him, the weight of the world bearing her down.

He hands her a glass of the light-colored red wine. "Talk to me. How are you feeling?"

"Relieved, in some ways. Ramon is an honest and hardworking man. I would've been honored to be his daughter. But he's poor. Which means there's still hope my father is an oil billionaire from Texas."

Enzo tilts is head back in laughter. "Let's not mince words."

Ada lifts a tanned shoulder. "Whatever. I'm so frustrated. My only hope is 23andMe. And that's such a long shot."

"You might be surprised. People are reunited on genetic websites every single day."

Ada rolls up a slice of prosciutto and cheese and nibbles on one end. "I'm tired of talking about me. What's up with you? How's the job search?"

"Over, as of Sunday. Starting next Monday, I'll be working at Foxtail Farm as Melvin Bass's assistant."

Ada offers a high five. "Go, Enzo! I heard Melvin was back at Foxtail. He's the most renowned winemaker in Virginia. You'll learn tons."

"I can hardly wait," he says, lifting his glass to his lips.

"You've been out of work for a couple of weeks. If you need some money to tide you over, I can float you a loan."

His dark eyes become stormy. "I'm not the pauper you think I am, Ada."

Ada crosses her legs and shifts in her seat toward him. "I have no clue who you are, because you never talk about yourself. Tell me who you are, Enzo?"

"I was working as a field hand to learn about grapes, not to make money." He stares down at his wine. "I come from an affluent family in Italy."

"I figured as much. You carry yourself well, and your home is a designer show house for wealthy bachelors." She sips her wine. "I'm happy for you, Enzo. You're making your dream come true. You inspire me. Maybe I'll find my dream job as well."

"Are things getting worse at Love-Struck?"

"By the day. My relationship with my father is awkward, borderline hostile. I have no idea where I'll go or what I'll do. Planning parties and pouring wine is all I've ever done. I need for my biological father to be a rich landowner who will share his good fortune with me. Better still, if he has no other children."

"Stop selling yourself short. You don't need a rich daddy to take care of you." Enzo gets up and pulls her to her feet. "Let's go for a walk. I want to show you something."

They take the wine and prosciutto tray to the kitchen and leave the house through the front door.

Ada's long stride matches his as they stroll down the sidewalk toward town. "I'm serious, Enzo. I'm a product of my father's making. I was raised with wealth and privilege. I don't know how to be any other way."

"If you start thinking of yourself as Ada instead of Daniel Love's daughter, you might like what you discover."

"That's what I'm trying to do. But I need the missing piece to the puzzle. How can I discover who I am until I know who I come from?"

Enzo takes hold of her hand. "You're going to find him, Ada. Just be patient."

They walk the rest of the way to Magnolia Avenue in silence. Enzo stops in front of Abbey Lane, an upscale women's boutique where Ada frequently shops. "This building will be available for lease in a few months."

Ada admires a white silk blouse in the window. "No way! Is she going out of business? Abbey's is the only decent dress shop in town."

"Apparently, she's moving to that new shopping strip being built at the other end of Magnolia Avenue. I'm thinking of opening a wine and cheese shop here."

Ada whirls around to face him. "I love that idea. But do you think a wine shop will survive in our tiny town?"

"Look around you, Ada. New buildings are going up all over this town. Rumor has it, construction on a posh boutique hotel will begin this fall. The world is changing. People are leaving cities en masse. Lovely has much to offer. Fresh air, hiking trails, fishing streams, and plenty of land to build their monster houses on."

"Now that you mention it, our restaurants and bars have been more crowded lately."

"Lovely is no longer a wedding destination. It's on the list of up-and-coming desired places to live in Virginia. Do you wanna be my business partner?" His mischievous grin lights up his face.

"With what? My measly savings account?" As the words leave her mouth, a brilliant idea strikes Ada. She smacks Enzo's toned abs with the back of her hand. "You're a genius, Enzo."

He frowns. "What'd I do?"

"You just renew my hope in the future," she says and heads off at a fast pace down Magnolia Avenue.

"Where are you going?" Enzo asks, catching up with her.

She cast a sideways glance at him. "Nowhere in particular. I'm just walking. My legs are trying to catch up with my brain. I'm excited, Enzo. I have a plan. If it works, I might be able to go into business with you."

Enzo grabs her arm to stop her. "Wait a minute. I wanna hear about this plan," he says and listens carefully while she explains. "That's a drastic move, Ada. Don't go off half-cocked until you've really thought it through."

"Don't worry. I will. But it's the solution that makes the most sense." They start walking again. "Why do you want me for a business partner? I know little about wine, except that Love-Struck wine sucks."

"Which is why you'll handle the cheese end of the business. You have impeccable taste. You're a gracious host, and you're ballsy. You don't put up with disgruntled customers."

Ada plants a hand on her hip and narrows her eyes. "What happens if I don't invest in your venture? Will you get someone else?"

Enzo shakes his head. "I don't need a financial partner, Ada. I'll move forward regardless of what you decide. I thought it'd be nice to have someone in the trenches with me."

"What about this thing between us? Whatever it is."

Enzo pulls her out of the way of a group of pedestrians. "By thing, do you mean chemistry?"

"Yes. That." She leans against a brick building. "Aren't you worried our chemistry might present problems in our partnership?"

"I'm not gonna lie. I'm attracted to you. We started off on the wrong foot with our drunken hookup. But this friendship that's developing between us means a lot to me. We need each other's support right now while we figure out our lives."

Ada drops her chin to her chest. "Especially me."

"You definitely have a lot going on. And I want to be here for you." Enzo lifts her chin. "As much as it pains me to say this, I suggest we table the romance for now. We'll reassess the situation in a few months once you've found your father and we've opened the wine shop."

"Deal." Ada flashes him a broad smile. "We're friends without benefits and potential business partners."

Ada loops her arm through his as they walk back to his house together. She has a renewed kick in her step. She's not entirely convinced the wine shop is the right path for her. If she can make her plan work, she'll have options.

CHAPTER 23
ADA

Ada is torn between playing it safe and taking a chance on life. She weighs her choices carefully. Once implemented, her plan is a final and drastic move. There will be no turning back. If she never finds her biological father, she'll be all alone in the world. Enzo is quickly becoming the center of her universe. But there's no way of knowing what will become of their relationship in the long run. Will they be business partners? Romantically involved? Will they even stay friends?

Thursday afternoon, her father summons Ada for an impromptu meeting in the company's boardroom. When she arrives, her brothers are stooped over the conference table, examining their mother's jewelry—diamonds and sapphires and emeralds set in gold and platinum. A collection fit for royalty.

When her father notices Ada in the doorway, he motions her inside. "Good. You're here. We can begin. Listen up! Here's how this process will go."

The siblings gather around Daniel for instruction.

"You will take turns making your selections. We will go through however many rounds it takes to divvy up all the jewelry." He eyes Ada's pearls around her neck. "Ada got the pearls. We'll consider that her first choice."

Anger rolls through her, and she presses her lips thin. *Keep your mouth shut,* she tells herself. *No good will come from arguing with him.*

Daniel squeezes Sheldon's shoulder. "You're up next, son. Make your pick."

"That's not fair," Hugh says with flushed face. "I'm the oldest. I should go first."

"Sorry. But we're doing this my way. Sheldon's first. Then you. Then Charles. Now, let's get on with it," Daniel says, and gives Sheldon a nudge toward the table.

Standing next to her, Hugh mumbles near Ada's ear. "This is a racket. He's playing favorites again."

Ada fights back tears when Sheldon grabs the velvet ring box that houses their mother's three-carat flawless diamond. As the only daughter, the ring should rightfully have gone to her.

Hugh and Charles pick Ada's second and third preferences— sapphire and diamond teardrop earrings and a gold Cartier Pasha watch, respectively.

Ada remains silent during the process, which takes over an hour. Ada's favorite choices are ruby stud earrings and a gold necklace with an emerald and diamond encrusted pendant. When all the jewelry has been divided, she rakes her stash off the table into her purse and leaves the conference room without saying a word to anyone. She doesn't need a rearview mirror to know her father is smirking at her retreating back. He just won another battle in their war.

With head held high, she marches past her office, down the stairs, and out the winery door to the parking lot. Her inner debate has ended. Her days here are numbered. She will soon begin a new life free of the Love family drama and dysfunction.

She starts the engine but takes a moment to compose herself before putting the car in gear. With the air conditioning blasting cold air on her face, she opens her inbox and scrolls through her emails. Her heart skips a beat when she comes across the notification she's been waiting for. The sender is 23andMe. The subject line lets her know her results are in.

Ada peels out of the parking lot and breaks the speed limit on the way to town. Enzo's pickup is in the driveway, but he doesn't answer the door when she knocks. When she tries the knob, she discovers it unlocked and lets herself in.

"Enzo!" she calls, but he doesn't answer.

When she steps into the living room, she hears water coming from the back of the house. She paces in circles around the room while she waits for him to get out of the shower. A red leather photo album on the custom-made bookshelves catches her eye, and she pulls it down. The first page features the cover of a British magazine. A much younger Enzo is photographed with a man and woman who, based on the physical resemblance, must be his parents. Enzo is wearing white britches and a bright red coat adorned with medals and gold braid. The caption says *Italian Nobility Attend Wedding of British Duke.*

Ada thumbs through the album. The pages are filled with images of Enzo photographed with important-looking people— some she recognizes but most she doesn't. Enzo admitted to belonging to an affluent family, but royalty?

When she hears the shower turn off, she returns the album to the shelf and calls out, "Hey, Enzo! It's me, Ada. I let myself in. I hope you don't mind."

"That's fine. Make yourself at home," he yells back, his voice muffled by the closed door.

Ada goes down the hall to the bathroom door. "I got my results from 23andMe. I need you to give me courage when I access them on the website."

"Cool! Be out in a sec."

Returning to the living room, she sits down on the couch and picks up the most recent issue of *Wine Enthusiast* magazine from the coffee table.

A few minutes later, Enzo emerges from the back hall in linen shorts, a black polo shirt, and hair still damp from the shower.

Now that she's aware of his lineage, she scrutinizes him through a different lens. His jaw is strong and facial features chiseled. Do members of royal families have certain physical features?

"Are you ready for the big reveal?" Enzo asks.

"I'm nervous as hell." She pulls her phone out of her purse and unlocks the screen.

"You can't see anything on your phone. Let me grab my laptop. It's in the kitchen." He disappears into the kitchen and returns a minute later with the computer and two lime flavored sparkling waters.

He hands Ada the lap, and she signs into the 23andMe website.

"Well?" he says, peering over her shoulder.

"I'm afraid to look. You do it," she says, depositing the computer in his lap.

"Hmm. Let's see." He narrows his eyes as his finger moves across the mouse. "Here we go. View your relative list." He clicks on a link. "Let's sort the names by strength of relationship. There is no match for parents, but you have a first cousin."

"Let me see that," Ada says, snatching the computer back. "Riley Hudson. I don't know anyone by the last name Hudson. But he's kinda cute in a rugged way."

"Geez, Ada. He's your first cousin. Your children would have genetic disorders."

"I don't want to marry him. Or even date him. I'm merely pointing out that he's good looking. Like me."

Enzo rolls his eyes. "I wonder if he's an egomaniac, too."

"Shush." She clicks on Riley's profile picture and reads his bio. "Born in 1992, which makes him three years older than me. Darn, he's from Hope Springs. There goes my dream of being a Texas oil heiress. His purpose for joining the website is to research his family's genealogy."

"Look! You can message him," Enzo says, touching the computer screen where it says *message*.

Ada clicks the link, and a chat box appears. She types out a message. *Hi. I'm new to the website, and I've just learned we're cousins. I live nearby in Lovely. I would love to talk sometime.* She presses send. "It'll probably take him a week to respond. I'm not sure I can handle any more waiting."

"Hopefully you won't have to."

Picking up her phone, Ada accesses her Facebook App and searches for Riley Hudson in Hope Springs, Virginia. "Here he is. He teaches history at Jefferson College. Check out his profile picture." She points at the screen. "He's obviously the outdoorsy type. He's at the top of a mountain with a friend."

Enzo glances at the screen. "That's not a friend, Ada. That's his partner. I think your cousin is gay."

Ada looks more closely at the profile image. "Really? How can you tell that from this picture?"

"Guys know these things," Enzo says nonchalantly.

The computer pings with a message from Riley. *Hey, cuz. Glad to make your acquaintance. Can you come to Hope Springs? I have class until 4:20. I can meet you at Caffeine on the Corner at 4:30.*

Ada responds: *I'll be there. Can't wait to meet you.*

She grabs her purse and jumps to her feet.

"Where are you going?" Enzo asks, following her across the room.

"To my apartment. I have just enough time to freshen up before I need to hit the road."

"I'm coming with you?" Enzo says, snatching his keys from the chest beside the door.

Ada pauses with one hand on the knob. "You're coming with me to Hope Springs?"

"Yep. You shouldn't be alone when you find out who your father is." Enzo walks her out to the front stoop and locks the door behind them. "You don't have to introduce me to your cousin. I'll sit at a separate table. We'll take my car in case you're too upset to drive home."

"Fine. I doubt I'll be upset, but I'd appreciate the company."

———

Ada's stomach is in knots on the drive over to Hope Springs. When they arrive at the coffee shop, Ada says, "Why don't you walk down to Town Tavern and have a beer? I'll join you there when I'm finished."

Concern crosses his face. "Are you sure?"

"Positive." She pats his cheek. "Don't worry. I'll be fine. I know where to find you if I need you. Having you spying on us from another table will make me nervous."

He hangs his head. "Okay. I get that. Where's Town Tavern?"

"Two blocks that way," she says, pointing him in the right direction down Main Street.

Ada is the only customer in the coffee shop. She purchases a cappuccino from the barista and sits down at a table by the window. Riley arrives promptly at four thirty. He's cuter in person with a scruffy beard and twinkling blue eyes. He calls out to the bartender for a black coffee and sits down across from her.

He unrolls his family tree on the table. "This is crazy! You don't fit on my tree. Which means you're—"

"Illegitimate. I know that much already. Do you know who my father is?"

"There's only one possibility." Riley studies her face. "You have his golden-brown eyes and square jaw."

Ada strokes her jaw. "Don't remind me. It's the least favorite of my features. So? Who is my father?"

"Because my dad is an only child, we have to be related on my mother's side." Riley taps the family tree. "Your father is my uncle, my mother's only sibling, Bud Malone."

Ada's mouth falls open. "No way. Bud Malone is my father's best friend. He's like an uncle to me." Her mind reels as she thinks about all the time she spent with Bud when she was growing up. "Wait a minute. It can't be Bud. I found letters from my mother's lover. He signed them with the initial *R*."

"Bud is a nickname for Robert."

Ada presses a trembling hand to her mouth. "I don't believe it."

The barista delivers Riley's coffee, and he sits back in his chair to sip it. "Are you going to confront him?"

"I assume so. How do you think he'll take the news?" Ada asks and holds her breath while she waits for the answer.

Riley holds his hands out, palms up. "I can't answer that. I guess, a lot depends on his relationship with your mother. But you'll have to wait awhile to find out. He left yesterday for Europe. He won't be back for two weeks."

CHAPTER 24
CASEY

Casey's heart beats in her throat as she waits for Daniel's reaction to her latest logo designs. His steely expression reveals nothing. But Casey's gut tells her he hates it, like all the others. She's worked hard on this concept all week. She has nothing else to give him.

Daniel stands abruptly. "This is garbage, Casey. Your worst proposal yet. Either you don't understand our brand, or you're too inexperienced for the position. I'm disappointed in you. I've been patient long enough. Since you're clearly incapable, we'll have to engage an outside design firm to do the job. And soon if we want to implement the new brand this fall."

In a tight voice with tears near the surface, Casey says, "I've hired a new graphics designer. She starts on Monday. Her portfolio is impressive. Can we at least see what she comes up with?"

"Fine. I'll give her one week." Daniel wags a finger at Casey. "Tell her to give me her best shot, because this is it. Let's skip the formal presentation. She can email me the graphics," he says, and strides angrily out of the room.

Tears stream down Casey's face as she closes her laptop and gathers her belongings. She's looking at the floor, not paying attention to where she's going, when she collides with Ada in the hall.

"Hey!" Ada gives Casey a shove. "Watch where you're going!"

Startled, Casey looks up, her face damp with tears. "Sorry," she mumbles and continues down the hall.

Ada follows on her heels into her office. "Wait up, Casey! I can tell you're upset. What's wrong?"

"As if you care," Casey says, depositing her laptop and files on her desk.

"Regardless of what you think of me, I'm not completely heartless. Looks to me like you could use a friend," Ada says in an uncharacteristically concerned tone.

Casey snatches a tissue from the box and blows her nose. "You hate me because I stole your life. And now you want to be my friend?"

A pained expression crosses Ada's face. "That life was never mine to steal. Maybe friend was the wrong choice of words. But I sympathize with you. Daniel is a difficult man to work for. I just thought maybe you'd want to talk about it. But never mind. Figure it out yourself," she says and saunters out of her office.

Casey yearns for the floor to open up and swallow her whole. Ada, her nemesis, was offering compassion, and Casey responded like a total jerk. A fresh round of tears stream down her cheeks. She's worked overtime this week, and she needs a break from her office, the winery, her father.

Leaving her computer on her desk, she grabs her purse and hurries out of the building. The warm sunshine offers a welcomed relief from her frigid air-conditioned office. But she's not sure where to go. She's a prisoner at Love-Struck Vineyard. She's a partner in Daniel Love's business and a guest in his home. For the first time since moving to Lovely in April, she longs for the streets of New York. And she's not even a fan of the city. Fortunately, there are plenty of places for her to get lost on the property.

Casey drives back to The Nest, changes into her swimsuit, and hides out by the pool with a romance novel. Late in the afternoon, when the urge to paint strikes, she throws on exercise clothes and heads down to the rose garden with her art supplies.

She's lost in her work and doesn't hear Sheldon approach. "There you are!"

She startles at the sound of his voice. "Sheldon! You scared me. What're you doing here?"

"Looking for you. I haven't seen you in a while. And I wanted to check in, to see how things are going."

Casey sets down her brush and wipes her hands on her smock. "Just peachy," she says in a sarcastic tone. "I think Daniel's going to fire me."

"That's ridiculous. What makes you say that?"

"Because I failed to come up with a design for the rebranding. I've tried everything, Sheldon. I've shown him dozens of potential logos. He hasn't approved of a single one."

"Right. He mentioned something about the logos this afternoon. But he didn't seem upset about it. He can be harsh sometimes, but he doesn't mean any harm."

"Harsh? He was downright nasty to me. I'm not used to being treated that way."

Sheldon's gaze shifts to the left. Noticing her painting of the water fountain, he says, "Wow! Look at that." He brushes her aside so he can study the watercolor more closely. "This is fabulous. You have serious talent. Have you done more paintings of the vineyard?"

"A whole portfolio of them. Why?"

"I need to see them. Now. Where are they?" He looks around, as though expecting to find them in the rose garden.

"In my room," she says with a flick of her wrist toward the house. "Can't it wait until later?"

"Nope. This is important. Come on. I'll help you carry your stuff."

He folds up her easel while she stows her paints in a canvas tote. On the way to the house, Sheldon says, "Tell me more about the other paintings."

"I've painted a little of everything. The field of wildflowers. The bridge over the trout stream. The view of the vineyard from your lot. There's no shortage of inspiring scenes around here."

When they reach the terrace, Casey says, "Wait here. I'll be right back." She takes the easel from him and darts up the back stairs to her study. She stores away her art supplies and retrieves the large folder that houses her portfolio from the closet.

When she returns to the terrace, Sheldon is resting in a lounge chair with head back and eyes closed. "Here!" She drops the portfolio in his lap and sits down next to him.

Sheldon flips through the paintings once, and then goes through them a second time, lingering over the ones he likes the most. "These are amazing, Casey. You really captured the beauty of the vineyard. Show them to Dad. I have a hunch this is the brand he's looking for."

Casey's heart flutters, but she warns herself not to get too excited. "Don't hold your breath. He's impossible to please."

Tugging his phone free of his pocket, Sheldon clicks on a number and holds it to his ear. "Dad! Where are you?" He pauses while Daniel responds. "Cool. I'm on the terrace. Get down here, now. I need to show you something."

When Casey moves to get up, Sheldon grabs her by the arm, pulling her back down. "Where're you going?"

"To my room. I've had enough disappointment for one day." She wrenches free of his grasp and gets to her feet.

Sheldon stands to face her. "Don't go, Casey. Wait and see how he responds. *I'll* be shocked if Dad doesn't go nuts over your paintings."

"Go nuts over what?" Daniel asks, emerging from the house. He smiles at Casey as though their earlier exchange never happened.

"These," Sheldon says, opening the portfolio on a nearby table.

Casey stands off to the side while they discuss her paintings. She's grateful she can't hear their lowered voices. Her ego can't bear the criticism.

When Daniel faces her, his smile is wide and his pale olive eyes bright. "These are brilliant, Casey. Why didn't you show them to me? They are exactly what I've been hoping for." He chuckles. "I love them all. Choosing which ones to use for the labels will be difficult."

"I'm sure we can find other uses for the rest," Sheldon says.

Daniel embraces her, but she doesn't hug him back. "I'm glad you like them," she says in a deadpan tone.

He holds her at arm's length. "I wish I could take you two out to dinner to celebrate, but I have a prior engagement."

Casey realizes for the first time he's dressed in black tie. "It's fine."

He kisses her forehead before letting her go. "Great job. Let's meet in my office first thing on Monday and get the ball rolling," he says and disappears inside.

"We'll celebrate without him," Sheldon says. "We could drive over to the Inn at Hope Springs and have dinner on Jameson's terrace."

"I'm sorry, Sheldon. But I'm not very good company tonight."

"I can fix that." Taking her by the arm, he leads her through the house to his Range Rover in the driveway. He opens the passenger door. "Get in."

"Where are we going?" Casey looks down at her jean shorts and paint-splattered shirt. "I'm not exactly dressed to go out."

"You're dressed fine for where we're going. It's peaceful and picturesque." A smirk tugs at his lips. "You might even want to paint it."

"In that case, what're we waiting for?" she says, and climbs in the car.

They drive several miles down the highway and make a left onto a bumpy dirt road. They continue for another quarter mile until a small log cabin comes into view.

"Is this your cabin? Where you live?"

He grins. "It is. What do you think?"

"It's charming. But you said it was a dump."

"It won't be a dump when I'm finished. I've decided to buy it and fix it up."

She looks from the cabin to him. "What about the house you're building at Love-Struck?"

"I'm putting that on hold for now," he says, reaching for the door handle.

She jumps out after him. "Does Daniel know this?"

"He knows I'm buying the cabin. I haven't told him I'm holding off on construction at Love-Struck. Come on. There's something I want you to see." He takes her by the hand, and they go behind the cabin to where a wide rocky stream flows beneath a canopy of trees.

"It's incredible. And so serene. You're right. I want to paint it."

"You can come here anytime. I didn't realize how attached I've become to this place. When my landlord told me he was thinking of selling, I made him an offer on the spot. Most nights I sit on the porch listening to crickets chirp and the gentle flow of water over rocks. I've already hired a decorator. I have big plans for my man cave. When I get around to building my big boy house, I'll use this as my fishing cabin."

"Your man cabin. I love it." Casey tilts her face to the filtered sun, relishing the gentle breeze on her skin. "What changed your mind about building at Love-Struck?"

"Something tells me Ollie won't be eager to live at Love-Struck after we're married."

"You, dog!" Casey punches his arm. "That happened fast. I didn't realize you two had gotten so serious."

"We haven't. In fact, we're currently not speaking to each other. We had a silly misunderstanding. Bottom line, she needs some time to herself. But she'll come around."

They walk over to the screened porch and sit down in rockers. "Where will you live when you and Ollie get married? In her farmhouse at Foxtail?"

Sheldon shrugs. "Wherever she wants."

Casey giggles. "You've got it bad, bro. I'm happy for you."

"What's going on with you and Jamie? Have you made your move on him yet?"

Casey groans. "That was a disaster. I'm not sure what I ever saw in him in the first place. Maybe I felt sorry for him because of the way Ollie treated him." Resting her head against the rocker, she closes her eyes and thinks about how she ruined her chances with Luke because of Jamie.

Sheldon nudges her arm with his elbow. "Why so quiet? Is there someone else?"

Opening her eyes, she rolls her head toward him. "There *was* for about a minute. I met this really hot saxophone player. But it didn't work out."

"Is this hot saxophone player by any chance Luke Ellington?"

Casey straightens in her chair. "That's right. Luke mentioned he did some legal work for the vineyard. What kind of legal work was it?"

"Well . . ." Sheldon folds his arms and rests them on his belly. "A few years back, the EPA came down hard on us regarding some chemicals we were using on our vines. We hired Luke to represent us. He's very good at what he does. What happened between you two?"

"I was sorta seeing Jamie at the time." Casey tells him about how she lied to Luke and how Luke caught Jamie kissing her at the Fourth of July party. "Luke said I was too young and immature to know what I want."

"If you like him, you should—"

Casey's hand shoots up. "Fight for him. I know. Fiona already gave me that lecture. And I tried. I went to see his show at Blue Cosmos last weekend. But his old girlfriend was there. The bartender told me Brooke convinced Luke to give her another chance."

Sheldon shakes his head. "You have nothing to worry about with Brooke. That will never last."

"How do you know her?"

"When Luke won our lawsuit, I invited him to dinner at

Belmonte's to celebrate. He brought Brooke along. She's a real piece of work. She shamelessly hit on me. Luke got livid and caused a scene in the restaurant. He called the next day to apologize. He told me he'd broken up with her. He said their relationship was doomed from the start."

"And now they're back together. Luke is the one who's too young and immature to know what he wants." Casey stands and stretches. "I'm hungry. Wanna grab some dinner?"

"Sure. I'd offer to cook for you, but the cupboard is bare."

Taking him by the hand, she hauls him out of the chair. "Let's go to Ruthie's. I'm buying."

"Deal," he says, and twenty minutes later, they are seated at Ruthie's with cheeseburger platters on the table in front of them.

"Luke is a regular here," Sheldon says, his mouth full of food.

"How do you know that?" Casey asks, dragging a French fry through a puddle of ketchup.

"I met him here for breakfast several times. You should stage an accidental run-in with him."

Casey cocks her head sideways. "Why would I do that?"

"To remind him what a beautiful and intelligent catch you are. The timing's perfect. Right about now, he's wondering why the hell he agreed to give Brook another chance."

Casey stuffs another fry in her mouth. "Or they're planning their engagement party. I rarely eat breakfast. Am I supposed to suddenly develop a fetish for eggs over easy?"

"If you want a chance meeting with Luke, you will. Your graphic designer is starting on Monday. You could order a tray of Danishes to welcome her. Or you could just stop by one morning for coffee," Sheldon says and bites into his burger.

"It's a little out of the way for coffee, don't you think?"

Ruthie appears at the table. "In case you're interested, Luke comes in every morning at eight. He is so punctual, I can set my watch by him."

Casey stares up at the diner's owner. "Ruthie! Were you eavesdropping on us?"

Ruthie hunches her shoulders to her ears. "I overhear much of what is said in here. If you don't want me to know something, don't say it. Coincidentally, Luke and Brooke are officially over for good."

"Did you overhear that too?" Sheldon asks.

"Nope. He told me himself. He also told me the graphic designer you just hired is his sister."

CHAPTER 25
OLLIE

Ollie ponders the issue of children for days until she finally gives up on Saturday evening and texts Sheldon. *How do you feel about children?*

He responds right away. *I get along with most children except brats and bullies.*

Ollie: *Ha ha. I'm being serious. How do you feel about having children?*

Sheldon: *Serious questions deserve serious answers. In person. I'll be there in a few.*

Ollie is tempted to tell him not to come. She's vulnerable right now. She's home alone on Saturday night. Will she be able to resist him if he makes a move on her? She'll have to, because she needs an answer to her question.

Five minutes later, she hears tires crushing gravel in the driveway. Sheldon jumps out of his car and joins her on the porch, bending over to kiss her cheek before dropping into the chair next to her.

"You look good, Ollie. Really good. How're you feeling?"

"Great. I'm sleeping like a baby, and I haven't had a panic attack since . . ."

Sheldon deflates. "Since we broke up."

"I was going to say since dinner with your father."

"So, what's this about children? Are you pregnant?" he says with a mischievous grin.

She slaps his arm. "I'm not joking, Sheldon. This is important."

His smile fades. "Okay. I'll be serious. To answer your question, yes, I want children. I want to give my kids the happy childhood I was deprived of."

"I find it hard to believe you had an unhappy childhood," Ollie says, her eyes on the stone mansion on the hill. "You grew up in a fairytale land."

"My parents fought all the time. Nasty arguments that often scared us. They made our lives miserable," Sheldon says with a faraway look in his eyes.

"I'm sorry, Sheldon. I didn't know."

His lips curve in a sad smile. "If I had my way, I'd have a whole brood of kids. But that's up to God. I'll be happy with whatever he blesses me with." He angles his body toward her. "Do *you* want children, Ollie?"

"When I was little, I couldn't wait to grow up and become a mom. I wanted to be just like my mom. But somewhere along the line, I became adamantly opposed to having a family. I'm not sure why, honestly. I wish I knew."

"Have you discussed your feelings with Ronnie?"

Ollie smiles. "I've discussed plenty of feelings with her. Just not this particular one. But I will when she gets back from vacation next week."

Sheldon's brow shoots up. "Ronnie Mason took a vacation? I'm shocked. Good for her. She deserves some time off."

"She does, indeed."

They sit for a minute in silence, watching the sky thickening with storm clouds.

Sheldon strokes his stubbly chin. "So let me get this straight. The purpose of this conversation isn't to find out if I want children. It's to tell me you don't."

"Maybe. Would your opinion of us change if I told you I don't want children?"

The mischievous grin returns. "Us? As in you and me? Is there a you and me, Ollie?"

Ollie lets out a sigh. "I miss you, Sheldon. This week hasn't been easy. I'd rather not be alone on a Saturday night. But I'm trying to figure out my life, for my benefit and yours."

His expression turns serious. "You're right. I'll cut the crap." He places his hand on top of hers. "If we get to be an *us* again, my loyalty will be to you, first and foremost. Not our unborn children. That's not to say I won't try to convince you to have children. I'll just have to spoil my nieces and nephews more."

Ollie looks out over the vineyard. The sky has grown ominous. She's always been afraid of thunderstorms. She longs to ask Sheldon to stay. To take him to her bed and make love to him all night with the wind howling and rain beating against the windows. But she's not ready yet. When it happens, it will be special. It will be forever.

Sheldon's phone vibrates the chair's arm, and he glances at the screen. "This is Dad. I need to answer."

Daniel's voice is loud and angry, and Ollie hears enough to get the gist of what he's saying. Love-Struck is hosting a wedding, and the bride's family was too cheap to pay for the tent. With the storm approaching, they need all hands on deck to move the reception indoors.

"I'm on my way." Sheldon stands and pockets his phone. "I'm sorry, Ollie. I've gotta go. Dad needs me at the vineyard."

"I heard," she says, rising out of her chair.

"I hate to leave you alone with this storm coming. It's gonna be a humdinger."

"I'll be fine. Melvin's around here somewhere." Ollie walks with Sheldon off the porch. When they reach the driveway, she sees Melvin heading their way. "Speak of the devil. There he comes now."

Sheldon waves at Melvin before getting in his car and driving off.

"Where's he going in such a hurry?" Melvin asks, watching Sheldon's Range Rover retreat down the driveway.

"To Love-Struck," she says and tells him what she knows about the doomed wedding reception.

Melvin turns to her. "Do you want me to wait out the storm with you?"

"Yes! Please. I need to secure the porch furniture and get the dogs inside."

For the next few minutes, they overturn chairs and tables and take down the hammock. Melvin calls for the dogs and they gather in the kitchen as the first drops of rain fall.

"Are you hungry?" Melvin asks. "I can make dinner."

"I'm starving." She opens the refrigerator. "I have a couple of chicken breasts. Obviously, we're not going to cook them on the grill in this weather."

Melvin peers over her shoulder at the contents of her refrigerator. "I'll rustle us up some pasta?" he says, removing milk, butter, and chicken broth from the refrigerator.

While he sets a pot of water on the stove to boil, Ollie cuts up vegetables for a chopped salad.

"I was encouraged to see Sheldon here," Melvin says, putting a pot of water on the stove to boil. "Are you two lovebirds patching things up?"

Ollie gives her head a solemn shake. "We were just talking about having children. He wants a whole brood of kids. He claims he can live without them, but I can't ask him to make that sacrifice for me."

Melvin melts the butter and whisks in flour and chicken broth. "Sounds to me like you're overthinking the situation. In my experience, these things usually have a way of working themselves out."

"It's not just that. Everything was happening too fast. Six weeks ago, I thought of Sheldon as my enemy."

Melvin looks back at her over his shoulder. "Sheldon is definitely not your enemy."

"I know that now. But within a span of two weeks, I broke up with Jamie, underwent extensive mental therapy, and fell in love with Sheldon. We didn't start dating like normal people. We jumped headfirst into a serious relationship. Don't you think we were rushing things?"

"Not when you find the right person." Melvin dumps the pasta in the boiling water and turns to face her. "My wife died from cancer at age fifty-four. That might seem like a long way off to you now, but time flies, and it'll get here before you know it."

Ollie's fingers graze his arm. "I'm sorry, Melvin. I didn't know."

"Anne was too young with too much living left to do. Don't waste a single day, Ollie. If you love Sheldon, be with him. The two of you will figure all this other stuff out together. That's what being a couple is about."

"That's good advice, Melvin. Thank you." Ollie opens the silverware drawer and sets two places at the breakfast counter. "Have you ever considered dating again?"

"Nah. Anne was my one and only." Melvin returns his attention to his simmering sauce. "But she left me a special gift. I see parts of her in my sons. Jerry has her warm brown eyes and Carl her dimples and laid-back attitude."

Unexpected tears well in Ollie's eyes, and she waits until she trusts her voice again. "You obviously love your sons very much. You should be with them. Why are you here instead of in Arizona?"

"Because I have to look out for myself. I was floundering out there. I felt myself slipping every day. This farm is in my blood. I need the fresh air and manual labor for my physical and mental wellbeing. I plan to visit them often, but this is where I need to be."

"Well, I'm grateful you're here." Talking to Melvin is like talking to her father. Countless times since his death, Ollie has picked up the phone to call her father. When she remembers he's gone, the letdown always hits hard. She misses his advice. He always had her best interests at heart. If he were alive now, he would help her make the right decision about her future with Sheldon.

Hearing Melvin talk about his sons touches her deeply. How can she deprive Sheldon of the opportunity to experience such unconditional love? Her next thought takes her breath. How can she deprive herself of the same?

CHAPTER 26
ADA

"You really screwed up this time, Ada," Daniel says, his face flushed red with anger. "This is a disaster. Our guests are soaked to the bone, and the food is all soggy. We have way more people in this building than the fire code requirements allow. If the fire marshal shuts us down, I'm blaming you."

Ada grits her teeth. "What was I supposed to do? The bride's parents refused to pay for the tent."

"Back in the beginning phases of planning. I just spoke with the bride's mother. She's been trying to reach you all week, since the storm system first appeared in the forecast. She wasn't aware we own tents. She would gladly have paid for the tents. This is all on you, Ada."

She can't argue. Everything he says is true. She's been so distracted lately.

Daniel jabs his finger in her face. "Another screw up like this and you're fired."

An old friend of the family appears at Daniel's side. "Daniel, my good man. How wonderful to see you."

Ada sneaks away while the two men are talking. Her job is on the line. Daniel is eager to get rid of her. She'll have to be more careful. She can't afford another screwup. Not until she finishes executing her plan. Daniel will get what's coming to him in the end. And she can hardly wait to see the look on his face when he realizes he's been duped.

———

Ada waits until after noon on Sunday to put the first part of her plan in motion.

She parks on the curb in front of Hugh's two-story brick colonial. As she's approaching the front door, she hears shouting coming from within. She hesitates before knocking. She doesn't want to interrupt their argument. When she hears a loud crash, the sound of a large object breaking, she spins around to leave. She's gripping the railing, descending the brick steps, when the door swings open and Hugh's wife blows past her. Laney crosses the lawn to the driveway, gets in her Suburban, and tears off down the road.

"How long have you been here?" Hugh asks from the doorway.

Ada turns back around to face him. "Long enough to hear you screaming at each other. I heard a loud crash. What broke?"

"The Ming Dynasty vase I gave Laney for Christmas last year. I bought it at Sotheby's auction. She smashed it against the wall."

"Ouch. I hope your kids aren't here," Ada says about his two preadolescent daughters.

"They're at a birthday party sleepover. Laney's going to pick them up now."

"I hope she calms down before the girls get in the car. She's liable to wreck and kill all of them."

Hugh glares at her. "Why are you here, Ada?"

"I need to discuss a business matter."

He steps aside and gestures for her to enter. "Come on in."

Ada admires the stylish decor as she follows him to the back of the house. Laney is the most put together woman Ada knows.

Despite having excellent taste, she's an expert gardener who often designs flower arrangements for weddings.

When they reach the kitchen, Hugh gathers dirty plates from the pine farm table and takes them over to the sink. "Sorry. We were having brunch when Laney flew off the handle."

"No worries. Are you and Laney okay?"

"We're fine. All marriages have issues." He holds up a coffee carafe. "Want some?"

"No, thanks."

He fills a mug, and they sit down across from each other at the table. "You mentioned a business matter?"

Ada explains the purpose of her visit.

"You've got my attention," Hugh says, straightening in his chair. "Why me and not Charles or Sheldon?"

"I may approach them as well. I haven't decided yet. But Charles's heart isn't in the vineyard. I'm not sure where his passion lies. If he even has one. And Sheldon is Dad's pet, which makes him the enemy."

Hugh lets out an audible breath. "There's no need to involve them. We can work this out, just the two of us."

Ada sits back in her chair and crosses her legs. "I'm calling the shots here, Hugh. We'll do this my way or no way."

"Oh? And what way is that?"

"Daniel is not to know about this until after the deal is done. When the time comes, I will be the one to tell him."

"Fine." Hugh lifts his coffee mug. "So he's Daniel to you now?"

Ada's gaze shifts from her brother to a cluster of beautiful blue hydrangea bushes in the backyard. "He's not my father. He certainly hasn't been treating me like his daughter."

"I'm sorry, Ada. I honestly thought he'd come around. You're smart to get out. Have you given any consideration to leaving town?"

"Lovely is my home. I have no desire to leave."

"You could always go back to school and get your degree," Hugh suggests.

Ada tears her eyes away from the backyard. "I'm not going back to college. But don't worry about me, Hugh. I always land on my feet."

He narrows his navy eyes at her. "What're you up to, Ada? There's something more you're not telling me."

Ada stands abruptly. "That's for me to know and you to find out."

Hugh walks her to the door. "Can I trust you not to tell Sheldon and Charles?"

"Yes. Unless you try to rip me off."

"I won't do that. You have my word," he says, drawing an imaginary *x* across his chest.

Hugh's word isn't worth much to Ada. She doesn't trust her brother. She knows him too well. But if he wants this deal to work out, he'll have to play by her rules.

Ada's spirits soar as she leaves Hugh's house. Step one is taken care of. Now onto step two. When she reaches the center of town, she turns left on Magnolia Avenue and drives five miles toward Hope Springs. She takes a right at the entrance to Malone Equestrian Center and proceeds another quarter mile to the stable complex.

Bud Malone was the town's primary doctor until he sold his medical practice and established the equestrian center. In the last ten years, he's built his business into the largest breeding and training facility in Virginia.

Bud's only child, Stuart, is standing at the railing watching a little girl trotting on a pony around the riding arena, her blonde braids trailing from beneath her helmet. The Malone and Love families were close when the kids were young. During the summers, they got together for barbecues on major holiday weekends. They had oyster roasts and skeet shoots in the fall and booked suites at the Homestead Resort every New Year's Eve.

Ada gets out of the car and moseys over to the ring. Stuart

doesn't notice her at first, giving her an opportunity to study his profile. She never noticed it before, never had reason to look for a resemblance. But the shape of his face and golden-brown eyes are so like her own. Stuart and Ada's brother Charles were best friends until they had a falling out their senior year in high school. Ada has always wondered what that was about.

Ada inches down the railing toward him. "Hey, Stuart. Is that your daughter?"

Stuart appears surprised to see her. "Hey there, Ada. She's my youngest. Molly ganged up with Dad against me. They insisted she have riding lessons. But it scares me to death. I'm certain if I take my eyes off her, she'll fall."

Ada chuckles. "I've fallen off my horse too many times to count. It'll make your daughter a better rider. Who's the trainer?" she asks about the attractive middle-aged woman wearing riding britches and offering the little girl instruction.

"Her name is Erin Burch. Dad's fortunate to have her. She's one of the best in the state. But that doesn't make me any less nervous watching my child ride around on the back of a powerful animal."

Ada places a reassuring hand on his shoulder. "Molly is doing great. Your father obviously never turned you into a horseman."

Stuart grunts. "Not for lack of trying. What brings you out this way?"

"I'm thinking of moving my horse, and I'm curious if there are any openings here," Ada says and is relieved when he doesn't ask why she wants to move her horse from Love-Struck.

Stuart's eyes remain on his daughter. "I wouldn't know. And Dad's currently in Europe. I would tell you to talk to Ernie, the stable manager, but Dad likes to vet potential boarders himself. I'm sure it won't be a problem since he already knows you. But I'm hesitant to speak for him. I can text Dad. His schedule is hectic, and it may take a while for him to get back to me. Can I let you know?"

"Sure!" Ada says, digging a business card out of her wallet

and handing it to him. "What're you up to these days? Are you still working at the bank?"

Stuart pockets the card. "Nope. I ventured out, started my own wealth management firm. Things are going really well. Lovely is growing so fast. So many people with truckloads of money moving here from up north."

"I keep hearing that. I hope Lovely doesn't get too big. It might lose its charm."

"I can't imagine that'll happen," Stuart says.

"Do you mind if I look around?"

Stuart casts her a sideways glance. "Not at all. Make yourself at home."

Ada leaves the ring and walks to the stable where the scent of horse dung and saddle oil embrace her like old friends. She's always found the barn at Love-Struck dreary and a little creepy. But Bud's facility is bright, with an abundance of natural light flowing in from rows of windows running beneath the peak of the roof. A handful of women of various ages chatter as they tack up their exquisite animals. These aren't ordinary horses. Some of them easily cost six figures.

As she makes her way to the opposite end of the barn, she pauses occasionally to stroke a muzzle and compliment its owner.

Standing at the back entrance, she stares out at the riding arena and grazing paddocks. There must be miles of riding trails in the woods surrounding the enormous expanse of land. Ada inhales a contented breath. She belongs here. She senses it with every fiber of her being.

Ada's mind reels with questions. Did Bud and Lila have a fleeting fling while Daniel was in California that summer, or did their affair go on for years? Did Lila tell Bud she was pregnant with his child? If so, did Bud willingly agree to let his best friend raise his daughter, or did he put up a fight? According to Riley, Bud will be home from Europe a week from Wednesday. Ten long days before she gets answers.

CHAPTER 27
CASEY

A box of Ruthie's famous cream cheese pastries and a large take-out container of coffee are waiting for Casey when she arrives at the diner at ten minutes past eight on Monday morning. But Ruthie's expression is grim when she delivers the news. "I'm sorry, hon. Luke didn't come in today."

Casey looks around at the occupied tables. "Maybe he's running late."

Ruthie shakes her head. "Luke is the most punctual person I've ever met. I'm guessing he has a court case this week. He usually tells me these things. He probably just forgot."

Casey tries not to let her disappointment show. "Whatever. It was a dumb idea anyway." She pays for the pastries and coffee and leaves the diner.

With an hour to kill before work, Casey drives through the neighborhood streets around town in search of a small cottage or garage apartment for rent. She can't stop thinking about Sheldon's cabin. Working with Daniel is enough. She can't continue living in his house. She needs her freedom, her own living space.

On her way back through town on Magnolia Avenue, she spots a sign in the second-floor window of the Abbey Lane building. She pulls to the curb and taps the listed number into her phone. A youngish sounding man answers on the second ring. "Toby Myers."

"Hi! I'm calling about the Abbey Lane building. What exactly is for sale?"

"Condominiums. Two of them on the second and third floors. I'm at the building now, if you'd like to take a look?"

Casey glances at her dashboard clock. Eight forty. She can be a few minutes late to work. "Sure! I'm right out front. How do I get in?"

"Drive around to the parking lot behind the building. There's a small vestibule with an elevator. You can't miss it. I'm on the third floor."

"Awesome. I'll see you soon."

Casey's mind races as she makes a sharp left onto the side street and parks her car in the designated lot. She was hoping to rent. Even though Daniel is paying her an obscene salary, she's not sure she can afford a condo. Then again, she's built up a respectable savings account while she's been living at his house rent-free. Maybe, if the price is right. There's no harm in taking a peek.

Toby Meyers greets her at the door. She guesses him to be in his early forties, bald head with a full beard. "I just bought the building," he explains. "I'm in the process of renovating, converting these two floors from storage into condos. Come on in." He steps out of her way. "I'll give you the tour."

The rooms are few but spacious, with warm pine floors and sunlight spilling in from oversized windows. Each of the two bedrooms has its own bath featuring marble countertops and walk-in showers. At the front of the condo, overlooking Magnolia Avenue, is a large living space and adjacent area that will serve as the kitchen.

"The cabinets will be installed next week. The appliances have been ordered and are scheduled to arrive soon." Toby gestures at the bare drywalls. "I've scheduled the painters to come in two weeks. If things work out, you can choose your own colors."

Casey pauses at the window to admire the view. She can see the mountains over the tops of the buildings on the other side of Magnolia Avenue. She can easily imagine herself living here, but her heart sinks when he tells her the asking price. Even if she got a roommate to help pay the mortgage, it would still be a stretch.

"Are both condos the same size?" Casey asks, hoping the one on the floor below is smaller and therefore less expensive.

"For the most part," Toby says. "The view is better from here, and there's not as much noise. But they're the same price."

She turns away from the window. "I need a couple of days to think about it."

"Of course. Do you work here in town?"

Casey realizes he's digging for information. He wants to know if she can afford the condo. "I'm the marketing director at Love-Struck Winery. I'm sorry. I should've introduced myself. I'm Casey Hobbs. Daniel Love's daughter."

This last bit of information has its desired effect, and his face lights up. "Nice to meet you, Casey. We'll soon be renovating the first floor as well. You may have heard that Abbey Lane is moving to the new shopping center down Magnolia Avenue."

"I didn't know that. Have you leased the space downstairs?"

"Not yet. I'm talking to several interested parties."

"Good luck in finding the right tenant." Casey glances at her watch. "I need to get to work. Thank you for your time."

On the drive back to the vineyard, Casey does the mental calculations and comes to terms with reality. She can't afford to buy a condo. She has little furniture to furnish it with anyway. She can hold out a little longer while she saves more money. In six months or a year, she'll be able to buy a condo or a small house.

The past few weeks have been stressful. But things should be easier now that they've identified the concept for the brand. Daniel may be difficult to please, but the perks are worth it. Fat salary. Free rent in a luxury resort setting.

Casey's new graphics designer is settling in at her desk when Casey enters the office. "I'm sorry I wasn't here when you arrived.

I stopped for refreshments to welcome you." She sets the pastries and coffee on the community worktable.

"That's thoughtful of you. These look delicious," Julia says, helping herself to a pastry.

Casey pours two coffees from the take-out container and hands one to her new employee. "Tell me about yourself, Julia. Do you have family in the area?"

"I do. A brother, Luke. Our parents are deceased. I've lived most of my life in Richmond. I divorced my husband last year and wanted a change of scenery."

Casey furrows her brow. "I'm sorry to hear that."

"Divorce is never easy, but it was for the best," Julia says, sipping coffee.

"Do you have any children?"

"I have a daughter. She'll start kindergarten in the fall. The public schools are much better in Lovely."

"What does your brother do?" Casey asks nonchalantly.

"He's an attorney by day. But he plays the saxophone some Saturday nights at Blue Cosmos. You may have heard his band. They call themselves Twilight Groove."

"I've heard them play. They're very good." Casey feels Julia's eyes on her as she pinches off a piece of pastry. "So, I hope you're ready to dive right in. We have a meeting with Daniel in an hour, and we need to prepare."

Casey opens the portfolio on the community table, and they sort through the paintings one by one, choosing their favorites and making a list of potential applications.

Daniel appears thrilled when they share their ideas with him later in the conference room. After a lengthy discussion about executing their brand, Daniel adjourns the meeting and asks to speak with Casey alone. Julia gathers her belongings and hurries from the room.

"I'm really pleased with the campaign, Casey. Excellent work."

"Thanks," Casey says, unable to look him in the eye.

"I get the feeling you're upset with me about something."

Casey braces herself. This is her chance to tell him how she feels. But when she opens her mouth to speak, no sound comes out. A gut feeling warns her not to rock the boat. He's done so much for her. So what if he was rude to her on Friday? He was frustrated she couldn't come up with a brand. She's still a novice at her job. She has much to learn about the professional world. She'll let it slide for now. After all, he's her father. The man she dreamed about from a very young age is finally a part of her life.

CHAPTER 28
CASEY

On Thursday morning, Casey arrives at work to find Daniel leaning against the window in her office. She deposits her belongings on her desk and joins him at the window. "This is a surprise. What's up?"

"I wanted to invite you to a dinner party tomorrow night. I'd like you to meet my top candidate for winemaker."

"I'd rather not. I'll embarrass myself and you with my lack of knowledge of wine."

Daniel chuckles. "You'll do fine, sweetheart," he says, holding her at arm's length. "You're more intelligent than you give yourself credit for."

Sensing eyes on them, Casey glances over at the door. Ada is glaring at them from the hallway. Despite the bad blood between them, Casey's heart goes out to her. Ada must be devastated at having lost her father to Casey.

Daniel kisses her forehead. "If it makes you feel better, there will only be four of us—you, me, Sheldon, and Bruce."

"Shouldn't you include your other children?"

"They'll eventually get to meet him. Yours and Sheldon's opinions matter the most. Seven o'clock on the terrace at The Nest."

Sounds to Casey like an order, not an invitation. "I'll be there."

She gathers her files and computer from her desk. "I hate to cut this short, but I'm late for a meeting with Julia."

"By all means, don't let me hold you up."

Casey and Daniel part in the hallway, each going in opposite directions. The door to the marketing office is ajar, and as she approaches, she hears Julia talking on the phone.

"Have you lost your mind, Luke? The Greenbriar's expensive."

Casey presses herself against the wall and eavesdrops.

"I thought you and Brooke broke up. You realize she's using you."

Casey can't bear to hear more. She clears her throat as she enters the office.

"I've gotta go. I'm at work." Julia slams her phone down on the community table. "My brother is a fool. He broke up with his girlfriend last week, and he's taking her to the Greenbriar this weekend. I don't understand why he allows her to jerk him around. He doesn't love her."

"Does she love him?" Casey asks, easing down in the chair beside her.

"Definitely not. The sex must be hot. That's the only thing I can figure."

"I'm sorry, Julia. I wasn't completely honest with you the other day when you asked if I'd ever heard Luke's band. The truth is, Luke and I had a . . . a thing a few weeks ago." Casey's hand shoots up. "We didn't have sex. It didn't go that far. But we shared an attraction."

Julia's hazel eyes grow wide. "So you're the pretty little blonde he told me about. What happened between you two? I got the impression he was really into you."

"We had a misunderstanding. I guess it's for the best. Sounds like he and Brooke belong together. I should've told you sooner."

Casey sits down at the community table and opens her computer, forcing Luke from her mind as she focuses on her work. She wants nothing to do with a man who can't make up his mind about a woman.

———

On Friday around noon, Casey drives to town to pick up a prepackaged salad from Delilah's. She usually goes for kale, but today, the Cobb with pulled roasted chicken tempts her. She's studying the ingredients on the label when a familiar voice says, "Hey there, Casey."

She cranes her neck to see Luke standing behind her, his sexy smile creeping across his lips.

"Oh. Hey," she says and returns her attention to the label.

Luke moves in closer. "What're you doing?"

"What does it look like I'm doing? I'm trying to decide which salad I want for lunch." She eyes his plastic basket, filled to the brim with wine and nibbles and chocolates. "What're you doing? Looks to me like you have a hot date lined up for the weekend."

He ignores her. "It's good to see you. Where have you been hiding?"

Returning the Cobb to the refrigerated shelf, she grabs the kale salad and faces him. "I haven't been hiding anywhere. I stopped by the jazz club a couple of weeks ago when your band was playing. I was disappointed to see your girlfriend had taken my seat at the bar. I'm curious, Luke. Is Brooke still your girlfriend? Last week, Ruthie told me you two had broken up. But yesterday, Julia said you're treating Brooke to a weekend at The Greenbrier. Based on the contents of your basket, I'm guessing Julia is right."

Luke deflates. "It's complicated."

"Right. Like it was complicated with Jamie and me. Personally, I think romance is pretty straightforward. You're either into someone or you're not."

Luke grimaces, as though she struck a nerve, which fuels her fire to keep going.

"Take my situation, for example. I had a ginormous crush on

Jamie, but once I went out with him a few times, I realized there's no chemistry between us. I also realized I had fallen for a certain saxophone player." She walks away from Luke and gets in line to pay.

Luke grabs a jar of macadamia nuts and comes to stand behind her in line. "Why didn't you tell me this before?"

"I tried at the Fourth of July party. But you blew me off. Then I came to the jazz club to see you. Of course, you'd already moved on. Oh wait! You weren't moving *on*. You were regressing by hooking up with an old girlfriend. A relationship that, according to Sheldon, you deemed doomed from the start."

Casey moves forward in the line. When the cashier tells her the amount, she swipes her debit card. She turns back toward Luke for one last word. "I may be young and immature, but at least I'm not fickle like you," she says and hurries out of the gourmet shop before he can come after her.

Casey floats through the afternoon on a cloud. Even the upcoming dinner with the winemaker can't spoil her exuberant mood.

Turns out, Bruce Wheeler is not the intimidating wine snob Casey expects. He's friendly and engaging, and he talks about wine making in simple terms. His bright emerald eyes mesmerize Casey as he discusses the transformation of the Love-Struck varietals. She notices Daniel watching Bruce with obvious admiration. She's certain he will offer him the job as head winemaker before the night is over.

After dessert, when Daniel drags Bruce to a far corner of the terrace for cigars and brandy, Casey and Sheldon head down to the pool. They kick off their shoes and sit on the edge of the pool with feet dangling over the side.

"I heard you put Luke in his place," Sheldon says.

Casey grins. "Who told you that?"

"He did." Sheldon leans into her. "I ran into him today outside of Delilah's. He asked if I'd seen you, and he told me about your encounter. I'm proud of you, Casey. You're learning to fight back."

Casey flutter kicks the water. "I prefer to think of it as finding my voice. I can't believe I was so wrong about Luke. He seemed like such a cool guy."

"He is a very cool guy, Casey. He seemed deeply disturbed by the things you said to him. I think he really cares about you."

"Then why is he spending the weekend at The Greenbrier with Brooke? Whatever. I'm over it." Casey dips her fingers into the pool and flicks water droplets at Sheldon's face.

"Ahh . . . that feels good." He closes his eyes and lifts his chin. "Do it again."

"If you're sure." This time, instead of flicking droplets, she splashes him with a wave of water.

Sheldon laughs out loud. "You asked for it." He slides into the pool fully clothed, taking her with him.

Casey tilts her head back to wet her hair. "You're right. It does feel good."

With heads above water, they swim breast stroke to the far end, climb out, and lie flat on the pool deck, staring up at the starry sky.

"I've been thinking about your man cabin all week, and I admit I'm more than a little jealous." She rolls her head to the side to look at him. "Prior to coming to Lovely, I spent three years nursing my sick mother. Which was a major setback for someone my age. I'm only twenty-seven years old, and I have no idea who I am. I feel like I'm in over my head, and I need my own space. Daniel's building me a house for crying out loud. If I let him control too much of my life now, I will forever be a prisoner of his kingdom."

"That's very astute of you. You know yourself better than you think. It took me years to figure out what you have concluded in a couple of months."

A breeze sends chill bumps across her skin. She shivers and wraps her arms around herself. "What am I supposed to do?"

"Be honest with him. Tell him how you're feeling."

Casey frowns. "Easier said than done. Why can't I stand up to him like I stood up to Luke?"

"Because he's been good to you, and you're worried you'll hurt his feelings."

"Exactly," Casey says.

"I know you're tired of hearing me say this, but you'd better toughen up. Prison orange would not be a good look for you."

"Ha ha. Aren't you the wise guy?" Casey catches sight of Daniel and Bruce on the upper level of the terrace. "I wonder what they're talking about. Do you think Daniel will hire him?"

"For sure. The man is a genius. Dad is probably making him an offer as we speak."

"Do you think men with ginger coloring are attractive?" she asks, her eyes still on Bruce.

"How would I know?" Sheldon chuckles. "I saw him eyeing you. He's too old for you, Casey."

"No kidding. He's easily forty. And he wasn't eyeing me. He was being polite to me because I'm Daniel's daughter."

Sheldon props himself on his elbows. "Are things better at work now that you've identified the rebranding concept?"

Casey sits up and pulls her knees to her chin. "Much better. I admit Bruce got me excited. The vineyard is already thriving, even though our wines are swill. Think of the growth opportunity if we can produce respectable, maybe even award-winning, varietals."

"Swill? What're you talking about?" Sheldon gives her a gentle shove. "Our wines may be subpar, but they aren't that bad. Where did you learn that word, anyway?"

Casey giggles. "That's what Ollie and Fiona say about our wines."

Steely determination settles on Sheldon's face. "Game on. We'll show them who's boss. Ollie may have Melvin Bass back, but Bruce Wheeler is one of the most prominent winemakers in Oregon."

"I hate to say it, but Melvin has the advantage. He knows

Virginia climate and soil way better than a newcomer from Oregon."

Sheldon cuts his eyes at her. "Hey! Whose side are you on?"

"Ours, of course. Whose side will you be on when you marry Ollie?"

His face falls. "Good question. I haven't thought about that. Who says I have to pick sides?"

"Ha. You don't know Ollie as well as you think you do. She's one of the most competitive people I know. You'll definitely be picking sides."

Sheldon pauses a beat and then shrugs. "I'll cross that bridge when I get to it."

Casey wishes she could live in the moment like Sheldon. Her life would be so much easier if she weren't constantly worried about and planning for her future.

CHAPTER 29
ADA

On Monday, eight days after her visit to Malone Equestrian Center, Ada finally receives a text from Stuart. *Dad confirmed he has room for your horse but he wants you to wait until he gets home from Europe to move her over.*

The waiting is driving Ada insane, and she says as much to Enzo the next afternoon as they're walking to Magnolia Avenue to meet with the new owner of the Abbey Lane building.

"You'll soon have your answers. Bud is due home from Europe tomorrow."

"So? He'll need to settle in, sleep off his jet lag, and catch up with his life here. I doubt he'll get back to me until next week."

Enzo shrugs. "Who says you have to wait for him to reach out to you? Why don't you contact him if you haven't heard from him by midday on Friday?"

"I guess I could. I'll just tell him I'm eager to move Glory."

"Is your horse's title in your name? I'd hate for you to run into problems with Daniel when you try to move her?"

"I hadn't thought about that. The title is in my name, but it's in Daniel's files. I'll have to figure out a way to get it."

When they reach Abbey Lane's, the building's new owner is waiting at the front door. After introductions are made, Toby says,

"Thanks for coming on such short notice. I have several interested parties, and Abbey insisted on being here during the showings. To make it easier on her, I scheduled all the tours on the same day."

"No problem at all," Enzo says. "I'm eager to see the space."

"Then what are we waiting for?" Toby says and leads them into the dress shop. "As you can see, the floor plan is simple. Showroom out front with a small office and storage room in the back. I'll provide the space, and you'll be responsible for the fixtures."

Enzo turns toward Ada. "I was thinking I'd run wine racks down both walls with a sleek tasting bar in the middle."

"Or . . . you might have several smaller stations to accommodate private parties." Ada looks up at the tin ceiling. "You could paint the ceiling a dramatic color and add some funky light fixtures." She circles the showroom. "We'll do some research. There are so many cool ways to display wine. You'll also need to determine where the cheese display and checkout counters will be."

"What is your timeline in terms of availability?" Enzo asks Toby.

"Abbey has promised to be out by the end of August. I'll need to do some electrical improvements, but I should be able to turn it over to you by the end of September."

"Do you mind if we look around for a minute?" Enzo asks.

"By all means," Toby says, sweeping his arm at the showroom. "Take your time. The next showing isn't for twenty minutes."

Enzo pulls Ada aside, and they speak in hushed tones near the front door. "What do you think?"

"You won't find a more desirable location in Lovely. The small parking lot in the back is key. You should know that I'm not in a position to commit to a partnership yet. It might be weeks before I can make that decision. If you're pursuing this venture with or without me, I say go for it."

"Will you at least help me with the decor?" Enzo asks, his face pale and sweat beading on his forehead.

"Absolutely!" Ada gives his arm a squeeze. "You've got this, Enzo. You're going to be brilliant at running a wine shop."

"Thanks for your vote of confident." Enzo inhales a deep breath. "Okay. Here goes." He motions for Toby to join them. "I'm definitely interested in leasing the space. Can you tell me more about my competition?"

"The rent is too high for the woman who was here before you. The next candidate is considering opening a fast casual salad franchise. I doubt this space is big enough, but we'll see what he thinks."

"I'm in. If he passes, I'll sign the lease right away."

"Excellent. I have your number. I'll text you after I meet with him," Toby says and sees them to the door.

On the sidewalk out front, Enzo says, "I'm too nervous to go home. Let's go to Belmonte's. We can have a glass of wine and some appetizers while we wait."

Ada hugs his arm. "Don't worry, Enzo. It'll be fine. You heard Toby. He doesn't think the space will work for the other guy."

"Let's not talk about it. You'll jinx me," he says, and they walk down Magnolia Avenue in silence.

At Belmonte's, they ask the hostess to seat them at one of the small tables under the awning on the sidewalk out front. Enzo peruses the wine menu. "Belmonte needs to up his game. His wine list sucks." When the server arrives, he orders two tequilas on the rocks and a charcuterie board.

When the server leaves, Enzo says, "We need to decide about the ambience. I have a vision in mind for the shop, but I don't know how to describe it."

Ada laughs. "I thought we weren't talking about the wine shop."

Enzo grins. "I meant the location, not the decor."

Ada accesses her Pinterest app on her phone and searches for wine shops. She shows him the results. "The possibilities are endless. Minimalist. Rustic. Contemporary."

"Those are just words to me, Ada." He looks down at the phone's screen. "I want something like this." He points to a photograph of a wine shop with oak floors and white shelving. Extending down the middle of the shop is a custom-made tasting bar with a charcoal gray base and counter made of white marble with heavy dark gray veining. "This is what I want. My wine shop is not for the housewife looking for two buck chuck. I'm hoping to attract wine enthusiasts who come to sip and stay awhile."

"Elegantly handsome." She studies the photograph more closely. "They've back lit the shelves to highlight the wine."

The server arrives with their order, and they spend a minute examining the offerings on the charcuterie board.

Popping an olive in her mouth, Ada says, "You should consider hiring a decorator if money is no object."

"Who said money was no object?"

She sits back in her chair, cocktail in hand. "You never said it, but you gave me that impression. You haven't worked in weeks. You told me yourself you don't need a financial partner. What aren't you telling me, Enzo?" she asks, a smirk playing on her lips as she sips her tequila.

He furrows his dark brow. "What do you mean?"

"You're hiding something from me, Enzo. You never talk about your past. I need to know more about you before I agree to be your business partner. Was your father in the Italian mob?" She knows about his illustrious family. But she needs to hear it from him.

Enzo is silent for a long time before responding. "I'm a descendant of the royal Italian family. Which means nothing since we have no power. I'm technically a prince, but all that gets me is an invitation to the country's most elite parties, weddings, and funerals."

Ada pretends to be surprised. "That's amazing, Enzo. Why wouldn't you want people to know? I'd tell the whole world if I were a princess."

Enzo chuckles. "You don't need a title, Ada. You *are* a princess."

Ada places a hand on her chest. "That's the nicest thing anyone has ever said to me."

Enzo's phone pings with an incoming text. "This is Toby. The potential client passed. The space is mine . . . ours if you decide to become my partner."

"That's great news!" She offers him a high five. "We should celebrate. Let's order a bottle of champagne. My treat." She's excited for Enzo, but this victory is his, not hers. The wine shop venture only mildly excites her. This is his dream. She has yet to identify what she wants from life.

———

Ada is the first to arrive at the winery on Wednesday morning. Letting herself into the building, she takes her belongings to her office and continues down the hall to Daniel's office. She uses her phone's flashlight to locate the familiar antique box on his bookshelves. Hidden in the box's false bottom is the key to his fireproof filing safe. Opening the second drawer, she flips through the hanging files until she finds the folder bearing the official papers relating to Ada's life. Her birth certificate, health insurance policy, and social security card are all there. The last document in the file is Glory's deed of ownership.

Ada cleans out the file and locks the safe before leaving her father's office. She stops in the break room for coffee and returns to her office, locking the door behind her. Seated at her desk, she studies her birth certificate. How did her mother feel when she lied to hospital administration about her father's identity? Did she ever second-guess her decision to raise another man's baby as Daniel Love's child? Her list of questions is long, but she will soon have some answers. If she doesn't hear from Bud by lunchtime on Friday, she'll reach out to him.

To occupy her mind, Ada busies herself with finalizing the

arrangements of upcoming fall weddings. She takes a short break for lunch, and she's so immersed in her work, she almost doesn't answer the call from an unknown number midafternoon.

She immediately recognizes the man's voice. "Ada, Bud Malone here."

Ada is suddenly tongue tied. She's always called him Uncle Bud, but he isn't her uncle. He's her father. "Yes, sir. How was your trip?"

"Exhausting," he says with a sigh. "An old college friend lives in London. He's been hounding me to visit him for years. We hit all the hot spots in Europe. We're the same age, but I struggled to keep up with him. I'm glad to have returned to my quiet life here." He clears his throat. "Stuart tells me you're interested in renting a stall at the equestrian center. I'm on the way home from the Richmond Airport. Can you stop by later this afternoon? I have a couple of stalls for you to choose from. You can pick one and fill out your paperwork."

To her delight, Bud sounds as eager to talk to her as she is to him. "You must be tired from your trip. It can wait until tomorrow."

"I'm fine. I'm honestly ready to get back to work. Does five o'clock work for you?"

"Five is fine. I'll see you then." After ending the call, Ada stares at the phone in her hand. She's been debating how much to tell him about the situation, but she has a sneaking suspicion he already knows everything.

CHAPTER 30
ADA

Ada is parking her car near the stable when she spots Bud on his back porch. He waves her over, and she walks around the outdoor riding arena to his Lowcountry style home. When he greets her with a peck on the cheek, she notices the dark circles under his eyes. She's touched he took the time to meet with her despite being travel fatigued.

"I love your home," Ada says. "Did you design it?"

"No, the previous owner built it. She's originally from South Carolina, hence the Lowcountry style. Let's sit down while you fill out the paperwork." He motions her to a nearby table where two glasses of lemonade with slices of lemon and mint leaves await.

They sit down across from one another, and Bud slides a clipboard with the forms attached over to Ada. "This is a simple boarding agreement."

While she fills out the form, he explains the monthly fees and rules for horse owners. She slides the clipboard with the completed form back to him, and he gives it the once-over. "Excellent. Are you ready to choose your stall?"

"Absolutely," Ada says, draining her lemonade and pushing back from the table.

They stroll down to the stable and pause in the doorway, watching a group of women saddle up their horses for a trail ride. Ada longs to be one of them. Maybe she'll finally be able to make some friends.

"I sense such positive energy here," Ada says. "The facility is clean and bright, and your boarders all seem so pleasant."

He smiles. "We're blessed. They get along surprisingly well. They have an agreement to leave the drama at home. This is their time to relax with their horses."

Ada and Bud wait for them to clear out for their trail ride before entering the stable.

"You have your pick of two stalls." Bud shows her the stalls, and she chooses the one with morning sunlight exposure. He gives her a tour of the tack room, where he assigns her a locker and a saddle rack.

Leaving the tack room, they mosey to the far end of the stable, stopping to speak to horses along the way.

"Glory will love it here. And so will I," Ada says, gazing out across the lush green acreage of the farm.

"Does your father know you're moving Glory?"

Bud's question provides Ada the opportunity she's been waiting for. "I haven't told him yet. Things are tense between Daniel and me at the moment. Are you aware his daughter from a long-ago affair has come into his life?"

Bud nods. "I met Casey at the Fourth of July party."

Ada thinks back to that night. She doesn't remember seeing Bud on the Fourth. But there were so many people at the party, and she'd been distracted by Casey and Daniel. "Have you heard the other family gossip circulating around town?"

The lines on his forehead deepen. "I don't believe I have."

"I was suspicious of Casey, this young woman who appeared from nowhere claiming to be Daniel's daughter. When I suggested she have a DNA test to prove paternity, Daniel insisted we all take tests. Turns out, I'm not his daughter." Ada watches closely for Bud's reaction. He doesn't blink. This is not news to him.

"I'm sorry, Ada. That revelation must have been difficult for you."

Ada stares down at the ground. "I was devastated at first. Daniel raised me as his only daughter, and I assumed he wouldn't care about genetics. Turns out blood trumps love. He's been a real jerk."

Bud sighs. "I'm not surprised. I once considered Daniel my best friend. He stabbed me in the back one too many times, and I finally wised up to his antics, his unethical means of getting his way."

"He's a difficult man to love," Ada says, kicking at the dirt with her boot.

"Will you stay on at Love-Struck as head event planner?"

"No. It's too painful for me to watch Casey take everything that once belonged to me. But the winery is the only life I've ever known, and I have no other plans for my future. I need to know who I come from in order to discover who I am."

"I can understand that," Bud says in a soft voice.

"I sent my DNA sample to a genetic genealogy website. I matched as first cousins with your nephew, Riley. I drove over to Hope Springs and met with him. He showed me his family tree." Inhaling a deep breath, Ada levels her gaze on Bud. "Are you my biological father?"

A single tear spills from Bud's right eye and slides down his cheek. "Yes, Ada. I am your father. Keeping this secret is the hardest thing I've ever done. I loved your mother very much. I made the mistake of letting her call the shots. I was prepared to leave my wife for her. But Lila was terrified of losing the boys. In order to be a part of your life, I had to go along with her decision to let Daniel raise you as his own."

"How long were you and Mom lovers?"

Bud wipes his tear-stained cheek with the back of his hand. "Not long. Our affair started the summer before she got pregnant with you in September. I ended it immediately when she refused to leave Daniel. But I never stopped loving her."

Ada presses her lips thin. "That was the summer Daniel spent in California. When he had an affair with Beverly Hobbs, Casey's mother. I'd call that the summer of love."

"It was a confusing time for all of us. None of us were happy in our marriages."

"Why didn't you tell me the truth after Mom died?" Ada asks.

Bud hesitates before answering. "About a year before her brain aneurysm, Lila came to see me. I've often wondered if she had a premonition about her death. She begged me never to tell anyone I'm your father. She said it would rock your world if you ever found out. Sounds like she was right."

"She knew Daniel would kick me out of his life." A moment of comfortable silence passes between them. "Mom left a bundle of your love letters with Beatrice to give to me when the time was right."

Bud's lips part in a sad smile. "I remember those letters. It's how we communicated when we couldn't be together. I rented a post office box in town. I kept your mother's letters to me. I still read them sometimes when I'm feeling lonely."

"Beatrice also thought Mom sensed something was going to happen to her. If Mom never wanted me to know you're my father, why'd she leave the letters with Beatrice?"

Bud shrugs. "Because she knew if you ever found out about Daniel, you'd want to know who your biological father is."

"Will you tell Stuart about me?"

"When the time is right. What about Daniel? Will you tell him about me?"

"With your permission," Ada says.

"Of course. I'm here for you, Ada. Anything I can do to help."

Ada straightens. "I'm leaving Love-Struck, Bud. I'm currently working on my exit strategy. My goal is to humiliate Daniel as much as possible."

He chuckles. "I'd love to witness this exit."

Ada cuts her eyes at him. "You don't strike me as the vindictive type."

"When it comes to Daniel Love, I am. I'd love nothing more than to see him get what he deserves."

Ada smiles. She senses a camaraderie developing between them. "In that case, I'll keep you abreast of my plans."

Bud moves in closer to her. "This is surreal for me, Ada. I've spent the last twenty-seven years loving you from afar. I won't pressure you. We'll move forward on your terms. But I would very much love to be a part of your life."

Ada surprises herself by bursting into tears. She never realized how much she needed to hear him say this. Unable to speak, she nods her head vigorously. Bud opens his arms, and she steps into them. He holds her tight, whispering comforting words while she cries. She hasn't felt such an overwhelming sense of belonging since her mother died. This is the sign she's been looking for. This man is her biological father, her flesh and blood. She belongs right here, in his arms, sharing his life.

CHAPTER 31
CASEY

Late on Thursday afternoon, Casey and Julia are wrapping up a planning session when Julia says, "Do you have a minute? I need to talk to you regarding a personal matter."

Dread rolls through Casey. "I'm almost afraid to ask about what."

Julia laughs. "It's about Luke. I rarely meddle in people's love lives, but he begged me to talk to you."

Casey grimaces. "I'll pass."

"Please. Just hear me out. He told me about your encounter at Delilah's. You made quite an impression by standing up to him. You got through to him. He broke up with Brooke for good."

Casey rolls her eyes. "Yeah, right?"

"I'm being serious, Casey. He refused to take her to The Greenbrier."

"Good for him." Casey slams her computer shut and stands abruptly. "Your brother is fickle. I'm sure he'll change his mind about her again tomorrow."

Julia rises from her chair. "I agree with you. When it comes to Brooke, he is fickle. She has some kind of weird hold over him. But he doesn't love her. He doesn't even like her very much."

"Like you said. Must be the sex."

Julia comes around to Casey's side of the community table. "Luke realizes he made some mistakes. But he's truly over Brooke. He knows it won't be easy, but he's determined to win another chance with you."

"Tell him not to bother. I'm not interested," Casey says and leaves the office.

"I'll tell him," Julia calls after her. "But he won't listen."

Casey bypasses her office and leaves the building. She's ready to unwind after an exhausting day. If she hurries, she can squeeze in a few laps in the pool before she joins Daniel on the terrace for dinner. She strides across the lawn to The Nest and traipses up the stairs. When she enters her bedroom, the landscape outside her window catches her attention. Something's different. She moves closer to get a better look. Down below, an earthmover is digging trenches for footings on her property next door. A sinking feeling weighs her down. She's forever doomed to live on the Love-Struck property. She mentally reprimands herself. She should feel blessed for having a father who loves her so much.

After swimming for an hour, she quickly showers and dresses for dinner in a pink T-shirt dress. When she goes downstairs, she finds Daniel waiting on the terrace with an opened bottle of red wine.

He pours her a glass. "This pinot noir is from Bruce's current vineyard. He's accepted my offer. He's starting work next week."

"Whoa. That happened fast."

Daniel laughs. "When he turned in his resignation, his employer sent him packing. Which is a bonus for us. We have much work to do here, and he's eager to get started."

"He's definitely enthusiastic." Casey sips the wine, tasting notes of dark cherries. "This is delicious. I can't wait to see what he does with our wines."

"I'd like to have a reception for him, to introduce him to the community. Sooner rather than later. Like the end of next week. Can we make that happen?"

"Ada's the event planner. Have you talked to her about it?"

"Ada has been too distracted lately. I don't trust her to handle this. If she doesn't shape up, I'll have to demote her to a lessor position."

Chill bumps cover Casey's bare arms. He's not planning to demote Ada. He's planning to fire her. He wants her out of his life for good.

Casey forces a smile. "Sure! The marketing department can take care of the arrangements. We'll need to get the invitations out tomorrow. How many people were you thinking of asking?"

"Use the list from the Fourth of July party."

Casey's mouth falls open. "That's several hundred people."

"Exactly. The point is to stir up interest in our new wines. Obviously, we won't need a band or fireworks. Just heavy hors d'oeuvres and plenty of top-quality booze. Whatever you do, put up a tent in case it rains."

Arabella appears with their dinner—ahi tuna steaks served over mixed green salads. Casey says little while they eat. She's disturbed at the ease with which Daniel is expelling Ada from his life. He's been her father for twenty-seven years. Any man with an ounce of compassion would've adopted Ada, not turned his back on her. The more Casey gets to know Daniel, the less she trusts him. She hates feeling this way when he's done so much for her. When he's her father.

She declines dessert, claiming a headache, and returns to her room. She changes into her pajamas, and even though it's still light outside, she crawls into bed. But she can't shake the uneasy feeling brewing in the pit of her gut. What if she somehow upsets Daniel? If she falls in love with a man he doesn't approve of or makes a drastic error at work? If he fires her from her job and takes away her home, she'll be left with nothing.

Her phone pings with a text from Luke. *Hi,* he says with a funny face emoji. She laughs despite being angry at him. She could use some unbiased advice about her father. After all, Luke is an attorney. Before she can respond, she receives an audio message from him. When she clicks the play button, the bluesy sound of his saxophone emits from her phone in a seductive song that stirs something deep within her, moving her to tears. She closes her eyes and imagines herself sitting at the end of the bar at Blue Cosmos, watching Luke make love to his saxophone on stage.

Luke texts again. *What do you think? I wrote it for you as a peace offering. I'm calling it "Golden Girl".*

Casey doesn't hesitate. *It's lovely.*

Luke: *Does that mean you forgive me?*

Casey smiles as she thumbs off her response. *It means the song is lovely.*

Luke: *Can we start over? I'd like to be your friend.*

Casey: *Maybe. But only because I need a friend right now.*

Luke: *You sound sad.*

Casey: *Ha-ha. More worried than anything.*

Luke: *Talk to me. You have attorney/client privilege.*

Casey turns off the light and slides further beneath the covers. She confesses her concerns about becoming a prisoner in her father's world.

Luke: *You have good reason to be worried. Especially considering the way Daniel has treated Ada. Have you shared your concerns with Daniel?*

Casey: *No. I'm afraid of hurting his feelings. And I don't know him well enough to gauge how he might react.*

Luke: *Then proceed with caution. Give it another month or six weeks. If you still aren't comfortable with the situation, you should discuss your issues with Daniel. But be prepared to move out if the conversation doesn't go well.*

Casey: *That makes sense. I'll definitely have a better feel for things after another month.*

Tired of talking about herself, Casey texts: *Did you really write that song?*

This leads to a conversation about his music, followed by an even longer one about his relationship and breakup with Brooke.

They text until past midnight and all throughout the following day. He invites her to dinner at Belmonte's, but Casey isn't ready for a date. She's enjoying their flirtatious getting-to-know-each-other texting.

Casey: *Wish I could. But I have to work. I'm in charge of the welcome reception for our new winemaker. Did you get your invitation?*

Luke: *Yes! I'll be there!*

Casey's heart skips a beat at the prospect of seeing him again. *Yay! Say a prayer all goes well. Daniel dumped the event in my lap. He no longer trusts Ada. I wouldn't be surprised if he fires her.*

Luke: *I'm sorry. That sucks for her.*

Casey: *Yes, it does.*

Casey hopes Ada won't be blind-sided if Daniel fires her. Surely, she must realize something drastic is coming down the pike.

———

Casey works on the reception menus until late on Friday night. When she leaves her study for her bedroom, the soft glow of the full moon shining through the window catches her attention. Moving to the window, she looks down at the building in progress on her lot next door. Daniel has yet to show her the architect's plans, and she has no clue about the size or style of the house. Surely, he'll ask for her input about bathroom tile and kitchen appliances.

Casey tries to imagine living next door to Daniel. She's still at the window ten minutes later when she catches sight of head-lights down by the stable. *Who on earth could that be at this time of night?* Daniel has gone to a friend's son's wedding in Richmond. No one else has any business being on the property.

She hurries down the back stairs and out the kitchen door. A truck with small horse trailer is parked in the driveway. As she approaches the barn, she hears Ada's voice. And she's not alone.

The second voice, older and more distinguished, belongs to a man.

Casey presses herself against the side of the barn as she listens.

Ada says, "I never realized how gloomy this barn is until I visited your equestrian center."

"We went to great lengths to gain as much natural lighting as possible," the man says. "You may have noticed the row of lights along both sides of the A-frame roof."

"I did, and it makes an enormous difference. Glory is going to be so happy there."

Casey hears the clip clop of horse hooves on pavement, and before she can hide, Ada emerges from the barn with Glory in tow.

Ada startles at the sight of Casey, and Glory rears back her head in alarm. "Geez, Casey! You scared the heck out of me." She strokes the horse's neck to calm her. "What're you doing out here? Spying on me?"

"I live here. What're *you* doing out here in the middle of the night?"

Ada holds her head high. "I'm moving Glory to a new boarding facility."

Casey moves closer to Ada and her horse. "Does Daniel know this?"

"Nope. She's my horse. I'll board her wherever I want."

A familiar-looking man comes out of the barn, carrying a saddle with bridle and reins dangling from around his neck. "Hey, Casey. I'm Bud Malone. We met at the Fourth of July party."

"I remember. Nice to see you again, Mr. Malone." Casey looks back and forth between Bud and Ada. Who is this man to Ada? And why is he helping her move her horse? He's way too old to be her lover. They kind of look alike. They have the same almond-shaped, golden-brown eyes. Holy . . .

"Ada, is Bud your father?" she asks in a whispered voice.

Ada exchanges a look with Bud. He gives Ada the saddle and takes the horse's lead rope, walking her into the trailer.

"This is none of your business, Casey," Ada says, opening the truck's back door and tossing in the saddle.

"Listen, Ada." Casey grabs her arm and spins her around. "As much as you despise me, I'm on your side here. I understand a little of what you're going through. I spent my entire life wondering who my father was. If Bud is your father, you're fortunate to have found him so quickly."

Ada falls back against the side of the truck. "That's true. Bud and Daniel used to be best friends. Bud was having an affair with my mother around the same time Daniel was sleeping with your mother."

Casey leans against the truck beside Ada. "Think how different our lives would've been if they'd left their spouses and married their lovers."

"Right?" Ada says with a sigh. "If only . . ."

"I'm glad for you, Ada. You deserve better than the way Daniel's been treating you."

Ada pushes off the truck and faces Casey. "I have no right to ask for a favor after the way I treated you. But will you please keep this to yourself for now? Our families go way back. Bud and I should be the ones to tell them."

Casey drags her fingers across her lips. "I won't say a word. I never saw you here tonight."

Ada tilts her head to the side. "Perhaps I misjudged you a little."

"You misjudged me a lot, actually. I never meant to hurt anyone. But I don't blame you for hating me. I screwed up your life."

Ada's face softens. "Actually, you may have done me the biggest favor ever. I've been on a long journey, but I'm finally where I belong. Don't make the same mistakes I made, Casey. Don't let Daniel control your life."

Alarm fills Casey's face.

Ada grabs her hand and gives it a squeeze. "Don't worry. You'll be fine as long as you maintain your independence."

"Thanks for the advice." Casey flashes her a grin. "Did we just cross the line into friendly territory?"

"I wouldn't go that far," Ada says and climbs into the passenger seat. "But I can see us being frenemies in the not-so-distant future."

Casey laughs. "I'll take it. Frenemies trumps archenemies any day."

Bud starts the engine, and they drive slowly off with the horse trailer bumping on the road behind the truck.

Casey replays the conversation in her head as she watches the trailer's taillights disappear around the bend. That was not the same Ada who slashed her tires and vandalized her house two months ago. This new Ada seems less troubled, less resentful. Is Bud responsible for the sudden change? After a lifetime of living under her father's thumb, she's freed herself from the claws of Daniel Love. *You'll be fine as long as you maintain your independence.* Casey must figure out a way to stand up to him. And soon.

CHAPTER 32
ADA

Ada spends the day on Saturday organizing her tack and grooming supplies at the equestrian center. She introduces herself to the other boarders as they come and go, striking up conversations with several she'd like to know better.

Late in the afternoon, she and Bud tack up their horses for a trail ride. When she emerges from the tack room with her English saddle, Bud says, "I thought you preferred to ride western."

Ada stops in her tracks. "How do you know that?"

He winks at her. "I know a lot of things from watching you over the years. Mint chocolate chip is your favorite ice cream flavor. You chew on your lower lip when you're unsure of something. And the yellow flecks in your eyes shine like gold when you're excited."

His words deeply touch her. She doubts Daniel knows her favorite flavor of ice cream. Not trusting herself to speak, Ada returns to the tack room for her western saddle.

When the horses are ready, they lead them out of the barn before mounting them. As they're cutting across the farm toward the woods, Bud says, "Your cheeks are rosier today. Are you happy?"

She smiles at him. "I'm more than happy. For the first time in my life, I feel at peace."

His eyes shine with unshed tears. "I can't tell you how much it means to me to hear that."

"I'd like to get to know some of the other boarders. I hope they like me. I don't really do the girlfriend thing."

Bud chuckles. "Another thing I've noticed about you over the years. You're smarter than most women. You're serious, more intense. Their frivolity is beneath you."

"I never thought of it that way." All her life, Ada assumed the other girls didn't want to be her friend, when it was the other way around. "You're amazing, Bud. I think you know me better than I know myself."

"One learns a lot from studying his daughter from afar. You'll make fast friends with the other borders because you have one important thing in common with them. You all love your horses. That makes for easy conversation, which translates into friendship. One group rides together in the morning and the other in the afternoon. Figure out where you best fit in. And just be yourself. They'll love you."

"I hope you're right." Ada gives Glory a gentle kick, and she picks up a trot. Seconds later, Bud trots up alongside her. They enter the woods, but the trail is wide enough for them to remain side by side.

Bud says, "Coincidentally, I received an invitation to the reception honoring Daniel's new winemaker."

Ollie rolls her eyes. "Daniel had Casey's department organize that reception, even though event planning is my job."

"Why'd he do that?"

"He's either trying to make me mad so I'll quit, or he's getting ready to fire me. Either way, it's time for me to leave, especially now that Casey knows our secret. The reception will provide the ideal venue for me to make a fool out of Daniel."

Bud drops his smile. "I was debating about whether to go. But I wouldn't dare miss the show."

There's that vengeful streak again. Ada wonders what other character traits they have in common. "Are you sure? It means letting the world know I'm your daughter. Are you ready for that, Bud?"

"I've been ready since the day you were born on June fifteen, 1995. But I should break the news to Stuart before the reception. I wouldn't want him to hear this kind of news from anyone but me. Are you okay with that?"

"Absolutely. How do you think he'll respond?"

"There's no telling with Stuart. He can be a bit of a wildcard. Don't worry if he's upset at first. He'll eventually come around."

"I would be surprised if he's not upset. He was raised an only child. Having a sister suddenly appear in his life will take some getting used to." She straightens, bringing herself to her full height. "All right then. It's full speed ahead with my mission."

There's still one crucial element she must put in place. Her plan won't work if Enzo denies her this favor. Her request is sensitive, but she can no longer avoid making it. She'll talk to him tonight over dinner.

———

After leaving the equestrian center, Ada stops by her apartment to shower and dress in white jeans and a hot pink tunic. Enzo is mixing her favorite cucumber martinis when she arrives at his house.

"I bought salmon steaks," he says, handing her a martini. "We can eat now if you're hungry."

"Let's wait awhile. I have something important I need to talk to you about."

They take their cocktails out to the terrace, and Ada tells him about her first day at the equestrian center. "I'm going back tomorrow. The newness may eventually wear off, but for now, I can't get enough of the place."

"I'm so happy for you, Ada. Your face lights up when you talk about Bud." He shifts in his seat toward her. "What's this important thing you need to talk to me about?"

Ada inhales a deep breath for courage. "I need to ask a favor."

"The answer is yes," Enzo says with a smirk.

"You should hear what it is first. You're probably not going to like it."

Enzo sets down his drink and takes hold of her hand. "I've grown to know the real you over these last few weeks. I've fallen in love with you, Ada, and I'll do anything you ask." He snickers. "Although I draw the line at hiring a hit man to kill Daniel Love."

Ada brings his hand to her lips and kisses his fingertips. Forget the favor. She's been fighting her attraction to him for weeks, and she can't wait another minute to be with him. "Will you make love to me, Enzo?"

"I thought you'd never ask." He pulls her to her feet and scoops her up, carrying her inside to his bedroom.

Their lovemaking is exquisite. Ada never thought it possible to feel such intense passion. It's almost midnight when their hunger gets the best of them, and they take a break for dinner.

They return to the kitchen—Enzo in his boxer shorts and Ada wearing his discarded T-shirt. Enzo sears the salmon in a heavy iron skillet while Ada tears up lettuce for a salad.

When they sit down at the counter to eat, Enzo asks, "So what's this favor you need?"

Ada describes what she has in mind.

A slow smile spreads across his lips. "I'm in."

Ada's golden-brown eyes grow wide. "Are you sure? I'm asking a lot."

He runs his finger down her cheek. "I'm positive. I told you I'd do anything for you."

Ada looks away. "I'm still not ready to commit to being your partner in the wineshop. I may take some time to figure out what kind of career I want in the future."

"I totally support that." Enzo carves off a slice of salmon and pops it in his mouth. "I've told you a thousand times, Ada. I don't need a partner. If you opt out, I won't look for another investor. I'll go it alone."

Ada stabs a forkful of salad. "Partner or not, I'll still help you get the wine shop up and running. In a month or so, I may totally change my mind and decide to be your partner."

"Whatever you decide is fine by me. You have a lot going on, professionally and personally, and I respect that. These are important decisions. Take all the time you need."

"Thank you for being so understanding," Ada says, and they eat for a minute in silence. "We should talk about us . . . about what happened here tonight."

"What happened between us tonight was amazing. I'd go as far as to call it earth shattering," he says with a naughty glint in his eye.

Ada smiles. "But it changes things between us. I want more than friendship now. Do you?"

"Hell yes," he says in a husky voice. "These past few weeks haven't been easy. Many times, I've had to stop myself from tearing your clothes off. But I'm glad we took the time to get to know each other as friends. Our relationship is stronger because of it. I meant what I said earlier. I love you, Ada."

She throws her arms around him, smothering his face with kisses. "And I love you too, Enzo."

CHAPTER 33
OLLIE

Ollie finally scores an appointment with her therapist late afternoon on Wednesday. "I'm sorry you had to wait so long to see me," Ronnie says when Ollie enters her office. "I'll never go out of town again. I'm having to work overtime to get all my patients in for counseling."

"You deserve a break, Ronnie. From the look of your golden tan, a week at the beach did you some good."

Ronnie smiles sheepishly at Ollie. "I spent seven heavenly days reading romance novels on the beach. My head is clear and my passion for my work renewed."

They leave the doctor's office and go out onto the terrace. Ronnie fills two glasses of sweet tea from a pitcher and settles back in her chair. "So tell me, how are things going?"

"Things are going well, for the most part. I've enjoyed these past few weeks to myself. I feel stronger every day. The panic attacks are mostly gone. As for the vineyard, we are growing a healthy crop of grapes, and Melvin is working with his intern to create our new rosé." Ollie smiles. "I can hardly wait for our first harvest."

"Wonderful! You seem to be getting your life on track. But something's bothering you, otherwise you wouldn't be here."

Ollie pauses a beat before blurting, "I miss Sheldon like crazy. But we can't be together. He wants children, and I don't. I love him too much for him to sacrifice something so important to be with me."

"Who gave you the power to make such an important decision?"

Ollie is taken aback by the sharp edge in the doctor's voice. "Isn't that what you do when you love someone? Melvin says we should make these decisions together, but Sheldon would readily give up having a family for me."

"Melvin is a wise man. You should listen to him." Ronnie crosses one long tanned leg over the other. "Let's talk about the real issue on the table. Why don't you want children? Is it the lifestyle change that scares you?"

"A little, I guess. Sheldon would be a hands-on dad, and we would probably get a nanny. I've given it a lot of thought. I can hardly think of anything else, actually," Ollie says with a dreamy expression. "I can picture a little boy with Sheldon's golden curls and easygoing nature toddling around." She folds her arms over her chest. "I can almost feel his little body in my arms and taste his sweet skin on my lips."

Ronnie places her hand on Ollie's forearm. "I wish you could see your face right now. If ever there was a woman who wanted a baby to love, it's you. What's stopping you?"

A sudden realization hits Ollie. She gets up and walks to the edge of the terrace. "The baby I described is Sheldon's. He'll be perfect, just like his daddy. I'm terrified of tainting it with my genes."

"I don't understand. You're beautiful and intelligent and driven. Those are admirable qualities to pass down to your offspring."

"I came to you because of my anger management issues. What if I'm prone to violet tendencies? What if I carry my brother's evil gene? What if I create a murderer?" A sob catches in her throat, and she bursts into tears.

"Oh, honey." Ronnie comes to stand beside her, placing an arm around her waist. "Is that what this is all about?"

Unable to speak, Ollie nods. Ronnie produces a box of tissues from nowhere and offers it to Ollie. She snatches a tissue and presses it against her eyes.

"I'm not a genetics expert, but I'm pretty sure there's no such thing as an evil gene. Were your parents good people?"

"Yes! The best. They were loving and hardworking and honest."

"What about your grandparents and great grandparents? Your aunts, uncles, and cousins? Do you have any sadists or pedophiles on the family tree?"

Ollie coughs up a laugh. "Not that I know of."

"Something most likely happened to your brother when he was young that scarred him. We will probably never know what it was. Perhaps his evilness stems from a lack of faith in God. But it has nothing to do with you."

"How can you be so sure?" Ollie asks, her shoulders heaving.

"I can't. There are no guarantees in life, Ollie. But people adopt babies all the time. More often than not, they know little about the children's pasts. But they shower them with love and affection and mold them into healthy adults."

"That's a good point," Ollie says.

"Those of us with obsessive-compulsive disorders like you and me tend to overthink situations."

"That surprises me. You're the most put together person I know."

"I've learned to control it, just as you're doing. But it takes time. Whenever I get stuck on an issue, I turn it over to a higher being and let what happens happen."

Ollie stares at Ronnie with eyes wide. "I don't think I can do that."

Ronnie laughs. "Trust me. If I can do it, you can do it."

"But how?"

"Let's sit back down," Ronnie says, guiding Ollie back to their chair. "I'll give you some tips that have worked for me."

———

When Ollie arrives home from her session, she grabs her sunhat, calls the dogs, and heads out to her favorite spot in the vineyard where she can see the mountain range on all sides. She may be biased, but she's certain her farm is one of the most spectacular places on Earth. And it belongs to her. But what good is it if she has no one to share it with? No husband to watch the seasons come and go over the vineyard. No children to share the joys of winemaking, to pass the business on to after she's dead.

While the dogs run in and around the rows of vines, Ollie replays her conversation with Ronnie in her mind. *Whenever I get stuck on an issue, I turn it over to a higher being and let whatever happens happen.* Her anxiety problems stem from worrying about things she can't control. She can choose what she'll eat for breakfast in the mornings and make all the important decisions regarding her business, but from now on, she'll turn all matters of the heart over to a higher being.

Tilting her head heavenward, she spreads her arms wide and calls out, "Lead the way, higher being. And I will follow."

A sense of profound peace settles over Ollie. She relishes in it for a long while, letting the evening sun warm her face, before turning back toward home.

At the farmhouse, she finds Melvin in the kitchen with a carafe of pink wine and a platter of cheese, olives, and hummus.

"What's all this?" Ollie asks, removing a bottled water from the refrigerator and guzzling it down.

"This is our first stab at our rosé. I thought we'd have a little tasting." Melvin pours a splash from the carafe into two stemless glasses, handing one to her.

Ollie takes the glass to the window and holds it up to the light. "Women will love the soft salmon color. It's perfect for a Syrah blend rosé." When Ollie sniffs the wine, her stomach rolls, and she turns up her nose.

Melvin's brow pinches in concern. "What's wrong, Ollie? What do you smell?"

"I'm not sure." She brings the glass to her lips and takes a tiny sip. Her stomach heaves, and she swallows back bile.

"You don't like it," Melvin says in a disappointed tone. "Enzo and I were sure we'd nailed it."

She sets the wine on the counter. "It's not the rosé. My stomach's been acting weird all day. Maybe I'm getting a bug or something."

He looks more closely at her. "You're pale. Should you call the doctor?"

"I'm fine. I'm great actually. I've just come from an enlightening session with Dr. Ronnie." Suddenly dizzy, Ollie lowers herself to a stool. "As of today, I'm turning over a new leaf. I will no longer obsess about things I can't control. And I'm dumping this anger and resentment I've been harboring."

Melvin chuckles. "And just how do you plan to do that?"

"I'm going to start by going to the reception at Love-Struck tomorrow night. I want you to be my date, and I'm insisting Fiona come with us. We're going to extend an olive branch to the Loves. This feud between our two farms has gone on long enough."

"I can't argue with that. I'm certainly willing to try it. Now seems like as good a time as any to make amends. Since you and Sheldon are getting back together."

Ollie jerks her head up. "Who told you that?"

Melvin's eyes twinkle. "You did when you said you're going to stop obsessing over things you can't control. You and Sheldon belong together. Your reunion is inevitable."

CHAPTER 34
ADA

Ada spends her days at the equestrian center and her nights in Enzo's bed. She avoids all work-related calls and texts. She doesn't go near the vineyard until late Wednesday night, when she sneaks into the winery building and retrieves her personal possessions from her office.

On Thursday evening, Ada and Enzo are headed out of the door on the way to the reception when Enzo stops her. "You'll need a prop for the show."

Ada scrunches up her nose. "What prop?"

"This one." Enzo tugs a velvet ring box from his pocket and opens it, revealing an enormous emerald cut sapphire flanked by triangular diamonds.

Ada's eyes pop. "Is that real?"

"Of course it's real. It belonged to my mother. It was her engagement ring."

"I can't do this," Ada says, backing away from him. "I realize it was my idea, but deceiving people by pretending we're engaged is wrong."

"Then let's not pretend." Enzo closes the distance between them and drops to his knees. "Marry me, Ada."

Ada plants a hand on her hip. "Be serious, Enzo."

He appears wounded. "I am being serious. Do you love me?"

Ada lets out an exaggerated huff. "Yes, I love you. These past few days have been a dream come true for me. But it's too soon."

"Then we'll have a long engagement. I love you, and I just want to be with you."

Ada, realizing he's serious, softens. "I want to be with you, too. I want to be your wife more than anything. When the time is right. You promise we can have a long engagement?"

Enzo stands to face her. "You're in the driver's seat, Ada. You decide the where and when." He slides the ring on her finger. "It's a perfect fit. Do you like it?"

Ada holds her hand up, admiring the ring. "It's obscenely gorgeous. I love it." She throws her arms around his neck. "I can't believe this."

"Believe it." He swings open the door. "Now let's go share our news with the world."

Ada can't tear her eyes away from the ring on the drive over to the vineyard. "Will I be a legit princess when we're married?"

Enzo smiles over at her. "You will, for what it's worth. Which isn't much." He returns his attention to the road. "I'm sorry. That wasn't much of a proposal. But it was the best I could do on short notice."

"It makes for a good story, though."

"We'll do something special to celebrate this weekend. Maybe we'll spend Saturday night at the Inn at Hope Springs. We can book a day at the spa on Sunday. How does a couple's massage sound to you?"

"Divine. I like the idea of what might happen after the massage even better." Ada places a hand on his thigh and leaves it there during the rest of the drive to the vineyard.

Her stomach knots when they pass the Love-Struck entrance columns. "Am I doing the right thing, Enzo?"

"It's already done. Although, if you're having second thoughts, you could go easier on Daniel."

The mention of Daniel's name brings reality spiraling back. He deserves the blow she's about to deliver after the way he's treated her. Her back goes ramrod straight. "Nope. I'll never forgive myself if I don't see this through. Just promise me you'll support me regardless of what happens."

"I promise. You can always count on me." Enzo locates a parking space and turns off the truck's engine. Taking hold of her hand, he thumbs the ring. "This is my commitment to you. If you get freaked out on stage, I want you to look down at this ring and know my heart is with you."

She leans across the console to kiss him. "I don't deserve you."

"We deserve each other," he says in a soft voice. "And we're going to have a beautiful life together once we put all this messiness behind us."

Sucking in a breath, Ada says, "Okay, then. Let's do it."

They get out of the car and walk hand in hand to where the crowd is gathered around a small stage. Daniel is heaping accolades on Bruce Wheeler, his new winemaker. Five minutes later, he finishes his speech by inviting his guests to eat, drink, and be merry.

As Daniel is turning away from the microphone, Ada rushes onto the stage. "Wait! Please! If I can have a moment of your time," she says, adjusting the microphone to her height.

Daniel, standing slightly to her right, says in a low and angry voice, "What do you think you're doing?"

Ada flashes him her brightest smile. "You'll see." She turns back toward the microphone. "For those who don't know me, I'm Ada Love. I was Daniel's only daughter until six weeks ago when his bastard child, Casey, appeared on the scene."

As Ada looks out across the sizeable crowd, she fears her knees might buckle. She catches sight of Bud, who gives her a thumbs-up and the courage to continue. "It's not every day we're blessed to have so many friends gathered together. I wanted to take advantage of the opportunity to announce my engagement to be married. I'd like you all to meet Enzo." She sweeps a hand in Enzo's direction, and he joins her on the stage.

Daniel moves close enough to Ada for his voice to carry over the microphone. "Over my dead body. No daughter of mine is going to marry a field hand."

"Enzo isn't just a field hand. He worked that job to learn the trade as he studies to become a sommelier. Turns out he's Italian royalty. Prince Lorenzo Giovanni Dante Salvatore Medici." Ada looks up at Enzo. "Did I get that right?"

He places an arm around her waist. "Close. You got the Giovanni and Dante mixed up. But you'll get the hang of it in time."

Laughter erupts from the crowd. Someone calls out, "What do you think of that, Daniel?" And another guest yells, "Is an Italian Prince good enough for Daddy's little girl?"

"Listen up! I have more news." Ada claps her hands, and the crowd goes silent. "Some of you may already know this. When Casey entered the picture back in June, Daniel insisted we all get DNA tests." She thumbs her chest. "Turns out I'm the only illegitimate member of the fam."

Audible gasps spread across the audience.

"Right? You can imagine my surprise. Anyway, I did a little digging, and I discovered my biological father is none other than Daniel's best friend, Bud Malone. How's that for an interesting twist?"

She looks over at Daniel in time to see the color drain from his face. "Also, effective immediately, I'm resigning from my position as the vineyard's event planner. I've sold my share of the business to my brother Hugh. I'm uncertain of my professional future, but for the time being, I'll be spending my days riding my horse at Malone Equestrian Center."

A single clap sounds from the back of the crowd. Across the sea of people, Ada spots Casey with her hands in the air. Others join Casey in applauding as Ada and Enzo leave the stage.

Bud is waiting for them on the ground. "You were brilliant," he says, engulfing her in a bear hug. "You're trembling."

"Delayed nerves, I guess."

"We have much to celebrate. I have champagne chilling back at the house. I hope you and Enzo will join me."

"I'd like that." Ada spots Daniel heading their way. "Let's get out of here before Daniel causes a scene."

They hurry together to the parking lot where they part ways toward their separate cars. As Enzo speeds away, Ada's phone blows up with texts.

Daniel: *You can't sell your share of the business. It's not yours to sell.*

Ada: *Take that up with Hugh. My money's in the bank.*

Daniel: *You won't get away with humiliating me like this.*

Ada: *Looks like I already have.*

Daniel: *How can you be sure Bud is your biological father?*

Ada: *A genetic website matched me to Bud's nephew. When I confronted Bud, he confessed he had an affair with Mom the same summer you were sleeping with Beverly Hobbs. Bud and Mom were very much in love, but Mom refused to leave you for fear she would lose her sons.*

Ada is staring at her phone, waiting for a response from Daniel, when she receives a text from Casey. *You rocked that. I'm sincerely overjoyed for you.*

Ada: *Thanks. That means a lot. I'm sorry if I embarrassed you.*

Casey: *No worries. It was worth it.*

Ada: *I was nasty to you in the beginning, but if you hadn't come along, I never would've discovered my true identity. I've learned a lot about myself these past few weeks. I realize now how bitter I'd become from trying to live up to his impossible expectations. Be careful, Casey. Don't lose sight of who you really are.*

Casey: *I won't. You're a true inspiration in that regard.*

Ada: *If you ever need to talk, don't hesitate to call.*

Casey: *Will do. Does this mean we're friends?*

No way, Ada types with a wink face emoji.

The last message is from Avery with an attached image. In the picture, Ada and Enzo are standing at the microphone together, beaming at each other, with Daniel in the background, his face red with fury.

Avery writes: *What do you think of this caption? Ada Love drops bombshell on Daddy Daniel.*

Ada texts back. *Don't post that unless you're prepared to lose your job.*

When Ada looks up from her phone, they are pulling into the equestrian center. Bud is waiting for them on the porch with a bottle of expensive champagne chilling in an ice bucket. He pops the cork and fills three glasses with bubbly. "I've waited a long time to say this. Welcome to the family, Ada."

The threesome clinks glasses. "And congratulations on your engagement." Bud's gaze shifts from Enzo to Ada. "I didn't realize you were in a serious relationship."

Ada leans into Enzo. "We haven't been seeing each other long. But I'm certain Enzo's the one. We're going to have a long engagement."

"It all happened suddenly," Enzo says to Bud. "Otherwise, I would've asked you for her hand."

Bud winks at Enzo. "You can ask once we've gotten to know each other better."

Enzo's phone vibrates, and he looks down at the screen. "This is my uncle calling from Italy."

"Isn't it the middle of the night there?" Ada asks.

"He's an insomniac. If you'll excuse me." Enzo leaves the porch to take the call.

Ada and Bud sit down in rockers. "I was hoping Stuart would come tonight," Ada says. "How did he take the news?"

"As I predicted. His mother and I kept our marital problems from Stuart. He was deeply disturbed when we divorced. To find out I had an illegitimate child with my best friend's wife is a devastating blow."

"I'm sorry, Bud. I didn't mean to cause trouble for you with your son."

Bud places his hand over hers. "None of this is your fault, Ada. Besides, I'm not worried. He'll come around in time."

Ada sighs. "I hope you're right."

"What's up next for you, now that you're no longer employed at the vineyard? I hope you meant what you told the crowd about your plans to spend more time here."

"Absolutely." The lights are on in the outdoor riding arena, and a woman is exercising her horse on a lead line. She admires the woman's commitment to her animal. Ada rests her head against the back of the chair. "This place has such a calming effect on me."

"Good! I enjoy having you around."

"Enzo asked me to invest in his wine shop. But I haven't decided about that yet. I need some time to clear my head."

"You're wise to do that." Bud touches his glass to hers. "To your future. May your journey going forward be less rocky than the past."

She rolls her head to the side, smiling over at him. "One thing's for certain. With you along for the ride, the trip will be more enjoyable."

CHAPTER 35
CASEY

Fiona stares over Casey's shoulder at her phone. "Who are you texting?"

Casey stuffs the phone in the back pocket of her white jeans. "Ada. She's such a badass."

"Since when are you friends with Ada?"

"I never said we're friends. I said she's a badass. What she did tonight was epic. The way she stood up to Daniel took real guts." Casey drains her champagne and grabs another glass from a passing server.

"Easy there, girlfriend. How many of those have you had?" Fiona asks, eyeing her flute.

"Buzz off, Fiona. I'm celebrating Ada's victory."

Casey doesn't hear Ollie sneak up from behind until she's standing next to her. "Hey, Casey. Long time no see. How's your new life treating you?"

"Things are going well. Thanks for asking." Casey takes Ollie in. She's wearing white linen pants and a white silk sleeveless top. Her aqua eyes are bright and mahogany hair hangs loose, framing her lovely face. "You look amazing, Ollie. How're you feeling?"

Ollie snickers. "I would say like my old self, but I've been lost for so long, I remember little about that girl. My new self, however, is getting stronger every day."

"Whatever you're doing is working," Casey says.

Ollie's smile fades. "I owe you an apology, Casey. I treated you unfairly. The panic attacks made a monster of me. I hope I've seen the last of that angry, paranoid person."

"I hope so too, for your sake. You and I started off on the right foot. I really admire you, Ollie."

"Right back at you, Casey. Do you think we can be friends?"

A soft smile spreads across Casey's lips. "I'd certainly like to try."

Ollie holds her arms out to Casey, and the women embrace.

Jamie appears with two glasses of red wine. "Here you go, babe," he says, handing a glass to Fiona.

Casey's brow hits her hairline. "Wait, what? Did he just call you babe?"

Fiona bobs her head, a flush creeping up her neck.

Jamie hooks an arm around Fiona. "Funny how things work out sometimes. My dream girl was right in front of me the whole time, and I never even realized it."

Casey turns to Ollie. "Did you know about this?"

"Not until tonight." Ollie smiles at Fiona and Jamie. "You two make a cute couple. I'm happy for you both."

Casey's fingers graze Ollie's arm. "Speaking of cute couples, have you seen Sheldon tonight?"

Pink dots appear on Ollie's cheeks. "He's busy entertaining the guests, but we spoke briefly. We made a date for lunch at The Foxhole for tomorrow."

"Yes! Love is in the air at Love-Struck vineyards." Casey goes silent and her pale olive eyes light up when she notices Luke heading her way.

Fiona sends an elbow to her ribs. "Speaking of love, someone's got it bad."

Luke stops in front of her. "Hey, gorgeous."

"Hey, to you too." This is the first time Casey has seen him in person since they started texting. These past few days, their message have become spicy. Her face warms thinking about the things they've said.

"I'm sorry, I'm late. I got hung up on the phone with a client."

"No worries. I'm just glad you came," Casey says and lets out a hiccup.

Luke chuckles. "Someone's tipsy."

"I may have overindulged a smidge. I was nervous about seeing you."

"I'm flattered," Luke says in a throaty, sexy voice.

"You missed the showdown, Luke. Wait until I tell you about Ada's drama."

"Sounds juicy. Let's go sit down somewhere," he says, and drags her to a small table at the edge of the crowd.

When Casey recounts the showdown from earlier, Luke says, "Good for Ada. How did Daniel handle being publicly dissed?"

"He appeared furious. But I haven't talked to him. I'm trying to avoid him."

Luke touches his finger to the end of her nose. "What about you? How do you feel about Ada standing up to him like that?"

"Empowered." Casey stares over at The Nest. No matter where she is on the property, the powerful stone structure is always within view, like a spy watching her every move. How can she possibly have any freedom while living in Daniel's house?

Luke follows her gaze. "Which one is your bedroom?"

"Far corner window, the one with the light on."

"Show me," Luke says with a naughty twinkle in his eye.

Casey shakes her head, her golden waves skimming her shoulders. "No way."

"Where's your sense of adventure? Didn't you sneak boys into your house when you were a teenager?"

"No way! My mother would never have allowed it. Even though our apartment was large by New York standards, any movement from within was easily detected."

Luke nods his head at the crowd. "There's Daniel, surrounded by his guests. He's not going anywhere anytime soon. The coast is clear for you to show me the house." Jumping to his feet, he pulls Casey up and drags her across the lawn toward the house.

"Luke! Stop!" Casey digs in her heels. "You and I both know what will happen if I take you up to my room. I meant it earlier when I said I was nervous about seeing you. I didn't get out much while my mom was ill, and it's been a long time since I . . . you know, hooked up with anyone."

Luke tilts her chin toward him and kisses her lightly on the lips. "I'm interested in more than a hookup, Casey. I promise I won't attack you. We won't do anything you're not ready for."

The kiss stirs something deep inside Casey. Taking him by the hand, she leads him to the house and up the back stairs to the second floor. By the time they enter her bedroom, they are tearing at each other's clothes. Luke is a gentle but experienced lover, and he takes her to heights she's never known. After making love several times, they fall asleep in each other's arms. When they wake the following morning, bright sunlight is streaming in through the window.

Casey reaches for the alarm clock. "Ugh. It's already eight o'clock," she says, slamming it back down on the nightstand.

"Who cares? It's Friday." Luke pulls her close. "I could get used to waking up like this every day. He runs his toes down her leg, tickling the bottom of her foot.

Casey lets out a squeal and clamps her hand over her mouth.

Daniel's voice bellows from the hallway, "Casey! Is someone in there with you?"

Casey sits bolt upright, clutching the covers to her naked breasts. "Um . . . no. I'm watching TikTok videos."

"Well, get dressed and meet me downstairs for breakfast," Daniel says in a demanding tone.

She calls out to Daniel, "Sorry! Wish I could. But I have a meeting at eight thirty."

"Then stop by my office afterward. I need to talk to you."

"Yes, sir." Casey waits until she hears Daniel's footfalls

descending the stairs before she swings her legs over the side of the bed. She takes the covers with her as she crosses the room to the window.

Luke comes to stand behind her. "Does he speak to you that way often?"

"Only when he's in a bad mood. He's not an easy person, Luke."

"That doesn't give him the right to order you around." Luke's eyes narrow when he notices the cement mixer on her lot below. "What's going on down there?"

"They're pouring footings. Daniel's building me a house."

"A house? That's outrageous. Did you approve of this project?"

"Nope. I haven't even seen the plans."

Luke squints as he looks closer. "With a pair of binoculars, he'll be able to see inside your windows. Doesn't that creep you out?"

Casey's mind travels back to last night. She admires the way Ada stood up to him. Ada had texted, *Be careful, Casey. Don't lose sight of who you really are.*

Casey turns away from the window. "I can't live here anymore. I need to move."

"Where will you go?"

"I looked at a condo a few weeks ago. There were two available, the second and third floors of the Abbey Lane building. It'll be a financial stretch. But I think I can make it work."

Casey drops to her knees and crawls around on the carpeted floor, searching through their discarded clothes.

"What're you doing?" Luke asks.

"Looking for my phone. I'm going to call the building's owner." Locating her phone, she scrolls through her contacts and clicks on Toby's number.

"Toby Meyers," he answers in an abrupt tone.

Casey sits back on her haunches. "Toby, this is Casey Love. I apologize for calling so early."

"No worries," Toby says in a softer tone. "Good to hear from you, Casey."

"Are the Abbey Lane condos still available, by any chance?" With phone tucked beneath chin, Casey holds up her hands to show Luke her crossed fingers.

"The third floor is still for sale. Would you like to take another look?"

"Yes! Please! Do you have time this afternoon?"

"I'm flexible. How about four o'clock?"

"Perfect. I'll see you then." Casey tosses the phone on the floor and looks up at Luke. "I'm gonna do it, Luke. I'm gonna buy this condo. Who cares if I don't have any furniture? I'll sleep on the floor if necessary."

Luke sinks down beside her. Taking her in his arms, he eases her onto her back. "There are other things we can do on the floor, too."

"Yes, there are. Unfortunately, I have to get to work," Casey says, and struggles out from beneath his weight.

"I do too, actually," Luke says, sitting up and combing his fingers through his unruly sandy hair. "I'll be home from work around five. Why don't you come over after you tour the condo? I'll help you figure out your financing. We can have some dinner, and I'll play my saxophone for you."

"That sounds nice. But I insist on taking care of dinner."

"Do you like to cook?" Luke asks as he gathers up his clothes.

She shrugs. "I wouldn't say I enjoy cooking, but I can manage simple dishes. I'm also a pro at heating prepared meals from Delilah's."

Wrapping his arms around her from behind, he plants a trail of kisses on her neck. "Anything's fine with me. As long as you're on the menu for dessert."

Casey groans. "It's gonna be a long day."

"I promise to make the wait worth your while."

CHAPTER 36
OLLIE

A wave of nausea rolls over Ollie when she opens her eyes on Friday morning. She stumbles into the adjacent bathroom and empties the contents of her stomach into the toilet. She flushes the toilet but continues to hug the bowl as more vomit threatens. What brought this on? It can't be a hangover. She only had a few sips of wine at the reception. Come to think of it, she had little to eat either. She's been queasy from hunger before, but she's never actually thrown up. She felt icky on Wednesday night when she tasted Melvin's rosé sample. She must have some sort of lingering stomach bug.

Ollie is slowly getting to her feet when she notices the unopened box of tampons on the shelf above the toilet. Her last period was sometime around the middle of June. And it's now the second Friday in August. But she can't be pregnant. She's on the pill.

"Ugh!" She palms her forehead. How could she be so careless? She'd forgotten to take her packet of pills when she went to Tranquil Mind, Peaceful Heart. She thought little about it at the time. She and Jamie hadn't slept together in weeks.

Her mind races as she thinks back to that time. She got home from mental rehab on Sunday. She had to call her doctor to refill her prescription, and since Monday was a holiday, she didn't start the new packet of birth control pills until the next morning. The morning after the party at Love-Struck. After she first slept with Sheldon.

Returning to her bedroom, Ollie paces in circles as she considers her next move. "Don't get your hopes up, Ollie," she says out loud to the empty room. She stops in her tracks. Did she just tell herself not to get her hopes up? She places her hand on her belly. Is it possible a little boy with blond curly hair is cooking in there? Her heart skips a beat and excitement dances across her chest. Despite all her worrying and carrying on these past few weeks, she wants nothing more than to have Sheldon's baby.

Grabbing her wallet and keys, Ollie hurries downstairs, making a detour through the kitchen to grab a sleeve of Saltines, and drives to the nearest drugstore.

Thirty minutes later, in the safety of her bathroom, she pees on the stick and watches two pink lines appear in the results window.

Happiness and fear flood her at once. She can hardly wait to tell Sheldon at lunch. He'll be thrilled, won't he? He's reliable, as steady as a rock. She'll be able to count on him as they enter this next stage in life.

———

Wearing a blue linen tank dress with her hair fastened into a chignon, Ollie makes her way down to The Foxtail early to secure a table on the terrace before the lunch rush begins.

Steve brings her a glass of lemon water, which she guzzles down. But it makes her nauseated, and she worries she might be sick again. She fidgets with her phone, watching the clock's second hand approach twelve. When she spots Sheldon in the doorway, her pulse races, and she thinks her heart might beat out of her chest.

Sheldon kisses her forehead in greeting. "What's wrong, Ollie? You're pale. Do you feel okay?"

She jumps up to face him. "I need to tell you something, but I can't do it with all these people around."

Sheldon dips his head at the vineyard. "Then let's go for a walk."

"What about the table?"

He shrugs. "Let it go. We'll get another one when we get back."

"Okay. I'll tell Steve. Be right back." Ollie locates Steve and explains they are letting the table go. When she returns, Sheldon is waiting for her at the edge of the terrace.

Neither speaks as they walk down the hill, into the rows of vines. Sheldon stops to pick a grape. "So . . . What's on your mind?" he asks, popping the grape in his mouth.

Ollie blurts, "I'm pregnant, Sheldon. I took a test this morning." She raises her hand, palm out to him. "And before you ask, I'm absolutely positive the baby is yours. Jamie and I . . . Well, the timing is all wrong for it to be his."

Sheldon stares at her, his expression impassive. Perhaps she was wrong. He doesn't appear thrilled. Is he angry? After an awkward minute of silence, he finally says, "You know what this means, don't you?"

"I'm still trying to wrap my mind around all that it means. What does it mean to you?"

"It means you have to marry me." Sheldon removes a ring box from his pocket. "My siblings and I recently divvied up my mother's jewelry. I got first pick, and I chose this with you in mind." He opens the box to reveal an enormous brilliant-cut solitaire diamond. "It was Mom's engagement ring."

Ollie, her mouth agape, stares down at the ring and back at him. "Are you saying you were going to propose, anyway?"

"Yep. When you asked me to lunch, I prayed you'd come to your senses about us. You know as well as I do we belong together. My goal was to marry you before you changed your mind again. But the baby seals the deal." He tilts his head heavenward and yells, "Thank you, Lord! We're having a baby."

"So, you're happy about the baby?"

"I'm overjoyed about the baby." He takes the ring out of the box and slides it on her finger. "You're aware of my parents' troubled marriage. If it freaks you out to wear her ring, I'll buy you something else."

Ollie admires the ring. The sun hits the diamond, shooting off rays of blue and pink and yellow. "It's spectacular. I absolutely love it. I know how much you loved your mother, and I'd be honored to wear it." She palms his cheek. "I invited you to lunch before I had any idea I might be pregnant. I asked you here today to tell you I love you with my whole heart."

"And I love you with my whole heart." Sheldon picks Ollie up and spins her around. "Wait a minute!" He sets her back down. "I thought you were struggling with the notion of having children."

"I was. I got some ridiculous notion in my head that I might pass on evil genes to my child, like the one that made my brother a murderer. But Ronnie set me straight."

"Ha. I'm the one who should worry about passing on undesirable character traits. Look at my father and brother. Daniel and Hugh are as sinful as they come."

"Let's forget about genetics. Although I'm pretty sure he'll have your blond curly hair. We'll shower this child with love. But we'll also instill in him proper morals and values."

Sheldon places his hand on her abdomen. "Do you really think it's a him?"

Ollie grins. "I have a hunch, although it's way too early to tell." Her expression grows serious. "We should discuss where we're going to live. I know how excited you are about building your dream home on your lot at Love-Struck, but I don't think I can live in such close proximity to your family."

"I put my construction plans on permanent hold. If you'll let me, I'd like to live here with you."

"Really? Do you mean it?" Ollie bounces on her toes. "I would love having you here with me."

Wrapping his arms around her, he pulls her close. "I've bought the cabin I was renting, and I'm turning it into a fishing camp. Casey calls it my man cabin. I hope you won't mind me sneaking off from time to time to fish."

"Fine by me. I need my space sometimes too. I admit I'm curious, though. Will I ever get to see this man cabin?"

"Of course. I may even teach you to fly-fish."

"Don't bother. My father tried when I was a child. But I never really got the hang of it. I'll let that be your thing. Yours and our son's."

"I like the sound of that." Sheldon chuckles. "So, when are we getting married? Considering the circumstances, the sooner the better."

"How does the Sunday of Labor Day weekend sound? If it suits you, I'd like to have a private ceremony in the vineyard in the late afternoon, with the reception immediately following at The Foxtail."

"That sounds perfect," he says, tightening his embrace.

She rests her head on his chest, listening to his heartbeat. She's no longer alone in the world. This amazing man will be her partner for life. She won't take advantage of him. She'll cherish him and give him all the love he deserves.

CHAPTER 37
CASEY

Midafternoon on Friday, Casey is relaxed back in her chair with eyes closed and feet propped on her desk, reminiscing about her night of lovemaking with Luke, when Daniel bursts in.

"I can't believe you're taking a nap on company time. So much for your busy day." His voice is thunderous. No doubt the other employees can hear him down the hall.

Casey throws her feet off the desk and sits up straight in her chair. "This is the first break I've had all day. And I wasn't taking a nap. I was resting my eyes for a minute."

"I asked you to stop by my office when you were free. I've been waiting all day for you."

Getting up from her desk, Casey crosses the room and closes the door. "Well, we're both here now. What did you want to talk to me about?"

"What happened last night," he says, his tone still angry. "I'm sure the whole town is talking about what a skeptical Ada made of herself. We need to be on the same page if anyone should question you about it."

Casey goes to stand face-to-face with Daniel. "I'm not sure what you mean. What page?"

"You know, about Ada's proclamations."

Casey narrows her eyes at him. "Is anything Ada said untrue?"

"She's probably lying about Bud being her father. Not that I care. She's no longer my concern. I'm simply trying to save face. I don't like people gossiping about my family. If anyone asks you about Ada, you tell them we don't discuss family business in public."

The tense nerves that have kept Casey on pins and needles these past weeks finally snap. She remembers Ada's texts from last night: *Maintain your independence. Don't lose sight of who you really are.*

She inhales deeply, bringing herself to her full height. "I can't do this anymore, Daniel."

Daniel looks down his nose at her. "Can't do what?"

"Work with you and live in your house. You're like some crazed dictator, ordering me around, telling me what to say."

"I'm upset, Casey. After what happened last night, do you blame me?"

"What happened is between you and Ada. But you're taking it out on me. You were rude to me this morning. You demanded I get dressed and meet you downstairs for breakfast." Casey swallows past the lump in her throat. "I don't like the way you spoke to me. And that's not the first time either. My mother never treated me that way, and I find it offensive."

Anger flashes in his eyes, but his tone is joking when he says, "You're not a little girl, Casey. We need to toughen you up."

"I'm sick of everyone saying that. Fight, Casey. Toughen up, Casey. Well, that's not who I am." She turns her back on him and goes over to the window. "You've been good to me, Daniel. I'm grateful to you for welcoming me into your family and giving me a job and a place to live. But I can't be your puppet."

"Come on, Casey. I don't think of you as my puppet."

"It feels like it sometimes. We'd get along a lot better if you'd accept me for who I am instead of trying to make me someone I'm not."

Daniel comes to stand beside her at the window, placing his hand lightly on her back. "I'm sorry, sweetheart. I didn't mean to be overbearing. You're just like your mother in some ways. She was very much her own person. I need to do a better job of respecting that you are too."

Casey stares out at the mountains, unable to meet his gaze. "I lied to you this morning. I wasn't alone watching TikTok videos. I was with Luke Ellington. We've been seeing each other, and he spent the night with me. I was wrong to sleep with a man in your home. But I'm twenty-seven years old, and I need my own space. For your sake and mine, I have to move out."

Daniel hesitates, and Casey is sure he's going to fire her, when he says, "I can understand that. Unfortunately, your house won't be ready for months, maybe even a year. You could rent an apartment in town in the interim."

Casey turns to him. "I don't want the house, Daniel. I never asked for it. Living and working in the same place isn't healthy for me. I've found a condo for sale in town. I'm looking at it again this afternoon, and I'm probably going to make an offer."

"If that's what you want," he says with a dazed expression.

"I'm sorry, Daniel. Everything has happened so fast, and I feel like I'm suffocating. Sometimes, I wish I'd never come here."

"Don't say that, sweetheart. We can work this out. We're just experiencing growing pains. I thought I was doing something special in building the house for you, but if you'd rather live somewhere else, I'll buy the condo for you." He draws her in for a half hug.

"No! Daniel!" She pushes him away. "I want to do this on my own." Her lower lip quivers. "I feel awful about the house. They've already poured the footings."

Daniel tilts her chin toward him. "It's not a big deal, Casey. Bruce can have the house. He's renting in town now, but it would be more convenient for him to live on the property."

Casey's hopes soar. "Really?"

"Really." Daniel kisses her cheek. "Tell me more about this condo. I'd like to see it before you make an offer." His hands shoot up. "I'm not trying to control you. But I know a lot more about construction and real estate than you."

She can see how much this means to him. "That would be great. My appointment is at four o'clock."

He fingers a lock of her hair. "If you won't let me buy it outright, at least let me make a sizable down payment. I don't want you strapped for cash."

"Seriously, Daniel, it's time I take responsibility for my own life. Although I would appreciate guidance on how to go about getting a loan."

He gives her a nod. "I'm happy to do that."

She glances at her watch. "Gosh. It's three-thirty already. We should leave soon."

Daniel starts toward the door. "I need to grab something from my office. I'll meet you in the parking lot in ten minutes."

Toby is waiting for them in the vestibule, and the threesome ride up in the elevator together. Casey wanders about the spacious rooms while Daniel asks Toby pointed questions about electrical wiring and plumbing.

When he's finished with his inspection, Daniel says to Toby, "Can I have a minute alone with my daughter?"

"Of course. Take all the time you need. I'll wait for you downstairs in the vestibule," Toby says and leaves the condo.

Daniel's serious demeanor alarms Casey. Is there something wrong with the condo? She holds her breath while waiting for his feedback.

"Toby has done a solid job with the renovations. It's a sound investment. You'll get your money back when you decide to sell."

A gush of air expels from her lungs. "I'm glad you approve."

Daniel circles the living room. "It's a good fit. I can totally see you living here." He hands her a check. "I want you to have this."

Casey looks down at the amount. "I can't accept this, Daniel. I thought I made it clear. I'm buying the condo on my own." She tries to give it back, but he won't accept it.

"It's not a gift, Casey. It's a bonus for all the hard work you did on the branding. You earned it. Your paintings are worth significantly more than that," he says, jabbing a finger at the check in her hands. "Use it however you wish. You can make a larger down payment, or you can buy furniture, or you can put it in your savings account for a rainy day."

She stares at the check again. The bonus would ease some of the financial stress of buying and furnishing the condo. "Seriously?"

"Seriously. It's yours."

Daniel's smile is genuinely sincere. He is a man of many moods. But one thing Casey is certain of—he doesn't lavish grandiose gifts on his children to control them. He buys them cars and houses and horses because he loves them. While he'll never admit it, there's no way Daniel stopped loving Ada after being her father for twenty-seven years. He must be devastated to learn his wife had an affair with his best friend.

Casey knew her mother well. Beverly Hobbs would never have fallen in love with an egotistical maniac. Beverly saw something special in Daniel. Casey, too, has caught glimpses of that person. She'll cut him some slack. He just lost his daughter. He's not himself right now.

Casey's mother always taught her to never lose sight of herself. She's been so lost these past few months since Beverly's death. But she made great strides today. She stood up to her father and established some ground rules for their relationship. Daniel Love is only a part of this new life she's forging for herself. She has a new romance, a promising career, and she'll soon be living in a fabulous condo. At the end of every day, she'll come home to her small slice of heaven with views looking out on the town and mountains beyond. Casey is no longer looking in the rear-view mirror. She's looking forward to the road ahead.

ALSO BY ASHLEY FARLEY

Virginia Vineyards

Love Child

Blind Love

Palmetto Island

Muddy Bottom

Change of Tides

Lowcountry on My Mind

Sail Away

Hope Springs Series

Dream Big, Stella!

Show Me the Way

Mistletoe and Wedding Bells

Matters of the Heart

Road to New Beginnings

Stand Alone

On My Terms

Tangled in Ivy

Lies that Bind

Life on Loan

Only One Life

Home for Wounded Hearts

Nell and Lady

Sweet Tea Tuesdays

Saving Ben

ABOUT THE AUTHOR

Ashley Farley writes books about women for women. Her characters are mothers, daughters, sisters, and wives facing real-life issues. Her bestselling Sweeney Sisters series has touched the lives of many.

Ashley is a wife and mother of two young adult children. While she's lived in Richmond, Virginia, for the past twenty-one years, a piece of her heart remains in the salty marshes of the South Carolina Lowcountry, where she still calls home. Through the eyes of her characters, she captures the moss-draped trees, delectable cuisine, and kindhearted folk with lazy drawls that make the area so unique.

Ashley loves to hear from her readers. Visit Ashley's website @ ashleyfarley.com

Get free exclusive content by signing up for her newsletter @ ashleyfarley.com/newsletter-signup/

Made in the USA
Middletown, DE
26 July 2022

70058269R00142